A FORCE BEYOND GOVERNANCE

By: Tom Fox

New Generation Publishing

A natural force beyond
governance

which could not be created

and would not be suppressed

For Jennifer and Candy

with thanks for all your kindness
and support

Christmas 2014

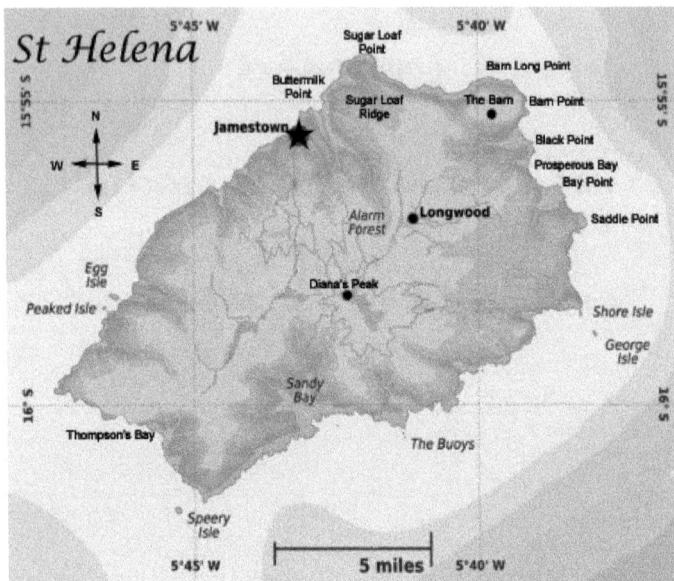

St Helena

5°45' W 5°40' W

15°55' S 15°55' S

Sugar Loaf Point

Barn Long Point

Buttermilk Point

Sugar Loaf Ridge

The Barn Barn Point

Jamestown ★

Black Point

Prosperous Bay

Bay Point

Alarm Forest ● Longwood

Saddle Point

Egg Isle

Diana's Peak ●

Peaked Isle

Shore Isle

George Isle

16° S 16° S

Sandy Bay

Thompson's Bay

The Buoys

Speery Isle

5°45' W 5°40' W

5 miles

N
W E
S

ST HELENA 1838

CHAPTER ONE

'He is probably the best offer you're likely to get.'

Ruth Morgan stood on the verandah of the timber framed shack she shared with her brother, watching Adam Fletcher walk across the garden to the cliff path, which led to the small settlement of Prosperous Bay. His gait was wide and slightly rolling, in keeping with his work as a fisherman. Her brother stood behind her in the doorway, barely visible in the failing light.

'I don't love him, Robert.'

'But you like him.'

'I've always liked him since Mrs Davies taught us to read and write together. He's steady and has always been kind and considerate. Is love too much to hope for?'

She heard a chuckle from the doorway.

'Dear sister, I'm afraid it probably is. Consider our situation; we're not wealthy. Prosperous Bay is a backwater with barely 100 adults of many nationalities and cultures, and some are freed slaves. We may be only ten miles from Jamestown, but the path through the hills is often impassable. The land King George gave to our grandparents provides an adequate living, but our parents never tried to retain links with Jamestown, which has left you poorly positioned when trying to find a husband. You live in a small isolated settlement on an island which is almost as far from Africa as it is from South America; I doubt there are more than seven thousand people on the island and the figure is only as high as that because of the West Africa naval squadron based in Jamestown. You might have hoped to meet an officer but, from what I hear, whenever a Jamestown girl has fallen for a naval officer the result is usually her ruin. Adam is English and from protestant stock, as we are; he shares our values. He gets some rent from the land he sub-lets to others. The profits from fishing aren't what they were when whaling was at its peak, but he still earns a reasonable living, although the work is hard. Some of the English criticise him for employing that Italian as crew, but if Ceruso is good I'd not hold that against him.'

'Quite the contrary, Robert, I know Adam did that out of a sense of duty when his father died. There is nothing to criticise, Adam is a fair and honourable man.'

'Then marry him, Ruth, perhaps love will grow out of the affection you already hold for him. I don't mean to belittle love or question your wish to find it, but I am afraid there can be few places where your choice of a marriage partner would be as poor as in Prosperous Bay, St Helena. Our father said 'old man' Lloyd made a big mistake when he didn't take the opportunity to marry Emma Lloyd off to George Jones, even though he was a good deal older. Now Emma, and her sister Dorothy, are spinsters with any hope of marriage long since gone. They're lucky the East India company allowed them to take on their father's franchise for the general store in Prosperous Bay when he died; and even more so for allowing them to retain it when the Island passed into the hands of the British Government five years ago, when the India act was passed in Parliament in London. If you leave things too long, opportunities will disappear.'

Adam was familiar with the cliff path and completed his short journey before dusk became night. A light shone through the single front window of his home, illuminating the covered front porch. He could see shadows moving on the curtains. Carmella Ceruso looked up as he opened the door. She was slim with long dark hair; an attractive women in her mid-thirties, undiminished by a life of toil,

2

scratching a living from the land she cultivated on behalf of her husband. Adam had grown up in her company and had a great fondness for Carmella. She had been his cook and housekeeper from the time of his parents' death, slipping into the role without being asked.

'I'm nearly finished, Mr Fletcher. There is a rabbit stew simmering on the kitchen stove and I've left you a couple of fresh loaves. I've put some fruit in the bowl in the larder.'

Adam's parents had both died in the typhus epidemic in 1835. Carmella and her husband, Francesco, were descended from Italian seamen who had been granted small plots of land after 20 years' service in the British Navy. The plots had proved to be of poor quality and insufficient to sustain even a small family. Her husband had crewed for Nathan Fletcher from the time of Adam's childhood. Adam had finished the rudimentary schooling Mrs Davies offered by the age of 15 and he had joined his father as crew of the sturdy, ocean lugger. Francesco had been retained, to the surprise of the villagers, and Adam learnt his trade from both men in the three years that followed. The decline in the whaling trade had produced local unemployment and Nathan Fletcher's decision to employ the Italian had provoked criticism from other Englishmen in the settlement, because he had not employed one of them. The typhus epidemic with the loss of his parents had brought that phase of Adam's life to an abrupt end. The young fisherman had been under even greater pressure to discharge Francesco and employ a young Englishman, Daniel Mott, who was a distant relative by marriage. The matter was considered to be a foregone conclusion by most of the small English community, who were outraged when Adam did not comply with their wishes. It had never been a difficult decision for Adam, as he did not hold the Englishman in high regard. Surprise was followed by anger and Adam's continuing employment of Francesco remained controversial in the settlement, particularly with Daniel's mother, Elizabeth Mott.

'Thank you, Carmella. How is Maria getting on in school?'

Adam knew Maria, an only child aged 12, was one of Mrs Davies's favourites.

'Good, I think. We're very lucky to have Lucy Davies looking after our children. What time do you want Francesco to meet you at the boat tomorrow?'

'Five o'clock should suit the tide and the wind looks as though it will be favourable.'

'I'll tell him. He'll bring more of the stew and a loaf that I put in the oven before I left home. Do you plan to stay out overnight?'

'It depends on the results of our fishing during the day, Carmella. If it's poor, we will probably stay out.'

'I'll warn Francesco. I'll see you later in the week, Mr Fletcher. There's a fresh bottle of rum on the dresser and a pitcher of cold water on the stone shelf in the larder.'

He escorted her to the door and kissed her on the cheek.

'Do you want to take a lantern, Carmella?'

'No, Mr Fletcher, I'll be fine.'

Adam returned to the house and surveyed the property with a more critical eye than usual. If he were to propose to Ruth Morgan, how would she feel about the accommodation he could offer? The house she shared with her brother was small. It had two bedrooms, achieved by having rooms that were a lot smaller than Adam's accommodation; he only had three rooms, a bedroom, a sitting room and a kitchen, but all were of generous proportions. Adam's father had designed and fitted an unusual addition. His house lay almost at the top of the cliff path close to a stream that ran from the interior of the island. The gradient was such that Nathan had run a pipe

4

from the stream to the roof of his house, supplying water to the kitchen and also to a cold shower in the bedroom. The lounge was large and dominated by an open fire, which backed onto the bedroom and would warm both rooms on the rare occasions when temperatures were very low. A dining table and six chairs stood against one side wall, next to a door which led into the kitchen. There was a cast iron stove with sufficient space on top for a kettle and a pan with the rabbit stew. A cast iron sink, served by a cold tap, lay under the window. One corner of the kitchen was filled by a small pantry with thick stone shelves. There was a covered porch at the front and the back. The house was on the edge of the village with the main settlement lying below. He walked out onto the rear porch. There were excellent views of Prosperous Bay with the small beach forming the focus of the settlement and the ocean beyond. The land rose steeply from the beach to cliffs which protruded out into the South Atlantic to the north and south, creating Prosperous Bay. Bay Point to the south was composed of weather worn volcanic rock. Black Point to the north was similar, but 100 yards beyond its tip in the ocean stood Sentinel Rock. It lay free of the cliffs and had not been subject to the gradual erosion of volcanic rock. It stood out from the cliff in the surf, perhaps 150 feet high and almost as wide. Adam had examined its structure in the past. The rock was jet black, shiny and of exceptional hardness so that it had the appearance of a gigantic glass obelisk. The fishermen treated it with great respect; the combination of current and prevailing winds had led many sailors to their death, at its base. The Sentinel at Black Point was always given a wide berth by the warships of the West Africa Squadron when they passed to and from Jamestown on anti-slavery patrols. Adam returned to the kitchen savouring the aroma from the stew that was simmering gently on the stove. He turned the tap in the sink and was rewarded with a plentiful flow of water. He hoped Ruth would approve of the home he had to offer.

Ruth was two years Adam's junior and she had joined Mrs Davies's school as a shy six year old. This respected teacher had helped in schools in England before her husband had been seconded to St Helena, at the time of Napoléon's incarceration in 1815. When Napoléon died, six years later, the British Government released most of the staff at Longwood House and granted Crown land around the island to those who were no longer employed. Edmond Davies worked his land near the settlement while Lucy offered her teaching services to the village. With help from the older students, she presided over 40 children from the settlement and the surrounding areas. The working language of the school was English but many other languages were spoken in the children's homes. There were two classes, the young'uns and the old'uns. Tuition took place in the community hall at the centre of the village. Lucy Davies often used some of the old'uns to help with new pupils. Adam had been asked to help Ruth settle in and they had remained friends throughout their schooldays. Their relationship had deepened when Adam's parents had died. He noticed in the months that followed the funeral that flowers often appeared on their grave. On the anniversary of their death, Adam and Ruth arrived at the grave simultaneously and grieved together. Ruth was slim with light brown hair, which she tended to keep short; she had blue eyes and a pale complexion. The shyness of childhood had evolved into a calm reserve, which Adam found particularly appealing. A couple of years previously Adam had noticed a feature which set her apart from all others. He enjoyed the company of the few young women in the settlement, but if the conversation slackened he could become nervous and tongue tied. This had never happened with Ruth; neither was ill at ease with prolonged silences and he felt content and at ease in her company.

Edmond Davies was celebrating his birthday in a couple of weeks and Adam knew that Ruth and he were both invited to attend. He would ask if he could escort her to and from the party and develop their relationship further.

The small table in the kitchen was set for dinner. He poured himself a generous portion of rum and savoured the spirit as it ran across his tongue. He ladled some stew into an earthenware bowl and cut slices of Carmella's bread. The meal was quickly consumed and the dishes cleared away. The remains of the stew went on the cool stone pantry shelf to await his return from fishing. He took the oil lamp through to the bedroom and carefully took off his best suit and shirt. Carmella had already laid out his fishing breaches and a rough linen shirt and tunic, which had been freshly laundered. He turned the wick on the lamp low and was swiftly asleep.

Adam met Francesco on the path down to the beach and they walked to the lugger. There were several smaller boats drawn up on the sand which would set sail later in the morning. They could only be used for close inshore work where the fish tended to be smaller and less plentiful. Only Adam's boat had the option of sailing further out and, if necessary, staying out overnight. There was a small area at the bow covered with a tarpaulin, which acted as a store room for equipment when the boat was beached, and for sleeping quarters if they chose to stay out overnight. Francesco untied the line which secured the bow and coiled the rope swiftly, securing it near the base of the main mast. Working together they eased the boat the short distance back into the sea. Francesco, being smaller and lighter, leapt aboard, opened the storage area and unrolled the main sail and jib. Adam, barefoot, pushed the boat into deeper water and slowly turned it such that its stern faced the beach. Francesco had attached the jib to the headstay but did not raise the sail. The main sail was then attached to the main mast. When all preparations were complete, Adam pushed off and lifted himself over the stern, taking control of the tiller and easing the bow slightly to port to catch the light breeze as Francesco ran up the main sail. The sail filled and the lugger began to pick up headway. Adam used his body to control the tiller bar as he reefed the lines controlling the boom. Francesco was raising the jib; both sails were swiftly sheeted home. They worked together to adjust the trim of the sails to suit the line of passage that Adam had chosen towards the sun, which still lay below the horizon. Neither felt the need to speak. Theirs was a time-honoured ritual and both preferred to work in silence at the beginning of a new day.

Francesco scampered back to the stern and sat next to Adam with the tiller bar between them. Adam inspected the boat in front of him. Their lunch had already been stowed in the bow compartment along with a thick jersey and wet weather canvasses. Francesco, as always, had left the coils of line neatly stowed. Each coil was stabilised by a quick release knot if sheets needed to be adjusted in an emergency. He held two bread rolls in his hand and passed one to Adam. He pulled a stone jar of cold water out of the stern locker and two wooden cups.

'From Carmella, for breakfast.'

Adam chuckled. This was usually the first statement of the day. Carmella's breakfast offerings were a pleasant part of the morning ritual. They were presented when the boat was underway and the sun was about to rise. The only sounds were of the waves slapping against the hull, and sometimes the wind in the rigging. Even the seabirds were quiet at this time of day. Adam enjoyed this period of their trip; all was in order and the boat was responding to the adjustments to the rudder. There was all the uncertainty of not knowing what the day's fishing would bring – success or disappointment. Carmella's rolls never disappointed. The exterior gave little clue as to the interior. She hollowed out the rolls and inserted a wide variety of different fillings, some sweet and some savoury. The rolls were long and sometimes came with two fillings with an end marked to indicate where the fishermen should start. Adams's father had never asked Francesco what the day's roll would contain and Adam had continued the same tradition. It was the first exciting uncertainty of the day; in this case with no risk of failure. Today's roll was marked at one end, thereby indicating two fillings. The roll felt slightly warm and even in the gentle breeze he could smell the freshly baked bread.

'Did she make them this morning?'

'Yes, she was up at 3 o'clock.'

'She works hard for us, Francesco. I have always considered her to be the third crew member. She helps our work in so many different ways.'

'I think she feels the same way, Adam. She has simple loyalties. She's never forgotten that your father gave me work and that he was criticised for it. She's always respected you, even when your father was alive. We both felt the pressure you were put under to release me and employ an Englishman. It was an expectation that would have been difficult to resist. As far as she's concerned you stood by me, but also stood by her and our daughter, Maria.'

Francesco laughed. 'I will tell her you consider her to be the third crew member. I think she'll like that.'

Adam bit in to the end of the roll; two rashers of bacon, still slightly warm from the pan. He grunted in satisfaction.

'The current is strong today, Francesco. I'll need to take her further to starboard, can you adjust the sheets?'

Francesco carefully replaced his bread roll in a small leather bag at his feet and moved forward as Adam pulled the tiller bar towards him and the lugger moved closer to the wind. Once the sheets were adjusted, Francesco returned to the stern but continued to stand as the boat slid past the Sentinel. The shiny black obelisk towered above them and Francesco shuddered and crossed himself.

'You fear that rock, Francesco, don't you?'

'I do, it's a graveyard, Adam. I knew men who died at its base, either caught on a lee shore or because they misjudged the currents, but, over and above that, the rock is not natural. I think it is sensible to fear it.'

'They say scientists have found that volcanoes can sometimes produce glass, as well as lava, Francesco. I don't know if that has anything to do with its appearance. Have you ever examined it up close?'

'No, and I would never want to, Adam.'

'I went once on a very calm day with an inshore fisherman in his small boat. It is like glass; nothing grows on its surface, above or below the waterline. The simple tools we had in the boat would not allow us to chip off any pieces from the surface.'

Francesco crossed himself again.

'That was most unwise, Adam. You should not tempt fate in such ways again. Taking tools to its surface can only bring you bad luck.'

Adam smiled. 'My good friend, I would not want you to worry. I don't plan to return there or ask you to go close. I do not fear the rock but I do respect it for the reasons you have given; the combination of prevailing winds, and especially the currents, which catch so many experienced sailors by surprise.'

The lugger had moved past the Sentinel and out onto the open sea. The breeze strengthened and the bow rose to the ocean swell. It never failed to excite Adam, although many would be daunted by the sheer immensity of the ocean they had entered. More than 1000 miles separated them from southern Africa to the east and to the north. The distance to the west (and South America) exceeded two thousand miles. The sea ice of the Antarctic lay a similar distance to the south.

Francesco moved forward without being bidden and readjusted the sails to the strengthening breeze. When he returned, they completed their breakfast as the lugger sailed to the first area that Adam had chosen to seek the ocean's harvest. He navigated by experience and the advice his father had given him before his untimely death. He had no compass, although he knew small portable compasses were now being used by the West African squadron. Close inspection of the relationship of the Sentinel rock to Diana's Peak, the island's tallest mountain, allowed him to judge the north/south line he wished to follow. The distance from Prosperous Bay to the east could be calculated by the height of the hills above the sea.

Francesco finished the remainder of his roll; the second filling had been honey. He took a final swig of water and moved forward to prepare the fishing lines and to bait the hooks. They were already well beyond the range of the smaller fishing boats from Prosperous Bay, which rarely strayed beyond the headlands.

Late in the afternoon Adam reviewed the fruits of their labour. The catch was reasonable, but not sufficiently large to justify sailing around the northern tip of the island to sell the excess to whichever of Her Majesty's men of war were re-provisioning at their base in Jamestown. The fishermen did not feel the need to stay out overnight and Adam brought the lugger about for the journey home. Francesco rewound the lines and hung them back up in the accommodation in the narrower part of the bow, where they would have slept if they had chosen to spend the night at sea. All was quickly restored to order and he returned with a fresh flask of water. They sat in the stern with the bow of the lugger pointing to the setting sun; St Helena and Diana's Peak rose up to meet them.

Adam cursed, 'I do believe these currents are getting worse, Francesco. I've not made enough allowance; we will have to go on an additional tack to get a better clearance of the Sentinel.'

It was not long before the manoeuvre had given them the sea room they required. A final tack brought them back on a safer run to the beach. They passed into the shadow of the Sentinel. Francesco stood by the mast, crossing himself and offering an invocation in Latin. Adam was surprised to find he was similarly affected, a momentary shudder and the feeling of non-specific anxiety. He forced a laugh.

'Francesco, your superstitions are beginning to get to me.'

Francesco smiled. 'We should talk of happier things. I think I see Carmella on the beach.'

The ever watchful Carmella was standing on the beach with her daughter, Maria, alongside the hand cart they used to sell the fish. Both waded out into the surf to meet the boat and Francesco dropped the sails as they neared the shore. All four pulled the boat higher onto the sand and Adam, Carmella and Maria transferred the fish to the handcart as Francesco stored the sails and restored the boat to order. He tossed the painter to Adam, who reattached the boat to the thick metal ring, which was securely fixed to a boulder. As the evening shadows lengthened, the quartet pulled the cart to the small square at the centre of the settlement to sell their fish and share out the proceeds of the day's work.

Adam and Maria took several rock cod to the house of Edmond and Lucy Davies. The schoolchildren had a simple lunch at the school and remained under Mrs Davies's supervision for most of the day, which allowed their mothers to work the land. Meat was relatively scarce and a fish pie was frequently on the menu. Adam completed their sale and walked back towards the square. They could hear voices, raised in anger.

A detachment of marines was permanently stationed in the settlement. Their deployment had been a precaution at the time of Napoléon's imprisonment in 1815. Until the time of his death there had been concern that his supporters would raid the island and release him from captivity, as had occurred from Elba. If an attempt were to be made, it was thought Prosperous Bay would likely be the site chosen for a landing. The bay could accommodate perhaps three frigates; if the settlement were approached at night in long boats, it could easily be overrun and its inhabitants taken prisoner. The trail to Jamestown and to Longwood House where Napoléon was held was tortuous and rough, but probably ideal for those seeking to free the Emperor. Forty marines were originally stationed in the settlement and a wooden barracks had been built on ground that had been levelled by the troops. At the time of Napoléon's death, the detachment was reduced to ten marines under the command of a sergeant. There had always been some friction between the soldiers and the settlers, with both sides considering they had grievances. The most recent sergeant, John Logan, was disliked by the settlers. He allowed drunkenness in his section of marines and crops were frequently stolen from the fields. Adam and Maria turned the corner into the square. A marine was arguing with Francesco.

Adam put his hand on Maria's shoulder. 'Stay back here, Maria.'

'If you want to buy those fish, that's the price.'

'They are rotten already. I'll pay you half your price.'

'If you think they're rotten, don't buy them.'

'You should be providing us with fish for free. You settlers are all the same, no respect for the soldiers of the Crown who protect you.'

Francesco laughed. 'From what? The only thing that needs protecting here are our crops and animals. You're the cause of the problem, not its solution.'

Adam attempted to defuse the situation. 'Marine, let it be. You know the price, we haven't raised it since you last bought fish and they are freshly caught today.'

The marine swore and paid for the fish.

Adam sighed. 'Why must there be so much unpleasantness?'

Any hope of resolution was dashed by the appearance of Sergeant Logan. His tunic was partly undone and he smelt of rum.

'I heard you, Italian scum. If you can prove any thefts, bring me the evidence. It's time you learnt to respect your betters.'

Adam was relieved that Francesco did not rise to the bait. Sergeant Logan looked over at Carmella.

'Charlie, I think you've been bidding for the wrong fish. You should come and visit the barracks, my lady, and find out what it's like to be looked after by a real man.'

Carmella gave him a withering look. 'Your invitation is declined, Sergeant.'

John Logan shifted his gaze to Francesco. 'I'm watching you Ceruso. Tread carefully around the marines.'

He turned back to Carmella and smiled. 'Believe me, I will have you and you may even come to enjoy it. Come on, Charlie, back to the barracks.'

Carmella beckoned her daughter over whilst speaking to the fishermen in a low voice. 'I loathe those men; they are not people I can respect. I think this section of marines is very ill disciplined.'

Francesco nodded. 'It comes from the top. Sergeant Logan is, without doubt, the worst we have ever had. If he causes you problems, Carmella, you must let us know.'

'Please don't worry, Francesco, I've handled worse than him in the past.'

She turned to Adam.

'Well that conversation took the shine off a good day. Why don't I bake us a fish pie, Adam, with some of the few fish we have not sold? By the time the two of you are cleaned up, it should be ready to eat.'

It had always amused Adam the way Carmella addressed him on different occasions. When working for him he was always addressed as Mr Fletcher. For social occasions she would use his Christian name. 'Thanks, Carmella, I can be back down to your house within the hour.'

CHAPTER TWO

On Sunday Adam donned his best clothes and attended the small church service in the settlement at 11 o'clock. They had no clergy. A short sermon was provided from within the community. Adam approved of the amateur status of those taking the service; the absence of clergy ensured a short, straightforward and practical sermon, which was appreciated by all. Edmond Davies usually organised the prayers and hymns, with Lucy Davies accompanying him on a well-travelled upright piano. Adam was occasionally asked to provide a sermon for the small congregation of all nationalities and religious persuasions. The Ceruso family attended most weeks, although the rota for preachers was restricted to protestant English stock.

Robert and Ruth Morgan were sitting in front of Adam. He spent a disproportionate amount of time during the service studying such of Ruth's features as were available, when viewed from behind. He considered she had nice hair and the short style she had chosen displayed the graceful lines of her neck to good effect. She was perhaps three inches shorter than Adam and her brother. He liked her dress which was sober, as the situation required, but nevertheless acknowledged her slim waist.

Matthew Draper, an elderly farmer in the settlement, moved forward to give the sermon. The congregation prepared themselves for advice on avoiding the sins of the flesh. It was a constant topic of interest to the farmer, who rarely felt the need to stray from his specialist subject when asked to preach. Adam suppressed a smile, recognising that today his search for salvation was playing second fiddle to a far more immediate search for a partner through life. He had never believed in an overly judgemental God to be feared, rather a more practical deity with a realistic appreciation of the weaknesses of his flock. Matthew Draper did not disappoint and gave a particularly vigorous sermon on the weaknesses of the flesh and situations that all should seek to avoid. On this occasion, Adam felt the sermon was perhaps more graphic than would seem appropriate to the more sensitive ladies of the parish. The Lloyd sisters were generally considered a barometer of acceptable social discourse. Both spinsters had their fans out earlier than normal and used them energetically; it was a sure sign farmer Draper had preached to the very boundaries of acceptability. Adam considered Mr Draper was perhaps a little more familiar with the practical aspects of the sins of the flesh than was seemly. Mrs Draper had died several years previously, to be replaced by a series of young housekeepers brought from Jamestown. Most lasted for a couple of years before being swiftly returned to the capital in dresses that were looser fitting than those in which they had arrived. Secrets are not easily kept in a small community. As usual, Mr Draper had nearly filled the village hall for the Sunday service and the congregation did not leave disappointed.

Adam, Ruth and Robert had been sitting near the front of the chapel and were delayed leaving by the congregation behind them, who were chatting as they slowly moved to the town square outside. The trio knew each other well and Adam felt he could tease Robert about the sermon.

'It must be difficult, Robert, to avoid carnal thoughts when you're surrounded by so many attractive animals. I can only respect your self-control.'

Ruth rose to her brother's defence. 'We've always thought you must be at far greater risk, out of sight from the land, with no witnesses and a boat surrounded by mermaids. Tell me, have you ever succumbed to the sins

17

of the flesh; perhaps a lonely night at sea and a beautiful mermaid looking for company?'

They all laughed. 'I keep looking, Ruth, but so far they seem more interested in mermen.'

He turned to Ruth. 'Ruth, I know we are both invited to Edmond's birthday party next Saturday, could I escort you there and back?'

Ruth smiled and curtsied. 'Certainly, sir. Thank you, Adam, I would like that a lot.'

'If I came at say six thirty, would that be alright?'

'I shall look forward to it.'

Adam enjoyed their company. All three knew that Robert was also invited but Adam was sure that Robert would leave for the party either half an hour earlier or later, to give his sister some private time with Adam. They left the church and walked slowly up the path to Adam's door. He kissed Ruth on the cheek and brother and sister moved on to their home a little further down the cliff path.

The week passed swiftly with good catches on most days. Adam and Francesco supplied about half the settlement with fish, with other farmers, who lived further away coming in to buy fish twice or thrice a week. If the catch was particularly plentiful early in the day it allowed time to sail round the north of the island and into Jamestown harbour, offering some of the larger fish to whatever frigates were moored in the bay for re-provisioning. This week they made two visits to Jamestown. Adam was concerned about the poor relationship with the marines in Prosperous Bay and suggested perhaps Carmella should leave the sale of the fish to the men for a while, but neither of the Cerusos felt the need to change their normal practice.

They fished in shallower water on the Saturday morning and the catch was sold by early afternoon. Adam walked home and showered in the cool water from the hill behind the settlement. He had decided this evening would be the time to make his proposal to Ruth. He was surprised to find he was not nervous; she was a good friend and must have some awareness that a proposal was likely. He knew she would treat his request with kindness and respect, even if her answer was in the negative. He tried to envisage how he would handle a rejection and hoped, if it occurred, it would not affect their relationship in the long term.

Adam arrived a little early but found Ruth was already waiting for him. Robert was nowhere to be seen. Adam kissed her on the cheek and they started to walk slowly towards the cliff path. He was not surprised to feel the tension rising within him as he steered the conversation around to his feelings for her and his desire to spend the rest of his days with her. They paused as they crossed a stile that marked the settlement boundary.

'Ruth, I'm glad to have the opportunity to talk with you privately. We've known each other since we were children and I've always enjoyed your company. My feelings for you have deepened over the last two years and I've felt emboldened by our close friendship to hope that you might consider becoming my wife. Life is challenging here and I would like to take care of you; we would both gain from each other's support. As you know, I do reasonably well from the fishing and with a wife I could, perhaps, take back the plot of land I rent out. I'm sure you could do better moving to a larger society in Jamestown and I would understand if you declined my proposal. Either way I hope my proposal will not undermine our friendship, which is of great importance to me.'

Ruth had listened to his proposal in silence and was about to reply when Adam was hailed from further back on the cliff path.   Matthew Draper, ignorant of the significance of the occasion, launched into a discussion on the feedback he had gained from last week's sermon. Ruth and Adam listened to the monologue, resigned to the fact that their discussion must remain incomplete.   As she stepped up on to the porch of the Davies's house Ruth turned to Adam.

'Thank you for what you said to me earlier, Adam. I look forward to talking about it later this evening. It is a matter which will receive my deepest thought.'

The Davies's parties were usually a high spot on the settlement's social calendar. Adam circulated among the guests and made small talk to friends and acquaintances, watching the hands of the grandfather clock in the corner slowly count down the minutes until he could safely withdraw with Ruth and escort her home.   They had a short period of time alone together as Adam replenished her glass of punch.

She smiled up at him. 'I am afraid we'll need to leave near the end, Adam, or we will again have company on the way home.'

Eventually, Matthew Draper left.   Robert shook Adam's hand and left shortly afterwards. Ruth and Adam bade farewell to their hosts and the remaining guests. Adam was sure his unease would be obvious to all present, but no one felt the need to question him escorting Ruth home, when a very obvious escort, her brother, had left barely 10 minutes earlier. They had company to the edge of the settlement, but eventually found themselves alone as they approached the stile. Adam helped Ruth over and passed her the lamp he had brought from his home earlier in the evening. She set it upon the top of the wooden post, illuminating both their faces.

'Adam, you sell your credentials too low. You're highly respected in this settlement. I'm honoured that you've asked me to be your wife. When I've imagined a proposal of marriage I've always thought it would be from someone I knew less well, as propriety usually dictates. The situation here is very unusual. It is almost like receiving a proposal from Robert. You've always been such a close friend, in effect, like a brother. If we were to marry there would be few surprises for either of us. Are you really sure this is what you want?'

'It is, Ruth. I've also found our close friendship for many years to be a confusing factor. I remember talking to Edmond Davies last Christmas and he told me that if your primary instinct in a relationship is to care and to give, rather than to receive, there is a good chance you would be happy and contented. That is how I feel about you. I want to care for you and share your love. As I said before, this is a harsh life and one that is better shared. The land alone would never support us, but we could do well with my fishing. Ocean fishing has its risks, but I've learnt well from Father and Francesco, and I am careful.'

'If you are sure, Adam, then I accept your proposal with great excitement and happiness. I shall enjoy working with you and caring for you. Friends will become lovers; we will rename this stile 'friends and lovers'. Do you have any plans for a possible date?'

'None but, as we already know each other so well, I see little need to delay.'

They had reached the path by Adam's house.

'Would it be too forward, given our changed relationship, if you visited me and had a drink to celebrate our decision? We could also try to choose a date for the wedding.'

'Believe me, Adam, I'm no prude, but I suggest you walk on to my house; there are few secrets in the village. May I share our news with Robert tonight?'

'Of course, I only hope he approves.'

'I think you'll find he is very enthusiastic, he has always held you in great affection.'

As they approached Robert was sitting on the verandah, smoking a pipe.

'Brother, you are to congratulate Adam on his singular good fortune; the most eligible young lady in Prosperous Bay has graciously consented to marry him.'

'Would that be Emma or Dorothy Lloyd, dear sister, or has Adam decided to take on both those vintage ladies?'

'Robert, you are a disgrace. Adam will think we're full of uncharitable thoughts about the Lloyds. He has proposed to me and I've accepted.'

Robert rose from his seat and kissed his sister. He seized Adam's hand and shook it firmly.

'I could not be happier for you both. You are ideally suited and it will be a pleasure to have you as a member of our family, Adam.'

'I've invited Adam back here, Robert, so that we might share the news with you directly and talk about a possible date for the wedding.'

'Come in, Adam, we have some port I picked up in Jamestown recently. Would you prefer me to leave you to yourselves for this discussion?'

'No, Robert, pour a third glass to toast us and help us with our thoughts on a date.'

Adam accepted a schooner of port and the marriage was toasted by the three friends.

Adam scratched his head. 'Where do you want to get married, Ruth, here or in Jamestown?'

'Here I think, Adam, but that means we will have to get the clergyman to come to us.'

'I agree it should be here. If you are happy with the wedding happening soon, I will sail over to Jamestown next week and ask who could officiate. I think they have to read the banns for about three weeks at their Sunday service. Are you happy for me to pick a date with the clergyman?'

'Yes, give me at least six weeks from today, Adam. I would like to make a new dress for the occasion. Should we keep our engagement secret until the wedding date is agreed?'

'I think so, Ruth. Robert aren't you due to preach the sermon next Sunday?'

'I am.'

'Perhaps you could announce the engagement and the wedding day, if I get the information I need from Jamestown next week?'

Robert smiled as he refilled their glasses.

'Yes, I'd like that. I will have to give particular thought to the theme of my sermon.'

Ruth turned towards him. 'Robert, if you stray anywhere near Matthew Draper's topic I'd be mortified.'

Robert brought his fingertips together, a mannerism used by Matthew Draper. He mimicked the farmer's Yorkshire accent. 'Brethren, it is at moments like this we should be aware of the risks of fornication and all the sins of the flesh. Temptation is all around us….'

Ruth groaned. 'Robert, please.'

Adam simply raised an eyebrow and growled at Robert.

Robert raised his hands in surrender. 'I'll be extremely discrete, dear sister, and will seek divine inspiration in the interval to ensure whatever I say will lift the congregation to greater spiritual awareness.'

Adam turned to his fiancée. 'Is he to be trusted, Ruth?'

'Probably, Adam, but I suggest we threaten him where we know he has a weakness, ocean fishing. '

'Of course, Ruth, I'd forgotten the only time he crewed for me several years ago. You're right. We could press gang him and take him far from the land, looking for mermaids.'

'You could not be so cruel?'

'If you embarrass your sister when our engagement is announced, I'd have to spring to her defence. You do want me to look after her interests, don't you?'

'My sister's wishes will be respected, Adam. I hope you two are not going to gang up on me in the future.'

'Only if you misbehave, brother.'

'Thank you for your hospitality, Robert. I will do everything I can to look after your sister.'

'I know you will, Adam. This is a very special day.'

Ruth followed him out onto the verandah. He held her in his arms. Both were exhilarated by the increased intimacy. Only a short while ago he had been looking at her profile from behind at the Sunday service, now his arms were around that slim waist. He kissed her on the lips. There was no tension between them. Her lips softened against his as she responded to the contact. He stroked her hair, an experience that he had been imagining for several months.

'Dear Adam, I look forward to an exciting new period of our lives. Go now, but I will walk with you and Robert to church tomorrow and then please come back here for lunch. Next week we will know when we can get a clergyman here for our wedding.'

The fisherman floated home in euphoric mood. He poured himself a glass of rum and sat on his verandah in the dark, thinking of the exciting times ahead.

Adam was standing on the cliff path the following morning when Robert and Ruth joined him on their journey to the church. He kissed his fiancée and they walked on into the settlement. On this occasion all three sat in the same pew and he revelled in the opportunity to sit by her side, close enough to appreciate the scent of her perfume. If any of the congregation noticed the change in

Adam's position, they did not comment. The trio chatted to the congregation in the square after the service and then walked back up the hill.

'So, Adam, would you care to give us your opinion on the quality of today's sermon?'

'I'm sorry, Robert, I really can't remember what was said. I was thinking of other things I must admit.'

'I hope it was not the sins of the flesh, my friend. Should I ask Matthew Draper to pray for your soul?'

'Robert, sometimes you go too far. I know we are all friends, but that is outrageous. Show Adam more respect and, come to think of it, also your sister.'

'He should make lunch, by way of penance, Ruth.'

'I fear we'd be the ones who'd suffer, Adam.'

'Apologies, sister, and to you, Adam. I will rein in my humour and I'm sorry if I've caused offence.'

Adam laughed. 'None taken, Robert, and I probably deserve it after last week's comments to you about yearning after some of your animals. However, in future, I will have to protect my fiancée's reputation and the threat of an ocean cruise for you is not forgotten.'

Ruth laughed. 'Consider yourself chastised, Robert. I will do the cooking but you'll do the washing up!'

'Yes, sister.'

The day passed easily; a lazy lunch followed by a leisurely walk on the headland. At Black Point they sat on the cliff overlooking the Sentinel rock, which shone brightly in the sunlight.

On the Tuesday that followed, Adam and Francesco set sail at four in the morning in the hope of catching sufficient fish early to justify a trip to Jamestown. The wind blew steadily from the north. The catch was plentiful and by late morning they had rounded Barnlong Point, close hauled and then travelled west with Sugarloaf Point off the port bow. They made swift progress and there was

25

no need to tack. Buttermilk Point was passed shortly afterwards at the northern tip of the island and Adam swung the tiller to port, allowing the lugger to cross Rupert's Bay and on to Jamestown, running before the wind. They did swift business with the only frigate re-provisioning in the bay before mooring at the wharf to sell more of the catch.

Adam had not told Francesco about his marriage plans, preferring to wait until there was a definite date and he had Ruth's agreement to share the secret. He excused himself with a need to visit the ship chandlers in town and left Francesco selling the fish on the quay. He went to the house of the Governor of the colony and sought the advice of the secretary. The Governor had arrived in Jamestown two years previously as a consequence of the island transferring from the ownership of the East India Company to the Crown. Adam had not met the Governor but he knew the official had a reputation for being ill tempered, abrupt and lacking in courtesy. The secretary was helpful. Jamestown had no church, but the naval squadron and the civil administration shared a Church of England vicar who had come out with the Governor's staff.

The Reverend Wilkes was summoned and escorted Adam to the garden for refreshments. Adam instantly liked the man. He was small, slim and enthusiastic, with a ready smile.

'You're the fisherman our cook prefers to buy from on the quay. She distrusts the local fishermen and is never happier than when your boat is sighted in the bay.'

'I never realised some of our catch was coming to the Governor's residence. Is she a fairly substantial lady of mixed race?'

'That sounds like Sarah, she chooses all the provisions that come to the kitchen and looks after us extremely well. I'll take you to the kitchen when our business is done and you can see if she needs any fish today, assuming you have brought a catch to the quay?'

'We have. My partner is selling our catch at present. I wanted to speak to you today about another matter. I proposed to a lady in Prosperous Bay a few days ago and she has accepted my offer. We would like to get married in the settlement's community hall in two or three months' time and hoped you might be able to officiate. We don't have a chapel, I'm afraid, but we do hold regular Sunday services in a community hall.'

'Don't worry about it, Adam; there isn't a proper church in Jamestown either. Most of our services are in the marine barracks, or in what has recently been called the Governor's ballroom; it is simply the largest room in the residence. I would be happy to officiate. How easy is it to get to Prosperous Bay?'

'I was thinking about that on the way this morning. Are you a good sailor?'

'I coped with the journey out here, Adam, and the weather was pretty wild on occasion.'

'In that case, I suggest my sailing partner transports you in both directions. At this time of year the seas are usually calm and the winds allow both journeys with the minimum of tacking. My wife to be would like a Saturday wedding in six weeks or more, so she can make a dress and sort all the arrangements.'

'I'm honoured to be asked, Adam. I have never been to Prosperous Bay and I like the idea of coming by sea. I've never seen the northern and eastern parts of the island.'

'Prosperous Bay is not as well-endowed as its title may suggest; I suspect it was named by sailors who compared it to the arduous life at sea! If Francesco, my partner, picked you up on the quay fairly early on the Saturday morning,

27

we could have you in our community for a noon wedding and we would want you to stay for the celebrations afterwards. Would you consider staying the night? If you left early on the Sunday, Francesco could have you back on the quay by noon at the latest?'

'That's excellent, Adam. It will be a chance for me to get to know the people in your settlement. I am keen to set aside some Sundays in the year for visiting outlying communities, if they feel the need for my services. I had not thought about it before but most of the settlements are most easily accessed by the sea.'

They settled on a Saturday in eight weeks' time.

'You'd better come to my office, Adam, and I will write down all the details.'

'It's Adam Fletcher and Ruth Morgan; both of Prosperous Bay.'

'I will read out the banns here, with the date we have agreed, at the next three Sunday services and bring the forms to sign with me on the day. We can sign the register in Jamestown sometime after you are married. I'm sure your boat is seaworthy, but I dare not risk taking the register on the ocean.'

'I understand, Mr Wilkes. Can I meet with you again in perhaps a month to finalise arrangements?'

The Reverend strode into the kitchen speaking in mock serious tones. 'Now then, Sarah, I've had complaints from a passing fisherman who says you've not been buying enough of his fish recently.'

Recognising Adam, she beamed at the Reverend. 'That's not true, Mr Wilkes, I only wish he would visit Jamestown more often.'

Adam shook hands with the portly cook. 'Sarah, I'd not realised you cooked at the Governor's Residence; I didn't know our fish was destined for such an exalted table. I'd prefer to make the visits on set days of the week, but that is not possible. A visit depends on a good catch by late morning and that can never be predicted. Would it help if I sent a boy up to the Residence when we arrive, to let you know we have fish on offer?'

'It would, Mr Fletcher. The Governor runs a large establishment here and the supply of quality meat is always limited. If you have completed your business with the Reverend, I'll walk back with you to quay.'

Adam turned to the cleric. 'Perhaps it would be sensible if you did not meet Francesco today, I have not told him of our plans; only Ruth's brother has been told so far and he will announce it at our service on Sunday. If Ruth agrees, I'd plan to tell Francesco and his wife during the week. They are my closest friends and the secret would be safe with them until Sunday. When we meet in a months' time, it would be helpful if you could come down to the quay to inspect my boat and its Captain for your trip!'

'I shall look forward to that, Adam.'

They parted on the steps of the Residence and Adam and Sarah walked to the quay.

CHAPTER THREE

They drew clear of Jamestown, but on this occasion close hauled to the wind travelling as far northwards as the wind would allow, until Buttermilk and Sugarloaf Points were astern on the starboard quarter. Adam then brought the boat about and they sailed east. There were still four hours to dusk and they were content to proceed slowly with the fishing lines rebaited, which produced a modest return for sale in the settlement.

When the final fish were sold, he walked up the path to his house. A fish stew simmered on the kitchen stove. Dinner would have to be delayed. He showered and changed and walked on to the Morgan's house in the dusk. Ruth and Robert greeted him on the porch.

'Did you manage to get to Jamestown, Adam?"

'Yes, the day has gone well. I met the Governor's chaplain. He'll come to the settlement and officiate. We settled on a date seven Saturdays from now. I have not discussed it with Francesco, but the plan at present is that he will pick up the Reverend Wilkes early on the Saturday morning from the quay at Jamestown, to be at Prosperous Bay well before a noon service in the Community Hall. He will stay overnight and then Francesco can take him back on the Sunday. You'll like him, Ruth; he's keen to make links with the outlying settlements and is probably open to leading three or four Sunday services each year.'

Robert poured them a schooner of port and they moved on to a discussion of the arrangements for the day.

'Would you be kind enough to accommodate Reverend Wilkes, Robert, on the Saturday night? You'll find him good company.'

'Of course. Francesco can tell me when he wants him down on the beach on the Sunday morning.'

Ruth placed some slices of fruit cake on a plate and offered one to Adam. 'Have you told Francesco about our marriage?'

Adam's reply was delayed by his first bite of the fruit cake. 'No, I told him I was visiting the ship chandlers and he seemed satisfied with that. Would you mind if I told him sometime during the week and asked him whether he would look after the Reverend Wilkes's transport?'

'Of course, Adam, I'm sure we can count on his discretion until Robert's announcement on Sunday. Let him know he can share the secret with Carmella. If she had the time, it would be nice if she could come for tea. I would like her to help me with the arrangements. I have most of the materials I need for my dress, but a visit to Jamestown would be helpful, perhaps with Carmella to offer a second opinion.'

'Would you be happy going by boat?'

'I'd love to. I think we'd have to leave that trip until after the announcement. If the pair of us set sail for Jamestown with both Cerusos, the whole settlement would know something was afoot. Any time in the next three weeks would be suitable, Adam; it would still leave me time to complete my dress.'

Adam told Francesco the following morning when they were far out to sea, with the island low on the horizon. The fishing lines had been baited and laid to eight fathoms. They ate their lunch as the lugger moved slowly under reefed sails.

'Adam, that's great news. Can I tell Carmella? She'll be very excited. I promise you your secret will go no further. I hope there'll be a good attendance at church when Robert makes the announcement.'

'Yes, tell Carmella. I know you'll be very discrete. If she has the time, Ruth would like her to visit for tea and help with the arrangements. She would also like to visit Jamestown with Carmella, looking for some extra fabrics and I suggest the four of us sail round sometime soon after the announcement has been made.'

Francesco laughed. 'Perhaps I should be taking you to look for a new suit at the same time, Adam. There'll be no problem looking after the clergyman. If I picked him up from Jamestown quay at 8 o'clock, we'd have plenty of time to reach Prosperous Bay, but I have no doubt the ladies will insist on an earlier start and I suggest we settle on seven in the morning. Do you think that will be too early a start for him?'

'No, Francesco, he is a very agreeable man and keen to see the island from the sea so I'm sure he won't object. I have to see him again in a month to make final arrangements and would like to bring him to the quay at Jamestown to see the lugger and meet the Captain for his visit.'

Maria had been with her mother to greet them on the beach and Francesco had made no mention of the impending wedding. Adam returned to his house and showered, aware a lamb stew awaited him on the stove. As he returned to the kitchen, he heard the sound of voices from the porch. He opened the door to find the two Cerusos holding an animated conversation under the porch lantern. Francesco passed him a bottle of rum and raised his arms helplessly.

'I'm sorry, Adam, Carmella refuses to wait until tomorrow to congratulate you and insisted on coming up tonight to hear all the details.'

An exuberant Carmella burst in to the room. 'I'm delighted for you, Adam, and it's an excellent decision. I have always hoped you would marry. Now tell me all the details.'

Adam winked at Francesco. 'There's not a lot to tell, we've just decided to get married.'

'Not a lot to tell! There's everything to tell. Start with the proposal; when did you ask her to marry you?'

Adam ushered Carmella to a seat. 'There is an opened bottle of rum in the kitchen, Francesco; you know where the glasses are. It seems this cross examination may take a while.'

Adam responded to her questions while Francesco poured drinks for the trio.

'She would like you to visit for tea, Carmella, and help her with the arrangements.'

'Of course, of course.'

Adam could see that Carmella was now surveying the room with a critical eye. She went over to the windows and drew the curtain fabric through her fingers.

'Hmm, there is more to consider than the wedding arrangements.'

She walked to the old stuffed armchair and with her finger traced the multiple cracks in the surface of the leather.

'Adam, this house is fine for a bachelor, but you can't bring a bride in here until it's refurbished. I keep it clean but Ruth will expect furnishings that match and that are in better condition than these.'

'Carmella! That chair is Adam's favourite. I am afraid, Adam, this is what happens when you propose – your whole world is turned upside down.'

'I understand, Carmella. Tell Ruth, when you see her that the pair of you are invited to inspect my house and draw up a list of changes she would like to make. However, it would be nice to be involved in the decisions.'

Francesco chuckled. 'Oh dear, Adam, there is much that you'll need to learn. The contribution wives require from you will be to nod your head in agreement and to pay!

Sunday morning found Adam sitting on his porch looking out for Ruth and Robert. There was no wind and the sea was calm with the sound of small waves lapping against the rocks at the base of the cliffs. The Morgans appeared on the cliff path; greetings were exchanged and they walked down the path to the settlement. The community hall was well filled; Robert was a popular preacher. Francesco and Carmella escorted Maria into a pew near the back.

As the second hymn came to a conclusion, Robert stepped up to the lectern. Adam wondered how Robert would announce their plans for marriage. Robert's opening sentences gave no clue of an impending marriage. However, he had chosen a topic which could be linked to the sacrament of marriage; a sermon on the importance of charity. There were numerous children in the congregation and he focused his sermon on the younger members. He spoke of the cycle of charity which so commonly occurs in life; to give is to receive. He drew on the example of Lucy Davies's school, where the young'uns were looked after by the old'uns when they first attended and were the beneficiaries of their kindness and friendship. As time went on, the role would be reversed and they were expected to give what they had previously received. He took the children through to adult life and how the community of Prosperous Bay depended on the skill and kindness of those around them. Farmers provided food but needed the services of Shaun Murphy, the local blacksmith. Matthew provided meat and vegetables but needed Adam Fletcher's skill to provide fish. None could live without the support of the others. Mutual support was seen at its best on a personal level; the sacrament of marriage, where a man and a woman came together to combine their skills and attributes for the creation and protection of a family.

Adam glanced at Ruth, her cheeks had coloured slightly. Both hoped the theme of procreation would not be developed much further. To their relief, Robert's sermon was almost run.

'The prospect of a marriage in a small community, such as ours, is always an important milestone. It is an investment in the future of the settlement; two young people linking their lives to a common future, and to the village in which they live. A marriage in the settlement is always to be celebrated by us all. I am pleased to announce that my sister Ruth has accepted Adam Fletcher's proposal of marriage. They are to be married at noon on the third Saturday in May by a Reverend Wilkes, who is the chaplain to the Governor General. Reverend Wilkes has kindly agreed to come to the settlement to officiate at the marriage. If we wished in the future to have him visit occasionally to lead our Sunday services, he is open to the suggestion. I hope you'll all join us on this special day at the service and the reception afterwards. I've known Adam, as you all have, from his earliest years. I am delighted that our two families will be united by marriage.'

Spontaneous applause broke out in the hall with good wishes offered to the couple. Robert returned to his pew, shook Adam's hand and kissed his sister. The congregation sang the final hymn lustily, conducted by a smiling Edmond Davies. Ruth, Adam and Robert stood in their pew as the remainder of the congregation spilled out on to the square, awaiting their arrival.

'I hope you approved of my sermon, sister?'

'It was very good, Robert, and you wove the wedding very neatly into your theme.'

Adam laughed. 'I don't think your sister was quite so sure when you started talking about procreation, Robert.'

'Ah, yes, it was put in to keep you on your toes. You'd better get out there and mingle with the congregation. No doubt the Lloyd sisters will want to sell you a wedding dress at a discounted price.'

Adam was amused by the way in which the community tended to seek out their own gender to offer congratulations. Men would shake his hand and compliment him on his choice of bride, coupled with dire warnings of loss of independence. The ladies sought out Ruth to congratulate her on her choice, and then moved swiftly to the important matter of arrangements for the day. What would she wear, had she met the chaplain from Jamestown, what help would be required for the celebration that followed; wasn't it time her brother settled down and took a wife?

Maria and her parents held back until most of the congregation had dispersed to discuss the matter in smaller groups. The Lloyd sisters had, indeed, invited Ruth to their store to see the bolts of cloth that had come most recently from Jamestown. There would, of course, be special reductions for such an auspicious event. Finally, the Cerusos joined Adam and Ruth Morgan on the steps of the hall.

Maria, bursting with excitement, gave the couple a kiss. 'Do you know what you'll wear, Miss Ruth?'.

'I have an idea, Maria, which I'll share with you soon, if you can keep a secret?'

Carmella smiled. 'She can be relied on to keep a confidence.'

'But just as important, Maria, will be the question of what you will be wearing. Would you agree to be my bridesmaid?'

Maria nodded with enthusiasm but looked to her mother for her agreement.

Carmella smiled. 'That is most kind of you, Ruth.'

'Maria, I think you should come for tea with your mother to discuss what I'll be wearing and then we can decide the most appropriate dress for you, so that we both look our best.'

'Oh, Miss Ruth, I'd be honoured. May I go and tell my friends?'

'Of course, but when we have made our choices they have to remain a secret until we arrive in church. Do you think you could keep our plans a secret?'

'Yes, Miss Ruth.'

Maria ran to tell her friends.

'That's very gracious of you, Ruth, she'll be so excited.'

'She's a beautiful girl, Carmella, and I want your family to be part of our wedding. I'm very conscious of the fact that I'm joining Adam's family – you, Francesco and Maria. Would you also be my lady in waiting?'

'I'd be honoured, Ruth. It'll be a very special day for all of us.'

'Carmella, I know it's very short notice, but Adam is coming for lunch and I wonder if your family might join us. We could start our discussion on the arrangements and perhaps draw up a list of matters to be agreed.'

A swift glance at Francesco produced a nod of agreement. 'Of course, we'd be delighted. Would you excuse me for a couple of minutes?'

Carmella beckoned her daughter and they walked briskly in the direction of their house. Within five minutes, the Ceruso ladies had returned bearing a copper container, one the fishermen commonly took with them to hold soup for lunch. Maria had a small bouquet of flowers.

'It's not very original, Ruth, I'm afraid it's fish soup; a speciality of the house!'

They walked slowly up the path, delayed by frequent conversations with the householders on the way.

Eventually the village lay behind them and they crossed the stile.

'When can the four of us go to Jamestown, Adam? It would be nice if it could be soon.'

Adam did not reply. He was standing near the edge of the cliff looking out over the sea. Francesco walked over and stood beside him. Ruth was about to repeat the question, but sensed it was neither necessary nor appropriate. Adam was frowning and ill at ease.

'You've been sailing for longer than me, Francesco. What is it that makes me feel apprehensive?'

'You may be younger than me, Adam, but your instincts concerning the weather are better than mine. Something is wrong, that's for certain.'

Carmella whispered to Ruth. 'We will not be going to Jamestown early in the week. I've seen Adam like this before; it seems he can almost sense bad weather approaching. His father had the same instincts. They're nearly always right.'

Adam laughed. 'It looks the same as usual, but something is not right. Could we plan for Friday if the weather looks reasonable on the Thursday night?'

'Of course, Adam.'

Robert led the ladies towards the Morgan's house whilst Adam and Francesco were still looking out at the sea.

'How do you want to fish tomorrow, Adam?'

'A later start, and closer in, Francesco, even if the catch is poor. I can't put my finger on it, but something has changed out there. The sea and the clouds look normal, but there's a feel to the air that disturbs me.'

Lunch passed easily after which the men returned to the porch with their glasses of port, while the ladies laid plans for the wedding. As the light began to fail, the group broke up and Adam and the Cerusos retraced their steps along the cliff path.

The fishermen met at the boat the following morning with the sun already risen. Carmella came with her husband to help move the boat the short distance to return it to the ocean.

'Do you still have the same feelings you had yesterday on the cliff path, Adam.'

'Yes, Carmella. I still can't explain my concern and nothing has happened overnight. We don't plan to go more than a couple of miles out from the bay. There is sometimes a good area to fish beyond Black Point and we'll probably try there. If there is any sign of trouble we'll be able to run downwind, back to the beach.'

Carmella stowed the copper canister of soup and the fresh bread in the covered area of the bow. She then stood with Adam in the water, her skirt wet up to her thighs, as they turned the boat with the stern facing the beach. Francesco was raising the sail as Adam and Carmella pushed the boat towards the open sea. Carmella released her grip and Adam climbed into the stern.

'Good luck, Adam. '

'Don't worry, we'll be careful.'

The breeze was gentle and the sea calm. 'I think we'll need the sails unreefed today, Francesco.'

They gave the Sentinel a wide berth in the light winds and sailed north and east, aiming for an area of the sea two miles off Barnlong Point. Francesco baited the lines.

'Would you prefer I shortened the lines to four fathoms, Adam?'

'Yes, that should be a good depth, Francesco.'

The lines were laid to the agreed depth and the sails remained un-reefed. The fishermen would normally sit and talk or carry out simple maintenance tasks before lunch. Francesco noted Adam was restless, standing in the centre of the boat.

'What is it, Adam?'

'I don't know. The hairs on the back of my neck feel as though they're standing up. Visibility has dropped a bit to the north, but otherwise it all looks normal. It's in the air, Francesco. I don't know what it is, but it's in the air.'

His glance fell on the brass plate of the tabernacle that supported the base of the mast. Moisture glistened on what was usually a shining surface.

'Not the right time of the day for dew, Francesco. Reel in the fishing lines, I'm taking her back to the beach.'

Adam's decision came too late. The gentle breeze died, visibility began to fall and the Sentinel was lost to view. By the time Francesco had retrieved the lines and coiled them away, the fishermen could barely see ten feet beyond the boat. Dew lay on every surface and dripped off the limp sails. They put on waterproof jackets.

'Francesco, I know we wouldn't expect it in fog but are the waves increasing in size?'

Francesco delayed his response for a couple of minutes. 'Definitely, I think I experienced something like this with your father many years ago. He said distant storms far out in the ocean can sometimes cause waves to spread very widely.'

'Let's take the sails down, Francesco. All they are doing is collecting water.'

When all the sails were stowed they returned to the stern, sitting with the passive tiller between them.

'This is a very bad combination of events. We are becalmed, but are still subject to the strong currents which are taking us towards the south and towards the shore.'

'To the Sentinel?'

'Precisely. If we strike the Sentinel with waves this size, we'll be destroyed. We can only move the boat by rowing. We've no terms of reference and are as likely to row into the Sentinel as away from it. Rest for now, Francesco. Give me a small amount of soup and bread. We'll need to conserve our supplies. I'll take the first watch. If I shout a warning, we'll not have long to try to save ourselves and the boat.'

They unlashed the oars and inserted the heavy brass rowlocks into the gunwale, so that they could start rowing at the first hint of danger.

Sometime later, Adam softly called Francesco. Within seconds the Italian had joined him in the stern.

'Have you seen anything, Adam?'

'No, but I do have something to report. I wasn't sure at first because the sound was very faint, but there is no doubt about it, I'm afraid. We have company. Somewhere in this impenetrable fog, there is another ship; perhaps a whaler or from the West Africa Squadron. They're ringing their bell every few minutes.'

'What direction?'

'I've tried to work it out, but it's impossible to tell. However, there is no doubt, the ship is getting closer. If it's a naval ship, their tall masts may mean it is still responding to the rudder. We've quite enough problems already without the risk of being run down by the Navy!'

The hours passed slowly, the swell increased and the bell gradually became louder. Francesco stood lookout at the bow, Adam at the stern. Even that short distance was partly obscured by mist, heavy with moisture. As the day wore on they retreated to the centre of the boat, sitting back to back staring into the impenetrable fog. It was easy to imagine half formed images of a ship or the Sentinel, only to find they disappeared in a bank of fog. Was it a little darker over there? Could it be the bows of a ship or the Sentinel's smooth rock face? And still the bell got louder. They had tried to hail the ship, but had got no reply and felt the sounds were likely soaked up by the mist.

Exhausted by the false alarms, Francesco failed to see the danger when it eventually came. Adam could feel his partner's back tense. He heard Francesco cry out in fear.

'God in heaven, Adam, all is lost.'

They stumbled to their feet and Adam turned to find Francesco dropping to his knees and crossing himself repeatedly. He was looking high above the bow. Suspended above them in the mist, stood a huge, stern, bearded man with his right arm outstretched.

CHAPTER FOUR

Adam seized an oar and stumbled to the bow.

'It's a man of war, Francesco, I'll try to guide us to one side of the bow. As soon as you have room, run out your oar and keep us clear of her side.'

As he spoke, the bow of the warship appeared through the mist on a collision course, slightly to the starboard of the lugger's bow. He braced his legs against the gunwale and laid the tip of the oar in a graze to the warship's bow. The pressure rose, the lugger tilted, but the massive bow, surmounted by the stern, unseeing figurehead, continued its remorseless advance.

'Help me, Francesco, I cannot hold her.'

Francesco joined Adam at the oar, on which their lives depended. The force increased and the bow of the man of war rose high above them in the mist. The oar began to bend. A voice above them cried out.

'Fishing boat under the starboard bow.'

Slowly the lugger began to swing to port and the pressure on the oar eased.

'I think I can handle it now, Francesco. Push off with your oar and then start rowing as soon as you have sea room.'

They heard the sounds of raised voices and running feet above them.

'We mustn't lose them, Francesco, they're in as much danger as we are. We stand a better chance together.'

A voice cried out from above. 'Ahoy in the fishing boat. Secure the rope and we'll draw you to the accommodation ladder.'

As he spoke, a rope fell across the boat and they were drawn aft to the narrow wooden steps that led to the deck.

'Secure the oars, Francesco, then come up and join me.'

Adam climbed the steps to the deck to be greeted by an officer. 'I'm Jason Hewitt, first officer of Her Majesty's Frigate, Intrepid.'

'Yes, I thought I recognised the figurehead, although it scared the life out of my crewman, when it appeared above us out of the mist. I'm Adam Fletcher, fisherman from Prosperous Bay.'

'Was your boat damaged in the collision?'

'No, we managed to fend your bow off and were clearing your side when you threw us the rope.'

'Do you know where we are?'

'I have an approximate idea of our position, because we've been in the mist only for the last few hours. We've been becalmed, but I fish these waters regularly and I'm aware of the effects of the current and the danger we're in'.

'The Captain needs to hear this. We've been fogbound and becalmed for three days. We've not been able to make a reckoning with the sextant and we're uncertain of our position. Aren't you a long way from the coast for such a small boat?'

'That's the problem, Mr Hewitt, you're a lot closer to the coast than you realise.'

They reached the door of the captain's cabin. The marine came to attention and stood aside. The captain rose from his desk and shook Adam by the hand.

'Captain Thomas Pickford at your service, Sir. I hope there were no injuries to your crew or damage to the boat?'

'Thank you, no, Captain, we managed to fend the bow off. There is no damage.'

'This is Mr Adam Fletcher, Sir, a fisherman from Prosperous Bay. He's only been fog bound for a few hours and has valuable information about our approximate position. He says we are not north of St Helena.'

'You are not, I'm afraid. We sailed from Prosperous Bay this morning. There had been something odd about the weather for the last couple of days, but I couldn't put my finger on the cause. I chose not to go too far out for that reason. Do you have a chart so I can explain?'

They stood around the captain's desk as a chart of the waters around St Helena was unrolled.

'When the mist came down, perhaps six hours ago, we were here. We've had no wind at all and have been at the mercy of the current since. They're exceptionally strong on this side of the island. As you probably know, the main drift is to the north but the promontory at Saddle Point or the contours of the seabed produces a counter current, and there's a very powerful north to south flow in this area. Any becalmed boat is carried remorselessly in this direction.'

'To Black Point?'

'Yes, Captain. There's a large black rock called the Sentinel, which lies just off the cliffs. The current from the north flows past it swiftly on both sides. At present I'd estimate our vessels lie here, almost two miles from Black Point and the Sentinel.'

'No chance that we'll miss it and pass to the south?'

'I doubt it, Captain. I thought Francesco, my crew and I would be lost if the fog did not lift. We could row, but we have no compass and ran the risk of rowing towards the rock, rather than away.'

'Will soundings warn us of our proximity to the cliffs?'

'No, Captain, nor can you drop anchor until the visibility and breeze have improved. It's the volcanic nature of the island; the bottom falls away very steeply in this area. You would get no warnings with soundings.'

'What if I use the longboat, the cutter and the gig and try and tow her off to the east?'

'It's the best chance.'

'Can I commandeer your lugger?'

'Of course, it's built for two pairs of oars, but I would imagine you could improve on that.'

The captain turned to his first officer. 'Jason, get the boats into the water, lines to the bow. Fetch the carpenter, I want a green light and a red light erected at the bow, so that the boats can see them. The green lantern should be 5 feet in front of the red – the longboat to take the middle position, keeping red behind green; the gig on the starboard, so that the green is to be kept on the right of the red, the cutter to port keeping the green to the left of the red. Mr Fletcher's boat is to follow the longboat. If the visibility gets any worse we'll call directions to the lugger and the rest will have to follow instructions from there. Take charge of the longboat yourself with good men in charge of the others. Explain the situation to the crew; they need to know they're rowing for their lives.'

The first officer left as a wiry, grey-haired seaman appeared by the door.

'Bates, go down to the lugger. How many rowing positions can you create swiftly?'

They walked back to the accommodation ladder. Francesco was on deck and stood by the rail. He wore a sea coat and sipped a steaming mug, which he cradled in both hands.

'Forgive me, Mr Fletcher. Call Jacob, - some refreshment and a coat for our guest.'

Adam had not had time to inspect the ship when he had arrived. The sails hung limply, the tops of the masts lost in the gloom. There was feverish activity as the three boats were swung out and lowered into the water. Boat crews assembled and tow lines were prepared at the bow. Lamps were being secured to spars and erected as the captain had instructed. The carpenter reappeared from below.

'Whatever you do, it has to be quick, Bates.'

Word clearly had travelled fast through the frigate and four seamen had appeared carrying a bag of tools and sections of wood. The carpenter turned to them.

'Get six brass rowlocks. We need two saws and a couple of augurs. We can bore extra holes in the gunwale for the rowlocks and bring planks for additional thwarts for the sailors to sit on when they're rowing.

He turned to Adam. 'I think I can put in six extra rowing points; it should not damage the structure of the boat, Sir.'

'Do what you need to do, Mr Bates.'

Two of the carpenter's mates had already disappeared over the side. The Captain turned to the First Officer.

'Six extra oars over here, Jason, and we need twelve seamen. May I suggest, Mr Bates commands the lugger and four of its crew are the carpenter's mates? They can start to create the new rowing positions as the boat gets into position. Mr Fletcher, would you mind if you and your crew member remain on deck with me; when it comes to endurance rowing these men are the best that there are, and there will not be much room down there.'

Jacob, the captain's servant returned with a ship's cloak and a tray with two steaming mugs of coffee.

'As you wish, Captain.'

'Thank you, Jacob.'

'Captain Pickford, may I introduce Francesco Ceruso to you. He's also fished in these waters for many years with my father, before we lost him to fever several years ago.'

'Mr Ceruso, your partner warns me of the risk of foundering on a rock nearby.'

'It's true, I'm afraid. Without wind, the currents will take us to Black Point and, even if we avoid Black Point, we would strike the Sentinel. To be safe we have to clear the Sentinel.'

'We plan to try and tow her clear; I can only hope your warning has come in time!'

The deck was quiet except for a group of sailors at the bow paying out lines to the naval boats that were already moving to their stations. Two of the carpenter's mates reappeared with extra sections of planking and wooden blocks to support the extra seats. The heavy brass rowlocks were lowered down to the lugger in a leather sack. The second officer walked over.

'How do you want us to signal direction to the boats, Sir?

'Flags I think, George. Have one flagman by the compass, one amidships and one at the bow, two flags each. If they're crossed, it means we're rowing due east, as planned. Two flags to the right side mean we need to veer to starboard. Two flags to the left mean veer to port. If visibility gets worse, make sure Bates at least can see the flags. Tell him to pass the information on to the First Officer in the longboat ahead of him and the other boats will have to follow their direction.'

The lugger had cast off and they saw that eight sailors were rowing using four of the larger naval oars in the conventional positions. The carpenters worked fore and aft with brace and bit, creating new holes in the gunwale and strengthening the holes with wooden blocks. Seats for the new rowing positions were being created. Adam and Francesco walked with the captain to the bow. As they arrived, the crew on deck were tossing a thin line to the lugger. Once this had been secured, a thicker rope was paid out and passed through a pulley which had been attached to the stern. The rope then ran forward between the rowers and was attached to the base of the mast. The lugger lay in the centre of the inverted 'V' and beyond them the longboat could be seen indistinctly in the mist. To the starboard they could see the gig, somewhat closer to the frigate than the longboat, with the cutter in a similar position to port. Adam thought the mist must have lifted slightly and at present all four boats would have sight of each other and of the frigate that they were towing. There was little noise to be heard beyond the occasional urging from those in command of the boats. The flagman, on instruction, pointed both flags to the left. Slowly the tow lines moved to port, drawing the frigate towards an easterly direction.

The captain and Adam walked back to the wheel. By the time they reached it, the flags were crossed and the frigate was on a course that might save them from foundering.

'How long can they last at the oars, Captain?'

'Normally I'd not have them rowing for more than a couple of hours without a crew change, but I think we'll have to carry on to exhaustion here. Perhaps in two hours I'll get the gig back to ferry water and food for the other boats. Then we will change a few crew members if they are completely spent. I think the crew will understand the need for such hardship. Now I'm afraid, gentleman, we simply have to wait and see if we're delivered from your rock.'

Two hours later the gig was recalled and the lugger moved off to starboard to take up the gig's previous position. Lamps, water, food and relief crew members were ferried out to the three remaining boats. They found that the crew changes occurred with minimal disruption. The gloom slowly darkened into night; a constant stream of crew filed over to the ladder as the gig slowly replaced all the rowers. The returning sailors went below for more food and water and to rest. Two hours later the process was repeated. Francesco had volunteered to row in the lugger and had not yet returned to the ship. Adam's offer to row had been declined.

'No disrespect, Mr Fletcher, but your knowledge is better used here than your muscle out there. I have many stronger men but they do not have the local knowledge.'

Adam liked the captain. He was caring of his men and wore his authority loosely. All officers and crew responded to his orders swiftly and it was obvious that he was well respected.

The marine captain approached as his sergeant hovered close by.

'Captain, my men are not sailors, but they can row. Can I tell them to join the line?'

The captain smiled. 'You're right, Ben, it's their home too. I know the crew will appreciate their help; mix them with the sailors.'

The marine captain turned to his sergeant. 'Carry on, Sergeant; they're to leave caps, tunics and boots on board.' He turned to the captain. 'Permission to join them, Sir?'

'Yes, Ben, and thank you.'

Thomas Pickford watched the marine captain walk back along the deck removing his tunic, while a private carried his belt and sword.

'I'm fortunate, Mr Fletcher, with my officers. They know how to lead their men. Ben Doyle has only been with the ship for a year. They're now the best sections of marines I've ever had the pleasure to work with. There's often some friction between sailors and marines, but there's none on this ship. The sailors respect him greatly, as do his own men.'

'Adam, with your knowledge of the current, show me on the chart where you think we might be now.'

They walked back to the Captain's cabin and studied the chart. After a short pause Adam pointed to the map.

'Eight hours ago, there's absolutely no doubt where my lugger lay.'

There were some thin wooden spills on the dresser that were used for lighting lamps. Adam took one and broke off the tip, placing it in the position he had indicated.

'At the time we arrived under your bow, I estimate we would have drifted to here.' The position he indicated with the second fragment of spill was less than two miles to the east and north of the Sentinel.

'I think that'll be fairly accurate, as we were becalmed and the only force acting on us will have been the current, which is very strong and predictable in terms of its drift.' He paused. 'I estimate it took about half an hour for your orders for towing to be actioned and that would place both of us here.'

He laid the third sliver of wood a little closer to the Sentinel. Adam took another spill from the dresser. He laid the remains of the first spill in an east west alignment and laid the fresh spill in a direction that was between west and south. 'This final spill indicates the direction of the current. What speed do you think we're making?'

Thomas Pickford frowned. 'It's difficult to say, we've been due a refit for a year. We've a lot of weed on the hull, which will create drag – perhaps one, or at best two, knots. I had not realised the current took us so far west as well as south.'

The captain studied the position of the spills on the chart and then looked up.

'If its two knots, we'll just pass west of the rock; if it's one knot we'll founder.'

They returned to the deck. The marines were returning from their quarters wearing only shirts and trousers. There was good humoured banter as the sergeant shared them through the line of sailors waiting to be ferried out to the boats. The marine captain laughed at a remark they could not hear.

'Yes, sailor, we do know which end of the oar to hold!'

The captain laughed. 'We'll need a bit of humour, Adam, I think we're all going to be tested to the very limit.'

The night seemed to go on forever. No one felt the need to sleep. The early good humour was replaced by a quiet, grim determination to save their ship. The captain paced the deck and passed the message out that the price of salvation for the ship was a speed of two knots. The gig continued to ferry the crew and marines to their boats for the two hour sessions at the oars. By the end of the middle watch, Adam thought he could hear the sound of surf on rocks and in the predawn gloom there was no doubt they were closing with the land. The fog appeared to be getting thinner and the lamps on the boats were seen more clearly. As the light increased, the crew knew their efforts had not yet delivered them from danger. The gig was now permanently engaged in ferrying exhausted crew to and from the boats and the duration of rowing had been reduced to an hour. Visibility was slowly increasing. The crew members on board now remained on deck, reluctant to return to their quarters in the deeper reaches of the frigate. A look-out at the mast head cried out above them.

'Cliffs on the starboard beam.'

All hands looked to starboard, but nothing could be seen at deck level.

'Have you ever been up a warship's rigging, Adam?'

'No, Captain.'

'Please call me Thomas. If we're going to meet our Maker, we may as well be on Christian name terms. Perhaps you'll be able to recognise our landfall. We'll take two seamen to assist. Hold on tight and do not look down.'

The captain swiftly moved up the rigging at the base of the main mast to join the look-out. Adam climbed slowly and deliberately, following instructions from the seamen.

The mist slowly faded and when they reached the crosstrees he found Thomas Pickford astride the topgallant spar. Cautiously Adam joined him and then looked around. They were above the fog in faint early morning sunshine. The captain turned to face him as the look-out made space for the new arrivals.

'Well climbed, Adam. I don't think I really need to ask you this but are we where you predicted?'

'Yes, I'm afraid that is the Sentinel.'

The look-out crossed himself. 'I called it as soon as I saw it emerge from the fog, Captain. That's as evil looking a rock as I've ever seen.'

The captain nodded. 'Jet black and shining in the morning light, Adam, it almost looks like glass.'

'Yes, my crewman thinks it's a rock from hell. I once rowed up to the other side of it, in the lea of the current. It feels like glass and when I tried to chip a piece off, it just blunted the chisel. It's so smooth even weed does not seem to grow on it.'

'Adam, is the forward edge the position we need to clear?'

'Yes, it's a sheer face down to the water.'

The captain turned to one of the seamen who had accompanied Adam up the rigging.

'Daniel, replace Matthew up here. I want you to give me regular calls on our position relative to that rock. I estimate the forward edge of the Sentinel is a ship's length ahead of the bow at present. To be safe, it needs to be 20 feet past the stern.'

The seaman nodded.

'How far do you think we are from the rock?'

Adam tried to remember the size of the upper part of the Sentinel.

'Not too much more than a cable length, sir.'

'We'll keep the estimate in feet, Daniel, because we'll inevitably come up close. So you think, at best, 600 feet? What's your estimate, Adam?'

'Probably about 550 feet, Captain.'

'I agree. If we do not clear it, how long do you think it will be before we strike?'

'If it was my boat, and we remained becalmed, perhaps an hour.'

'This will be close run. Daniel, call down regularly with our distance from the rock. Call it in feet and also give me the position of its forward edge compared to the Intrepid.'

He turned to Adam. 'I'll go ahead back to deck, take it steady, don't look down and let these two help you.'

For Adam, the return to deck was a lot slower and confidence only grew when he started on the final section of rigging. The rock was again hidden in the mist. Jacob stood waiting for him. 'Captain's compliments, Mr Fletcher. He's taken command of the gig and they've taken up the fourth tow rope. He asks that you remain on deck and assist as you see fit. The boats will return to the port side of the frigate, if we don't clear the rock.'

Adam walked to the bow. The boats were closer together now and the captain stood at the stern of the gig, exhorting his men in all the boats. An older sailor in his boat was slumped over his oar exhausted. The captain lifted him from his seat and laid him in the stern. He took off his coat, wrapped it around the sailor and started to row.

Adam noticed several of the sailors in other boats were too exhausted to row. All the officers were now at the oars, the flagman on the frigate's bow was clearly in view. His flags were crossed. A voice from above called down.

'Rock edge at 250 feet, in line with the bow; a ships length to clear.'

A young junior officer, the most senior remaining on deck, relayed the information to the captain through a speaking trumpet. The weakened crew redoubled their efforts at the captain's bidding. Adam could see Francesco rowing with other sailors and marines. His head was bowed, seemingly oblivious to what lay beyond the confines of the boat.

'Pull hard, lads, you'll not need to row for much longer. Give everything you've got. The next few minutes will decide whether we still have a home, or we go back to rescue the remainder of the crew. There's only a ship's length to clear.'

Adam heard agitated voices from the cutter on the starboard station. The officer called across the water. 'We have surf in sight on the starboard quarter, Captain.'

All eyes turned to starboard and there was a hint of darkness to the texture of the fog. The seamen on the frigate watched helplessly while the Sentinel slowly revealed itself, as the mist thinned. Adam noticed that even the exhausted seamen had crawled back to their oars and the blades continued to rise and fall. The absence of the mist seemed to have made the sound of the surf, crashing on the rocks, even louder. At the frigate's stern, some of the crew were hastily lashing a spar to act as a fender, protecting the stern if they should fail by only a few feet. One team was creating a hole in the bulwark, close to the stern. Another team was setting up ropes and pulleys, linking the inboard end of the spar to the bulwark. The Bosun hoped they'd be able to generate enough force to hold the stern free of the rock for a few crucial minutes.

'Rock edge at one hundred feet, now lying amidships, Captain.'

A second hole was cut in the bulwark, twenty feet forward of the first and another spar was being made ready to act as a fender. Ropes were swiftly passed through blocks and lashed to the inboard end of the beam.

Captain Pickford called up from the gig. 'On deck, recall the lookouts, their job is done.'

The sailors worked in silence, in awe of the daunting sheet of shining black rock that reared above them. Adam walked towards the stern. All the remaining sailors were clustering around the two improvised fenders. He joined several on the forward fender; its tip protruded through a hole in the bulwark, extending two feet beyond the hull. It was capable of being run out to twenty feet when they closed to within that distance of the rock face. It was now easy to see the painfully slow forward progress obtained by the flotilla of small boats and compare it to the shrinking gap between the frigate and the cliff.

'Steady, lads, wait for my order then run out fast and pull for your lives. The spar will likely buckle and shatter but we need to get as much force on the ropes for as long as possible, in the hope we start to push the stern off the last few feet of the rock.'

Adam's mouth was dry. They were still moving forward but the gap between the rock and the frigate was narrowing rapidly. The Sentinel was now so close they all realised they would fail to clear the rock. To their surprise the sailing master at the wheel announced 'Captain on deck'. They turned to see Captain Pickford striding across the deck, barefoot, a trail of water leading back to the boarding ladder.

'What's this, Bosun?'

'It's not much, Captain, but it might help if we fail by only a few feet. I've taken two spare yard arms to act as fenders if the stern fails to clear the rock. Did you swim back, Captain?'

'Yes, the gig might just make the difference to our speed.'

The Bosun smiled. 'Good to have you back on board, sir, I think we're getting close to advancing the first spar if you're agreeable, Captain?

Captain Pickford moved to the rail. 'Leave it a minute, Bosun, I don't want to slow our forward motion. Fetch grease to apply to the end of the spars, it might just make a difference with the rock surface being so smooth. All men to the forward fender. Do you think the face is sheer below the waterline, Adam?'

'All the parts I've seen are sheer below the water line, Captain, but I can't speak for this section.'

'I think we'll have to gamble on that. Bosun, we'll wait until the boat is five feet from the cliff, that'll probably still leave us with thirty feet of stern to clear, and then it's all hands on the forward fender. I want a maximum effort to try and turn the bow beyond the rock slightly to starboard. We need the greatest force for the shortest time, or we'll lose our forward motion. Adam, tell the boats what we're doing and that they are to keep pulling, even if we seem to be slowing.'

Adam sprinted forward and delivered his message. He ran back down the deck as the order was given to run out the first fender. Every available seaman took up the slack and the fender slid forward and came in contact with the rock's smooth surface.

'Now, lads, everything you've got.'

The ropes narrowed under the massive load. The pulleys groaned and the end of the fender slowly moved across the rock with a screech of splintering wood. The bulwark to the stern of the yard arm buckled as the forward motion of the boat forced the fender towards the stern. The gap between the frigate and the Sentinel narrowed but they continued to move forward.

'Release the ropes lads, we'll get no more benefit from that one. If the bulwark is damaged any further we'll lose the missen mast shrouds; take up position on the second fender.'

The sailing master stood by the binnacle. 'It's had some effect, Captain; the bow has shifted one point to starboard.'

The captain clapped the Bosun on the shoulder. 'Your fender might just be the saving of us, Bosun.'

The forward edge of the rock lay twenty feet from the stern. The gap between the ship and the cliff had fallen to two feet and they could feel a coarse vibration indicating the starboard hull had made contact with the rock underwater.

'One final effort, men.'

The second fender engaged the rock and slowly moved along the cliff wall. The stern did appear to move further from the cliff and the vibration ceased.

'Hold it. Hold it.'

The massive pressures applied to the spar proved too great;' it shattered in mid shaft and the sailors fell as the ropes abruptly slackened. The sailing master's voice broke the silence.

'That's two more points to starboard, Captain.'

Thomas Pickford stood by the stern rail on the starboard side. There was still six feet of the Sentinel, to clear. Forward movement was slower and the vibration returned. He heard shouts from beyond the bow as Jason Hewitt exhorted the rowers to one final effort. Abruptly the vibration stopped and their speed increased. There was a final crash as the extreme edge of the Sentinel struck the stern, shattering the bulwark. They had passed the Sentinel and the frigate slowly drifted across its eastern face, free of further contact.

CHAPTER FIVE

'What now, Adam?'

'You've saved the ship, Captain. She'll drift into Prosperous Bay. It'll be wise to take soundings in about half an hour and you can then drop anchor.'

'Recall the boats, George, and get the cooks back into the galley. All officers to my cabin when the boats have returned. Bosun, come with me to check the hull, and start soundings of the bilges. I want to know if we're stoved in and taking water. Adam, please go to my cabin, I'll see you there shortly. '

The officers had all gathered by the time the Captain's inspection was complete.

'Jacob, open the best wine I have. Oh and while I think of it, invite Mr Fletcher's crewman to my cabin. No man rowed harder to save the Intrepid and I'll not forget it.'

He turned to the sailing master. 'When the ship's carpenter returns to the boat ask him to attend me in my cabin.'

The officers were all barefoot and, to a man, exhausted. Their hair was matted with dried sweat. None wore tunics beyond a senior midshipman who had been left on deck throughout. The captain waved away their apologies for the state of their undress.

'Excused, gentleman. Please be seated. Jacob has bowls of water to wash your hands and some oil for the skin. Rub it in gently, it'll help your hands to heal. Adam, would you assist Jacob? Your leadership, gentlemen, has saved our ship. Mr Fletcher advises me we'll now drift into Prosperous Bay; the sailing master will take soundings shortly and then anchor. We'll spend the next two days here. Jason, I want a full inspection of the hull; my cursory examination suggests we're not holed, but the hull needs to be properly inspected from within and without. The bulwark to the stern section on the starboard side will have to be replaced. For the moment we will leave the boats in the water.'

There was a discreet knock at the door and the ship's carpenter entered and touched his forelock in respect. 'Ah, Bates, thank your men for their swift actions altering Mr Fletcher's lugger. How much damage has been done to his boat?'

'It's not the way I'd want to hand it back, Captain. The extra rowing positions have damaged the gunwales, and the extra planking for the thwarts will only obstruct its normal use as a fishing boat.

The captain turned to Adam. 'Would you be agreeable to returning to shore in the gig and we'll return the lugger to you, say, tomorrow evening. Can you work to those timescales, Mr Bates?'

'Yes, Captain. I'd like to do a proper job. The changes were made in haste but it should be ready by tomorrow evening.'

Jacob moved between them with a tray of empty wine glasses as the captain followed with a decanter of wine. 'Take one, Mr Bates, we've much to celebrate. Let us raise our glasses; first to our home, HMS Intepid. '

All stood and returned the toast.

'And a second toast to our saviour, Adam Fletcher. He warned us of the danger and, but for his lugger, we would never have cleared the rocks. Without his warnings we would not have even reached the Sentinel but foundered under the cliffs of Black Point. It was only his knowledge of the strong current that has saved us.'

As they raised their glasses, Francesco walked through the door. 'Welcome, Mr Ceruso, thank you for all your efforts. Jacob has fresh water and ointment for your hands, although I dare say the skin of your palms is a deal thicker than those of my officers! I hope you will join us for some wine.'

A midshipman appeared at the door. 'Compliments from the sailing master, Captain. The sounding shows a depth of ten fathoms, Sir, and falling. The water level in the bilge is not rising.'

'Excellent, he is to drop anchor at eight fathoms.'

'Aye, aye, Sir.'

'Mr Ceruso, I have agreed with Mr Fletcher that we'll need to repair the damage we've done to the lugger. You will be taken to the shore in the gig and the carpenter assures me all the repairs to the lugger will be completed by tomorrow evening. The Intrepid will remain in Prosperous Bay for the next two days to allow the men to rest and to carry out repairs.'

The captain turned to Adam. 'Would you and your wives care to join us for dinner tomorrow night?'

Adam turned to Francesco. His friend raised his wine glass in agreement.

'Thank you, Captain. Francesco and his wife have a twelve year old daughter. Would it be acceptable for her to be included?'

'Of course.'

'I'm engaged to be married. My fiancée, at present, lives with her brother.'

'Both must come along. Perhaps you would gather on the beach at seven and the longboat will come to collect you. And now, I should imagine, you will want to return to shore. Jacob, more wine for the officers while I escort Mr Fletcher and Mr Ceruso to the gig.'

As they walked out onto the deck, they saw the lugger being lifted aboard and lowered onto the longboat's cradle. Francesco patted its bow as they walked past. He shook hands with the captain and climbed down into the gig. The captain turned to Adam.

'Adam, you've done good work here and I will be always in your debt. I look forward to seeing you all tomorrow night.'

'Until tomorrow, Thomas.'

Adam descended the accommodation ladder and they were rowed ashore.

A crowd had gathered on the beach. They had watched the frigate being towed past the Sentinel and had seen the damage to the starboard side. Carmella stood at the water's edge as the gig grounded on the sand.

'Adam, Maria has gone to Ruth's with news of your return.'

He could see both running back along the beach, pushing their way through the throng. The five hugged each other with relief at their safe return. Carmella cradled Francesco's blistered hands.

'You were right, Adam, the weather was a threat. The mist came down so swiftly here in the bay.'

'It was the same out at sea, Carmella. By the time I realised what the threat was, the wind had fallen and the mist had cut us off from sight of land. Intrepid nearly ran us down – they at least had the benefit of a compass. Even then, we nearly ended up under the Sentinel.'

'Is the lugger lost?'

'No, there's some damage, but the carpenters promise it'll be ready by tomorrow evening. Which reminds me, Francesco, do you want to tell your family about the social engagement for tomorrow night?'

Francesco laughed. 'Indeed. The Ceruso family are to be guests of Captain Pickford of the Intrepid, for dinner. We're to be on the beach by seven o'clock.'

'Me as well, Papa?'

'The captain asked me to bring along the most beautiful of my daughters.'

Carmella feigned anger. 'I'm hoping, husband, that you only have one daughter.'

Adam had his arm around his fiancée's waist. 'Ruth, the invitation includes you and Robert. Do you feel he will be able to come?'

'I'm sure he'll be honoured, Adam.'

Adam turned to Francesco. 'I think a bit of rest is required, my good friend. No boat and no fishing tomorrow. Rest your hands and we'll meet on the beach tomorrow at seven in the evening.'

Adam and Ruth strolled through the village hand in hand until they reached Adam's porch. His proximity to death had affected them both and they kissed with a passion neither had previously experienced or allowed.

'I have a stew and fresh bread at home, Adam. If you want to wash and change I'll bring it back for you, along with the laundry from last week.'

Adam stripped off and showered under the cool mountain water. When Ruth returned with his fresh clothes, she found him in the kitchen drinking a mug of watered down rum. His body was still wet and he had a towel around his waist. The air was charged with excitement. Both had been aroused by the risk of death and their earlier, passionate embrace. Ruth stood close to him, intoxicated by his muscular frame. Concern crossed her face as she noticed a broad scar that started high on his loin and extended below the upper margin of the towel. She slowly traced its ragged margins with her finger, from his loin to the towel.

'A fishing injury several years ago, darling.'

His voice was thick with emotion.

'Oh, Adam.'

Ruth was surprised by her boldness. She felt reluctant to remove her hand from his body. Adam closed the little gap that remained between them.   The morning had been oppressively hot in the settlement and Ruth had not been expecting company when Maria had brought her the news of Adam's return. She was only wearing a simple shift, tied loosely at the waist.   There had been no time to change when Maria had run up the path. Adam could feel her slim body beneath the thin material, first her waist and then more widely. He was kissing her passionately and she could feel her shift being drawn up towards her waist. She wanted to arch her back and press her breasts against his chest. Only a small towel and her thin shift lay between them and she wanted to be free of both but a lifetime of training, prudence and rectitude overrode her emotions and she blurted out.

'No, Adam.'

He recoiled, confused and embarrassed. 'I'm sorry, Ruth.'

Such a short statement but it had a profound effect. Spoken as a reflex to her upbringing but regretted as soon as it had been uttered. There were tears coursing down her cheeks. Adam thought he was witnessing fear and disgust at his behaviour but Ruth's distress was caused by her frustration at her own words, which threatened the one trait she feared her marriage might not offer – a passionate love. The moment was lost. Her natural reticence did not allow her to tell him she wanted to trace the scar beyond the top of the towel, to let the towel fall to the floor and to raise her hands above her head so he could free her of the shift. She wanted him to carry her to his bed, to love, and to be loved.

'I'm sorry, Ruth. It was wrong.'

A voice inside her cried out, it wasn't wrong – you might have died today; live as if each day is your last. Tell him, tell him what is in your heart. She could not find the words.

'Thank you for the clothes and the food, I'll go and get changed. Do you want to walk down to the beach together tomorrow evening?'

The tone was formal, borne of hurt and embarrassment; she felt dismissed.

'That would be nice, Adam.'

'Until tomorrow then, Ruth. I'm sorry for what happened.'

He dared not reach out to kiss her for fear he would be rejected. She felt she had created a barrier where none had been before. She walked to the door and up the cliff path with tears still streaming down her cheeks.

Adam slept poorly and could not settle to any activity. He went for a long walk, south along the cliffs to Bay Point and on further to Saddle Point. By six o'clock he was washed and dressed, sitting on his porch looking out over the sea.

Ruth had also had a troubled night rehearsing the words she wanted to share with Adam, to explain her feelings and her regret that she had destroyed a moment of passion that was wholesome and proper for them both. She had made a foolish error, based on previous rectitude and had failed to realise that what was correct in the past did not apply in their new relationship. In the morning she had tried to stitch the bodice of her wedding dress, but then worried he might no longer want to marry her, and put the material away. She went to his house with a carefully rehearsed speech, but he was absent. In the afternoon she rested, lying on her bed, but could not sleep.

'Robert, do you mind going down to the beach early and telling Adam, when you pass his house, that I will follow you and walk with him.'

'Of course. Is everything alright, sister?'

'Yes, Robert, it just allows some time to talk in private, which is always nice.'

She slowly walked down the path to Adam's house. He rose from his seat to greet her. Embarrassment and confusion had been replaced by a cautious civility. His first remarks threw her off her prepared speech.

'Ruth, do you still want to marry me?'

'Yes, Adam. Do you still want to marry me?'

'Yes. Can we consider that matter closed?'

'Do you feel it would be helpful to talk about it, Adam?' The little voice, inside her head shouted, *No, don't give him the choice; tell him your thoughts.*

'No, I was wrong and there is nothing more to be said about it.'

He offered her his hand but she knew a barrier still existed.

'We should set out for the beach.'

She walked alongside him on the cliff path in silence. She would find a time to tell him what lay in her heart; the right moment would surely come.

They joined Robert and the Cerusos on the beach. They had been under observation from the frigate and the longboat pulled clear and set course for the Captain's guests.

'Uncle Adam, will we have to wade out to the boat?'

'I'm not sure what they will do, Maria, but I have no doubt your father will carry his ladies to the boat to keep them dry.'

The settlers had been watching the activities on the frigate throughout the day. The shattered bulwarks had been replaced and sailors had hung from gantries over the starboard side of the stern, inspecting for damage and re-caulking and painting the grazed woodwork. The longboat grounded on the sand and the oars were raised. A gang plank was manoeuvred over the bow. The sailors were in their Sunday best and four sailors in bare feet ran nimbly down the plank to the sand. Jason Hewitt walked forward from the stern and down the plank to join them. Adam introduced Robert and the ladies, who were looking at the gang plank with apprehension.

'Do not fear ladies, our sailors will assist you; I will go first to demonstrate.'

A sailor stood on each side of the gangplank with a boathook. Jason walked back up the gangplank holding one of the boathooks for support.

'If you feel the need for support on both sides, ladies, it is available.'

Carmella went first, using one boat hook for support. Maria preferred two and Ruth followed her example. Robert, Francesco and Adam joined them in the longboat without needing help and they set off for the frigate.

The whole experience was novel for the ladies and for Robert. The deck of the frigate rose slowly to a daunting height as they drew up to the accommodation ladder.

'I know two of you are familiar with the ladder, but it is not suitable for the ladies in dresses.'

A boson's chair was lowered from above and Carmella was lifted to the deck as the two fishermen climbed the ladder, followed by Robert. The captain greeted them, with Jacob in attendance holding a tray of glasses filled with wine. Maria and Ruth joined them and, when the party was complete, Jason Hewitt followed them up the ladder.

'May I present my captain of marines, Benjamin Doyle. We shall repair to my cabin shortly but I thought you might enjoy refreshments on the deck with views of your settlement at sunset.'

The evening was mild and they enjoyed the officers' company as the sun set behind Diana's Peak.

'Ladies, would you mind if I take Adam and Francesco to inspect their lugger? Jason, Benjamin, if you would escort the ladies, we'll not be long.'

The captain and the fishermen walked to the cradle, which normally contained the longboat. The ship's carpenter and his mates stood close by.

'Mr Bates, can you show Mr Fletcher the changes you have made and what you've done to make them right.'

'Yes, Captain. As you know we put in two extra thwarts for our sailors to use, Mr Fletcher. Now they've been removed and there has been no damage to the hull. I was more worried about the holes we bored in the top rail for the rowlocks. We were concerned it might weaken the bulwark; the holes have been plugged and glued, but I felt it needed more support so we've used brass plates on the inside to add strength. Better not to touch, Sir, we've rubbed her down and given her a new coat of paint. It won't be dry before tomorrow.'

'Thank you, Mr Bates, she looks beautiful. I did not expect this.'

'On the contrary, Adam, thank you, from the whole crew for helping to save our ship. Take him to the stern, Mr Bates.'

Intrigued, Adam was led to the stern. Neatly painted above the rudder, in gold letters he read 'HMS Bountiful – Auxiliary Ship'. Captain Pickford explained.

'Adam, the officers have decided your vessel should become an honorary supply ship to the Queen's navy, for the provision of fish. All ships of the Squadron will recognise your naval pennant.'

Adam had not noticed his mast now sported a pennant. Adam and Francesco laughed.

'You're very generous.'

Adam peered inboard at the base of the mast. A hardwood box had been attached with brass fittings. The lid was held closed with a padlock.

'What's that, Mr Bates?'

'Captain's orders, Sir, for the secure storage of valuables at sea.'

The Captain did not elaborate. 'Adam, I know you sometimes stay out overnight sleeping under the canvas cover at the bow. Mr Bates did have an additional suggestion which I asked him to action and I hope you will find useful.'

Mr Bates nodded to his men and they went over to an object which lay under a tarpaulin by the bulwark. They brought out a curved section of hardwood, shaped to the contours of the bow. Adam noticed small brass buckles had been placed on the gunwale so that it could be fixed securely. The carpenter's mates attached it to the bow – a solid roof for their sleeping accommodation.

'The sailing master was worried the additional weight would alter the sailing characteristics of the boat and Mr Bates has tried to keep it as light but as strong as possible. It should provide you with better cover; we hope you find it useful.'

'My thanks, Captain, and to you, Mr Bates, and your men.'

'It has taken longer than I thought, Mr Fletcher, and the paint is still drying. If you were to come to the beach at noon tomorrow we will have it back in the water for you.'

Adam laughed. 'I cannot thank you all enough and we have the bonus that we can enjoy the evening, knowing that we do not have to row the ladies home.'

Ruth walked the deck with Jason Hewitt whilst Benjamin Doyle escorted the Ceruso ladies.

'It's very kind of Captain Pickford to invite us to dine, Mr Hewitt. I've seen your ships at a distance over the years but never walked the deck of a warship.'

'Miss Morgan, this deck would not be here to walk on were it not for Adam Fletcher. His timely warning and the use of his lugger, unquestionably saved the Intrepid. We try to reduce the risks but I'm afraid danger is never far away.'

'Yes, I do worry for Adam. Sometimes, since our engagement, I rise early and walk to the cliff top and watch the pair of them setting sail for their fishing grounds. From that height it seems a very small boat on a vast expanse of water.'

Jason nodded. 'Yes, Jamestown is an unusual posting even for sailors. There is probably no other harbour that is so isolated from other lands. Most of our sailing, when hunting slavers, will have us hundreds of miles from shore. We usually hunt alone and the slavers are desperate men if cornered. You need to have confidence in your ship and its crew; for many weeks at a time it is our whole world. Self-sufficiency and mutual respect are essential traits if one sails these waters, Miss Morgan. We are fortunate with our Captain. He is clever and resourceful and encourages the officers and crew to speak openly.'

'I know Adam was impressed by the way he dealt with the crisis and also how he related to his men.'

'Yes, he has an easy style, but not to the point that undermines his authority. There are fewer discipline issues on the Intrepid than any of my previous commissions.'

They all gathered around the lugger and Adam pointed out the changes that had been made. The light was fading and a cool breeze sprang up from the ocean.

'We should retire to my cabin.'

They slowly walked towards the stern. Several sailors greeted the two fishermen as they passed. The Marine on guard, outside the Captain's door, had shared a thwart with Francesco in the lugger and touched his cap in salute.

'Good to see you again, Mr Ceruso.'

'And you, Nathan,'

The Captain shared his guests around the table seating Ruth to his right and Carmella to his left. Jason sat on Ruth's right with Francesco beyond. Benjamin Doyle sat with Adam and Robert, with Maria flanked by two young junior officers. As the first course was served Jason presented Ruth with a dark, red rose. Captain Pickford and one of the young officers presented Carmella and Maria with similar gifts. The evening passed too quickly for all the guests. Ruth enjoyed Jason's company, hearing of his experiences at sea and the countries he had visited. He was still a young man but one who had extensive knowledge of the world. She was fascinated, and wanted to understand what it meant to be part of a community who lived so much of their lives isolated from the remainder of humanity on the vast and unpredictable ocean. She also saw a new side to Francesco's personality as he exchanged reminiscences with Jason. Adam found Benjamin Doyle to be equally engaging. He was a more recent arrival on St Helena and was keen to hear about the Island and their lives.

As the evening drew to a conclusion, Captain Pickford rose to his feet.

'Ladies and gentleman, you have just heard six bells in the first watch; that to you ladies is 11 o'clock in the evening. Before we bring the dinner to an end I would ask you to raise your glasses in a toast to Adam and Francesco of HMS Bountiful, in thanks for their invaluable service to Her Majesty's ship Intrepid.'

All except Adam and Francesco rose for the toast. 'To Adam and Francesco.'

Jacob and a Marine brought cloaks for the ladies for the journey back to the beach. Robert chose the bosun's ladder to return to the longboat and all made use of the two boat hooks for support, as they walked the gang plank to the beach.

It was a jovial group that ambled back through the settlement.

'They've done us proud, Francesco, and it'll be interesting to see if the roof to the bow does affect how she sails. I'll meet you on the beach at noon and we can prepare her for fishing in the early afternoon, but I see no point in going out tomorrow.'

'I agree, but we'll need to get out in the market the day after with some fish to sell, before people forget we are their suppliers.'

Adam and Ruth walked hand in hand up the path to the cliff top with Robert.

'I had a marvellous evening, Adam. Mr Hewitt was excellent company. The roses they gave us are beautiful. I shall press mine between the pages of a book as a memory of a very special evening. It was nice to see Francesco having such a good time. He obviously impressed the sailors with his efforts in the lugger. I felt there was a lot of good will evident as we walked the deck.'

'Yes, and they've done an excellent job with the lugger. I must get used to her new title. I like the choice of Bountiful – very appropriate for one who sells the fruits of the ocean!'

As they neared Adam's house, Robert excused himself. 'Ruth, I'll wait a little further up the path for you.'

'Thank you, Robert.'

The couple stood looking out over the bay; there was a half-moon which showed the silhouette of the frigate, riding at anchor. The breeze had settled and the settlement was dark and silent. Adam stood behind Ruth with arms around her waist. In the distance, Ruth heard the sounds of the ship's bell; eight bells, midnight. The distance between the settlement and the frigate was short but they lived in different worlds. Adam kissed her hair.

'It was a special evening, Adam, and they're obviously very grateful for your help. It has been a chance to see a completely different life from the one we know in the settlement. It's not an evening I would ever wish to forget.'

'Yes, Ruth, they have to make their own world within the confines of the ship – it travels with them wherever they sail.'

'Jason Hewitt mentioned the words 'mutual respect'. It must be a very special experience being part of Captain Pickford's crew.

'Yes, Thomas Pickford would be a good man to sail under, Ruth, but it must be very difficult to live under a bad captain whom you did not respect. You should go, my love, Robert will be waiting for you.'

She kissed him on the lips and he stroked her hair. 'We still need a date for visiting Jamestown.'

'Francesco and I will fish for the remainder of the week, but will set Friday aside next week.'

'Thank you, Adam.'

He walked her up the path to Robert and they made their farewells.

The fishermen returned to the beach at noon in working clothes. There had been intense activity on the Intrepid as it prepared to sail. The long boat was no longer in the water and they were picked up by the smaller gig commanded by Mr Bates.

'The Captain would like to see both of you on deck before you take your boat, Mr Fletcher.'

The lugger was moored at the base of the accommodation ladder with sails reefed and the bow cover in place.

'She does not look any lower in the water at the bow, Francesco. Perhaps we should sail her out into the open water and test her performance before we return to the beach.'

The fishermen scrambled up the ladder. Captain Pickford was there to greet them, accompanied by his First Officer and Marine Captain.

'I see you are ready for the sea, Thomas.'

'Yes, we'll sail as soon as you are clear. We will return to Jamestown for provisioning and then, no doubt, be back on our slave patrol. Best wishes for your wedding. One of Mr Bates's men has made a gift to you and Miss Morgan, on behalf of the crew.'

The young sailor moved forward carrying an oak bowl.

Adam laughed. 'The last time we met, you were drilling holes in my boat.'

'Sorry about that, Mr Fletcher, needs must. It's a fruit bowl, Sir, we hope Miss Ruth will approve. I've carved an inscription on the base.'

'I'm sure she will love it. Please thank the crew on our behalf. We should not detain you, Thomas.'

The captain waved his hand. 'My sail maker wanted to thank the pair of you in his own way. He's run up a spare set of sails for HMS Bountiful.'

An old man stepped forward and touched his forelock. 'We've run them up the mast, Sir, and I think you'll find they're serviceable.'

The fishermen and the Queen's officers shook hands.

'Good luck with your fishing. We shall look out for your pennant in Jamestown harbour and inform the rest of the squadron of your new status.'

A sailor lowered the canvas bag with the new sails to the lugger and the fishermen returned to their boat. They cast off and Francesco raised the sails as they drifted out of the lee of the frigate's stern. The sails filled and they cleared the ship, as the capstan shortened the anchor chain.

Sailors swarmed up the rigging and the great sails unfolded. The capstan continued to turn and the frigate's bow turned towards the wide mouth of the bay. Slowly the frigate picked up way as the anchor left the seabed and emerged from the water. Both boats sailed together to the open sea although the frigate was rapidly gaining speed. Captain Pickford gave a final salute and then turned back to his command.

'The Intrepid is a beautiful ship, Adam.'

'Yes and I'm pleased we've been part of its life for these last few days.'

HMS Bountiful performed to their satisfaction, perhaps a little heavier at the bow, but Adam thought she could still tack as close to the wind. They returned to the beach and prepared her for an early start in the morning.

CHAPTER SIX

The weather on Friday was judged suitable for the trip to Jamestown. Ruth, Carmella and Maria helped the fishermen launch the boat from the beach and, once afloat, were carried through the shallow water to keep their skirts dry. A gentle, westerly wind took them out of the bay and then north and east past the Barn, a hillock Adam frequently used when taking bearings. He kept on the same tack, out into the ocean north of the island until Sugarloaf Ridge was on the port quarter.

'Is the swell out here a little too much for you? If you feel sick we can stay closer to land in Flagstaff Bay, but we would need to tack more frequently. If we stay on this run we'll tack just the once and then run west past Sugarloaf Point; that is only a short distance from Jamestown.'

Their passengers were coping with the modest swell without difficulty and they held their course to the north.

'I'm glad we've chosen to sail to Jamestown, Adam; I've never seen the island from the sea and I've often wondered what it must be like for you when you're out fishing.'

'This is calm, Ruth, and normally we'd fish a bit further out. We reef the sails to travel more slowly when we're fishing.'

Carmella stood by the mast. 'It's interesting for me as well, Adam. I sell the fish, but I've never seen them caught. Would you mind if I joined you one day?'

'That would be fine, Carmella, it would be nice to have you along.'

Maria was sitting next to Ruth, her dark hair tied back from her face. 'Could I come too, Uncle Adam, I'd like to see what my father does.'

Adam looked over at Francesco who smiled and nodded.

'We'd be happy to have you aboard, Maria; we'll pick a day that should be warm and calm. I think probably an early start would be best; the island looks beautiful in the early morning light. If we get a good haul of fish we'll take it to Jamestown, sell some there and get back early enough to sell the remainder in Prosperous Bay. Would you be interested, Ruth?'

'I can cope with this today, Adam, but I probably wouldn't come fishing.' She gave Maria a hug.

'Maria can tell me all about it afterwards.'

Sugarloaf Ridge was almost lost to view on the port quarter and Diana's Peak, the tallest point of the island, was now low on the horizon. They changed tack and started the run south and west towards Jamestown. As they approached the dock, Adam brought the lugger up into the wind and Francesco lowered the sails. The small town's existence had depended on its role as a re-provisioning stop on the route to India and beyond. Several whalers from the South Atlantic Fleet were in port and an East India Company ship which had been damaged by storms, when travelling round the Cape of Good Hope. Only one of the Queen's frigates was in port and looked due to set sail in the next few hours. They rowed to a low jetty that allowed the ladies to step out of the boat without negotiating ladders.

'I think the first thing we should do is visit the Governor's Mansion and speak to Reverend Wilkes. I sent a message to say we hoped to meet him mid-morning. Then it will be on to the shops.'

They walked down the main street of the island's capital. Life in Prosperous Bay did not prepare the ladies for the noise and activity around them. There were few women to be seen, but many men speaking diverse languages. The Reverend Wilkes was expecting them and took them through to the Governor's garden. Adam introduced the wedding party.

'You have almost all the participants here, Reverend. This is Ruth Morgan, soon to be my wife. Francesco is my sailing partner; he will provide your transport to and from Prosperous Bay. He has also agreed to be my best man. His wife, Carmella, will be matron of honour for Ruth and their daughter, Maria, will be the bridesmaid. The only person absent today is Ruth's brother, Robert, who will be giving her away and has agreed to host you for the night after the wedding.'

They planned the arrangements for the ceremony over a cup of tea. Francesco agreed the time to pick up Reverend Wilkes on the Saturday morning, so that they would arrive at the community hall in good time for a noon wedding. The pastor walked back to the dock with them and agreed, before taking his leave, a rendezvous point with Francesco. Ruth then took control of arrangements.

'Adam, there are four or perhaps five shops we'll need to visit.'

She turned to look at Carmella. 'Do we need the men in attendance?'

Carmella shook her head. Adam looked relieved.

'Shall we meet at the boat at 3 o'clock? That should leave us plenty of time to get back to Prosperous Bay before nightfall.'

Jamestown was a settlement built around seafaring needs and had as many ship chandlers as it had shops for women's clothes. Adam and Francesco spent a very enjoyable couple of hours examining the wide variety of maritime equipment. Francesco was inspecting an anchor that was claimed to reduce the risk of dragging on the seabed when Adam called him over.

'We could've done with this last week.' He held a small brass drum up in his hand. He lifted up the lid to reveal a thick glass window.

'It's a portable compass.'

Francesco frowned. 'I didn't realise they made portable ones. I saw the binnacle on the Intrepid and envied their ability to navigate in the dark or on the open sea in heavy cloud.'

'They're new. I'd heard of them but didn't realise they could be made that small.'

The shop assistant came over. 'They're beautiful aren't they, and said to be reliable, although we have not stocked them long enough to have had any reports. The navy is sufficiently impressed to have started ordering them for the fleet. At three guineas they're pretty expensive at present, but perhaps with time the price will drop. I'm afraid that one has been sold, but I have ordered more.'

Adam reluctantly handed it back. 'It would certainly be useful in our business.'

The two friends walked back to the quay and were sitting on a low wall in the sunshine when Maria advised them the shopping was taking longer than expected and a further hour would be required. A walk around the town brought them back at the appointed hour and they caught up with the ladies in the main street, carrying their purchases to the quay. An animated discussion between Carmella and Ruth ceased as they approached.

'I don't suppose we can have a look at what you've got?'

'Absolutely not Adam, but you can carry the heavier ones, providing you do not look.'

The Westerly breeze suited their return to Prosperous Bay, running down the wind for the first leg and then a tack to starboard to take them past Black Point and the Sentinel and up onto the beach.

'Are you happy with your purchases, Ruth?'

'Yes, it was helpful to have Carmella with me. I hope you'll feel all three of us look at our best.'

He carried her shopping up the steep path to his house. They sat on the porch looking out over the sea, sipping glasses of water from the kitchen.

'I'm not a good sailor, Adam, but I enjoyed the trip today. However when we sailed far out I really did feel daunted by the sheer vastness of the sea, not just in its width but in its depth. It's not a life I'd feel able to live easily.'

'I suppose it's in the blood. I'm actually exhilarated by the open sea; I respect it, but I do not fear it. I think you're probably better on the land. You'll have plenty enough to do maintaining the house and the allotment.'

They carried the parcels back to her house, as the sun sank behind the hills.

Lucy Davies gave Maria permission to take a day off class to experience fishing with her father. Carmella and Maria joined the fishermen on the beach at sunrise and they helped push the boat out into the bay. Maria and her father hoisted the sails and Carmella sat with Adam in the stern, one on each side of the tiller. Adam set them on their first tack out into the bay demonstrating how the sails should be trimmed and how subtle adjustments to the rudder allowed them to sail close to the wind. Carmella was to look for signs of the jib losing shape and flapping.

'It means we're sailing too close to the wind; ease the tiller back and you'll see the jib tighten up and recover its tension. It's a mistake to try to sail too close to the wind, even if it's the direction you want to take.'

He showed her how the boat slowed when they were close hauled to the wind and how they picked up speed when he let the bow ease off and the sails tighten. Maria and Francesco were preparing coils of fishing line on the starboard side of the boat. Each hook was baited with small fish that had been netted by an inshore fisherman the previous day. Carmella had control of the rudder. Adam pointed to her left.

'Take her further to port, Carmella, and we'll continue on this tack until we're a couple of miles out.'

'How do you know if you are in the area where you want to fish?'

'The contour of Diana's Peak gives us a fair idea and the position of the Sentinel with respect to the hills behind it. There is a very brisk, north-south current which we have to overcome if we're north of Prosperous Bay. I tend to work the waters to the north; if we get a good catch early in the day and we're up past Barnlong Point, it's an easy matter to tack west for Jamestown and sell the bulk of the fish.'

Half an hour later, Adam felt they were sufficiently north and east to justify going about and settling onto a long tack to the east. Maria and Francesco reefed the sails. Francesco turned to Adam.

'What depth today?'

'Five fathoms, Francesco, and let us see what that produces.'

'Maria, the lines are marked at one fathom intervals, unwind the line to the sixth marker.'

'How will we know if there's a fish on the line, Father?'

'The fish we catch are often quite big and it's very obvious when that's the case. I feel each line every few minutes. With experience, you can tell if even a small fish has been hooked.'

As he finished his explanation, one of the lines stiffened and a large kingclip was drawn to the surface and hauled into the boat with a gaff.

'Uncle Adam, I think there's something on this one.'

Adam checked the tension on the line and laughed. 'I think we should bring you two more often.'

Two frantic hours of fishing followed. Carmella sailed the lugger and Maria sat with her in the stern. Carmella showed Maria what Adam had taught her and they sailed the boat together.

'It's always difficult to know when to stop on a day like this. There is no point in pulling in more fish than we can sell. There are probably two frigates in Jamestown who would take some of the catch. Shall we say two more, Francesco?'

Within a quarter of an hour they had their quota and Adam guided Carmella onto their new tack north and west to clear Sugarloaf Point and swing south to Jamestown. Carmella watched from the stern as the fishermen worked and Maria walked forward to bring food and water for an early lunch.

'It's interesting to watch the pair of you fish. I thought there would be fishing lines and ropes all over the place, but throughout the hectic activity, there's never been any untidiness in the boat. Francesco is not like that at home, Adam!'

Francesco smiled. 'Desist, woman, you're lucky to have me. Adam and I were trained by his father; if there's untidiness, there's risk.'

'He's right, Carmella. You have to remember the boat is often bucking about more than today. It's very easy to trip over a loose rope or catch your hand on a fish hook. I'm not the tidiest at home either, but everything we do out here is designed to reduce risk.'

Adam and Carmella shared the tiller, as they ate their lunch. Maria then replaced her mother and Adam supervised her tack to port and the approach to Jamestown.

There were two frigates in port and the bulk of their haul was swiftly sold. Adam had noticed there was now less haggling over price since their involvement with HMS Intrepid.

'We've sold more to the frigates today than we would normally. I see little point wasting time selling more on the quay. We should be able to sell the rest in the settlement.'

'I agree, Adam. I know Mrs Davies wants quite a lot for the children's lunch tomorrow.'

Adam brought the lugger about and Francesco trimmed the sails as they set off on a north west tack.

'Carmella, if you and Maria take the tiller, I will help Francesco put the fishing lines away and get the boat ready for tomorrow.'

As a goodwill gesture, the second frigate had sent them down a basket of fruit with their payment. When they had travelled sufficiently far north to clear Sugarloaf Point, Maria tacked to starboard and they started the run across the top of the island. They sat in the afternoon sunshine and ate apples as Diana's Peak moved from starboard beam to starboard quarter and then astern.

'We've cleared Barn Long Point, Carmella, but we need to give ourselves a little more sea room for our final tack to starboard. It's a mistake to tack too early; we'd only have to tack again later to clear the Sentinel.'

The final tack to starboard brought them swiftly past the Sentinel and Adam took the tiller for the final run to the beach. Maria and her mother took some of the fish to Lucy Davies. Adam and Francesco had sold the remainder by the time they returned. Carmella kissed Adam on the cheek.

'Thank you, Captain, I really enjoyed today; to be part of what you do.'

'Francesco and I have enjoyed having you with us. Did you enjoy it, Maria?'

'Oh yes, Uncle Adam, I really enjoyed it.'

'No sea sickness?'

'None at all. I love the space and the freedom, it's been very special.'

Adam's voice took on a more serious tone. 'And now, Francesco, we have to consider how the days taking should be split. In these special circumstances I think an equal four-way cut would be correct.'

'That's extremely generous, Adam.'

'It's my pleasure. I've enjoyed the day and the ladies brought us good fishing. Seven o'clock tomorrow at the boat. Carmella and Maria, we'll miss your company.'

As the wedding approached, Adam found he was becoming more nervous. He saw little of Ruth and Carmella as dresses were made and the ladies of the settlement agreed the arrangements for the reception. Adam was by nature a private man and was ill at ease with a role that placed him at the centre of attention. He took Ruth back to Jamestown to purchase some additional items and bought a new suit and shirt with Ruth's guidance. The Reverend Wilkes joined them for coffee on the quay to finalise the order of service.

Adam had a restless final night as a bachelor; sleep would not come to him. He rose with the sun and put on casual clothes. He stood on the cliff top looking down over the silent settlement and the calm bay. The lugger was gone indicating that Francesco was already on his way to Jamestown. Adam walked along the cliff path to Bay Point and then on to Saddle Point beyond. The countryside was deserted with only birds to disturb the silence. When he returned to his cottage the settlement was awake and active. Smoke rose from the chimneys and three inshore fishing boats were moving slowly across the mouth of the bay, trailing their lines. He did not feel like eating breakfast but knew he should have some sustenance before the ceremony. Carmella had supplied a game pie for his evening meal the previous day and some was still in the bowl, but he opted for simpler fare – bread and cheese and a mug of tea. He showered and dressed and then sat out on the porch overlooking the bay. The lugger was on its final run in to the beach. The Reverend Wilkes was carried to the sand and met by Edmond Davies who escorted him to the meeting house. Francesco secured the boat and moved swiftly towards his house to change. Twenty minutes later Adam's best man trotted up the path, carrying his Sunday jacket.

'Francesco, come and sit down. You need to cool down and catch your breath. I'll fetch you some water.'

'Thanks, Adam; it will be nice to sit for a few minutes. Carmella drove me out of the house early and the chaplain was on the quay before the appointed hour. The winds have been light and the return trip was slow. I enjoyed our conversation on the way here. I hope he does hold occasional Sunday services, I'm sure they'd be well attended.'

They greeted Robert Morgan and he sat with them on the bench, hanging his jacket on the front rail. Francesco continued. 'Ruth is dressing at our house so I wasn't allowed in. My clothes had to be moved to the neighbours' and I changed there. I was not allowed sight of any of them; apparently that is very bad luck. But Lucy Davies did and said they all looked beautiful.'

Robert laughed. 'I can only hope they feel we are suitably debonair and match their elegance!'

'Have you got the ring, Adam?'

Robert reached inside his pocket. 'No, I have it, Francesco. Ruth wanted to wear her mother's ring. She has tried it on and it fits snugly.'

Francesco nervously looked at his pocket watch. 'We shouldn't be late, Adam.'

'Is that you speaking, Francesco, or can I hear Carmella's instructions?'

'I have to admit Lucy Davies did pass on an order from my wife that my prime responsibility is to get you to the meeting hall on time.'

Robert stood up. 'I suspect neither of you would survive a late arrival; we should start walking now.'

The three friends walked down the hill and past the Marine Barracks where several soldiers sat at a table cleaning their weapons. A barrage of cat calls and rude remarks accompanied their passing. John Logan mocked them. 'Are those the best clothes you've got? She shouldn't be wasting her time with bumpkins when she could be on the arm of a man in uniform. We'll be down later.'

Francesco stiffened but Adam quietly intervened. 'Leave it, Francesco, we've more important matters on hand. It's sad, no-one minds a bit of banter, but with this section of Marines it's always so unpleasant and the worst of all of them is the man who leads them – Sergeant Logan.'

Francesco shook his head. 'They should never have been invited.'

Robert disagreed. 'I know how you feel but we could not avoid inviting them; they're part of the settlement community whether we like it or not. Perhaps it will lead to better relations with them, but I doubt it.'

They entered the community hall and walked to the front with Adam receiving good wishes as he progressed. The entire community was in its Sunday best. The

Reverend Wilkes was in earnest conversation with the Davieses. They greeted the groom warmly.

'We think we're all organised, Adam. It's a pleasure to have met Edmond and Lucy and I would enjoy working with them, if the community would like me to visit each quarter.'

The chaplain called them to order. 'Francesco, you have the ring?'

Robert passed it over. 'I'll go to the back and await my sister.'

Lucy moved to the piano. The Reverend Wilkes turned to Edmond Davies.

'Edmond will you conduct the hymns, as normal? I will take care of the service.'

Francesco and the chaplain tried unsuccessfully to keep Adam relaxed with small talk. Edmond nodded to his wife and she launched into the introduction of the opening hymn. Adam felt hot and his collar had become too tight. He saw a movement out of the corner of his eye and turned to view his bride. She smiled nervously, as if seeking approval.

'You look beautiful, Ruth.' He turned further and saw Carmella and Maria. 'You all look beautiful.'

Francesco beamed and Robert kissed his sister's cheek as the last chorus of the first hymn died away. Their nervousness settled as the Reverend Wilkes took control of the situation and led them through the ceremony. Readings were performed by Robert, Edmond and Matthew Draper.

Adam risked a raised eyebrow to his bride as Matthew moved forward to speak. She mimed 'behave, Adam'.

Edmond had chosen the readings with Ruth in advance and the congregation was spared the usual moralising about carnal thoughts.

The exchange of vows affected Adam deeply. Ruth held his gaze as she spoke with emotion and sincerity. They were face to face. She was beautiful and was flanked by her brother, maid of honour and bridesmaid. He blessed his good fortune to be accepted as a husband to such a special person. Ruth's mother's ring passed to another generation.

After a nod from the Reverend Wilkes, Edmond started marshalling the congregation for the final hymn. They walked back down the church with the congregation singing enthusiastically and offering congratulations to the couple. They moved out into the sunshine and the congregation spilled out into the square with them. Trestle tables had been set up in the shade of an oak tree and the settlement's wives and husbands swiftly filled the surfaces with food and drink. The marines appeared in ones and twos and the community sought to include them in the celebrations. Adam and Ruth walked arm in arm for much of the time, enjoying the close proximity that was now permissible as man and wife.

Late in the afternoon, the wedding party was sitting in the shade. Francesco stood up and walked over to the drinks table to replenish their glasses with punch and tankards of beer for the men. As he returned, Sergeant Logan weaved his way towards them. He pointed to one of the tankards.

'Give me one of those, fisherman.'

Francesco paused and weighed up a variety of possible responses. Should it be a polite negative or a more conciliatory reply? He opted for the latter as he offered Robert and Adam their tankards.

'Take mine, Sergeant, I'll get another one.'

Sergeant Logan accepted the tankard and watched Francesco walk toward the barrel. He turned and stared at Carmella greedily. At first nothing was said, as tension mounted and Carmella held his gaze defiantly and with obvious disgust. The Sergeant waited until Francesco was back within earshot. The Reverend Wilkes walked past with Lucy Davies and the Lloyd sisters. Sergeant Logan sneered.

'I don't know why you waste your time with him, woman, he's a coward. One of these days you'll come looking for me. Don't wait too long or it'll be your daughter who has the pleasure.'

Francesco moved forward but Robert swiftly blocked his path. 'Touch any of my family, soldier, and I'll gut you faster than I would a fish.'

The sergeant laughed and turned his attention back to Carmella, occasionally glancing at Maria.

'Growing up nicely, isn't she? You wouldn't want her education to be too early, would you?'

He smiled again and touched the side of nose. 'So you know what to do, don't you?'

He smiled at Francesco. 'Only joking, want to get me another jug of ale?'

He bowed at Adam and Ruth and walked back to the barrel. Robert shook his head.

'Was that just a joke in bad taste or was it a threat?'

Adam sighed. 'It's a threat. I cannot see it any other way. He knows he's the only authority in the settlement and he thinks he is above the law. I just think we'll all have to be very careful to look after each other. It can't be too long before his section returns to Jamestown or onto a frigate. He's been here longer than most of the previous ones.'

Adam turned to his bride. 'Ruth, perhaps we should leave now and let the revellers carry on into the evening.'

'I will change into something simpler at Carmella's and I have a small travelling bag to take care of tonight's needs.'

When Ruth had changed, they made their farewells and thanked the Reverend Wilkes again for his kindness. His attendance had been greeted with enthusiasm and the Davies family were discussing dates for quarterly Sunday services. Adam and Ruth walked back up the hill, as the shadows lengthened.

Ruth lay on her back in the dark listening to Adam's breathing. It was slow and regular and he might be sleeping but she doubted that was the case. She had never slept in a bed with another person and the experience was disconcerting. She had not been sure what to expect when they made love, but had not found it enjoyable. Both were nervous which had not helped. Adam remained cautious and uncertain with her and the barrier, which she felt she had created after his rescue persisted. She bitterly regretted destroying the surge of passion they both had experienced that day; surely that passion would not be lost forever? She comforted herself with the thought that many newly-wed couples probably experienced these problems and overcame them. Tomorrow would be another day. She sighed, turned away from her husband and tried to sleep.

CHAPTER SEVEN

Maria's trip in the lugger had increased her interest in her father's work. If school was over she would come with her mother and help deliver orders of fish. If there were no classes, she begged to be allowed to join them; Francesco was less certain.

'Adam, I don't want to encourage her, if you'd prefer we fished on our own.'

'It's not a problem for me if she comes, Francesco. She's sensible and finds useful things to do. If you and Carmella are happy, let her come along. Talk to Carmella. As long as you're both content for her to come, I suggest you make it a condition that she learns to swim first.'

'That's sensible, Adam. Should we set a distance?'

'Yes, how about 50 yards and the ability to tread water for ten minutes.'

'I'll talk to Carmella tonight.'

Carmella did approve and Francesco enlisted the help of one of the inshore fishermen who was considered one of the strongest swimmers in the settlement. Maria attended every afternoon after school and practised frequently at other times.

Two weeks later Carmella, Maria and her instructor greeted Adam and Francesco, as they returned with the day's catch.

'We think she's ready for your test, Adam.'

They marked out 50 yards on the beach and her instructor rowed Maria and Carmella out of Maria's depth, in line with the first marker.

'Take it steady, Maria, don't put too much effort in at the beginning, I'll be rowing just behind you in case you have problems. Your mother will be in the bow and we can get you out if there are any difficulties. When Mr Fletcher waves, you've swum far enough, then just tread water for 10 minutes – I'll keep the boat very close.'

Maria slid into the water and began to swim. Adam and Francesco walked slowly between the markers. There was activity far out to sea.

'Those sails have to belong to a frigate from the West Africa Squadron.'

'I agree. It's unusual to see them on this side of the island. He'll have to change his bearing if he wants to clear Sugarloaf Point for Jamestown.'

The frigate did not change course and continued on a bearing which would bring them to Prosperous Bay. Adam frowned. 'He has to be coming here, Francesco.'

They reached the second marker. 'I reckon she's done 50 yards, Francesco.'

They waved and Maria started treading water. 'She's done well, Francesco. That must have tired her, but she still looks comfortable.'

They studied the frigate as it swept into the bay. 'It's the Intrepid, Adam. I don't think I'll ever forget that figurehead.'

Sailors manned the yard arms and the sails were furled as the frigate swung into the wind. The ship lost way as it moved against the north-south drift. The anchor was released when forward motion had ceased and they could hear the capstan reclaiming excess cable, holding the vessel firmly in the current.

'That's impressive seamanship, Francesco, I wonder what brings them back to Prosperous Bay?'

'Whatever it is, Adam, they're not wasting time.'

The longboat was being swung out and lowered into the water.

'That's at least 10 minutes for Maria.' They waved and Maria gratefully climbed into the boat and returned to the beach.

'Well done, Maria. If you have a day off school in the future I'd be happy to have you with us out in the boat.'

'Why do you think Intrepid is back in the bay, Father?'

'I don't know, but I think we'll find out soon. That's Jason Hewitt in the longboat and he's coming this way.'

The longboat grounded on the sand and the first lieutenant jumped down onto the beach.

'This is a pleasant surprise, Mr Hewitt, and very accomplished seamanship. What brings you back to Prosperous Bay?'

'You do, Mr Fletcher. Captain's compliments and would you join him on the deck? It'll not take long, sir, and I'm sure he'd wish Mr Ceruso to attend.'

Bemused, Adam turned to Carmella.

'Can you take care of the sale of the fish please, Carmella.'

They boarded the longboat and took their seats in the stern. The atmosphere was informal with a voice from near the bow asking Francesco if he'd like to do some more rowing. He laughed and declined. They came up to the side of the Intrepid and the oars were raised as a sailor in the bow hooked onto the accommodation ladder. They climbed to the deck to find Captain Pickford was in attendance surrounded by his officers and many of the crew. Jason Hewitt joined them. The Captain strode forward.

'Welcome, Adam, welcome Francesco. We've timed our arrival well with the pair of you still on the beach. The ship's company has a gift for you in appreciation of your recent efforts on our behalf. There was some discussion as to what the gift might be. I was struck by a remark you made when we first met. When you were becalmed in the fog and near the cliffs you said you could not make your way to safety, as you were as likely to row towards disaster as away from it. You were envious of our compass. A naval officer has recently designed a portable compass which is being brought into use in the service. We'd like you to accept this gift with our thanks.'

The second officer passed the Captain the brass compass.

'That's magnificent, Captain. I've seen one before, but never dreamt I'd ever own one.'

'It's from all of us, Adam, the officers and the crew; I think you'll find, if Mr Bates has got his measurements correct, it will fit snugly in that hardwood box he placed at the base of your mast.'

Adam laughed. 'Now I understand. Thank you, Captain, and all of you. We'll treasure your gift and it'll be of great benefit when fishing far out to sea.'

The Captain escorted them to the accommodation ladder. The compass was secured in a bag, which Adam wore round his neck for the descent to the longboat. Jason Hewitt shook their hands as the longboat's bow grounded on the sand. 'I hope it fits Mr Bates's box, Adam.'

'I'm sure it will.'

They climbed aboard the lugger, as the longboat returned to the frigate.

'That's clever, Francesco, the grooves in the wood match the contours of the compass. The box will hold it firmly and protect it from damage.'

They heard the sound of the capstan, as the anchor cable was tightened further. Seamen lined the yards and the longboat was being swung back onto its cradle.

'By Jove, Francesco, they don't waste any time, do they?' As he spoke, the anchor cable was lifted from the seabed and the sails were unfurled. The frigate was carried south by the current, but the sails filled swiftly and the frigate slowly picked up way across the bay. When Captain Pritchard had gained sufficient headway, the frigate swung onto a starboard tack for the open sea.

Maria joined Adam and Francesco frequently when she was not attending Lucy Davies's school. Some fishermen worked with their sons, but no other girls sailed on the boats and the women of the settlement observed the change with disapproval. They did not consider it appropriate work for a young girl on the threshold of womanhood. Carmella dismissed their concerns. Francesco and Adam had reassured her that Maria made a valuable contribution as a crew member; she worked hard and learnt fast. The fishermen taught her never to drop her guard when on the open sea and constantly to monitor wind and wave.

The justification for constant vigilance was emphasized on one of her earliest visits. They were far out to sea trailing deep fishing lines. Diana's Peak had already sunk below the horizon but they had a compass bearing for their return journey. The main sail was reefed to slow their passage through the water. Adam was ill at ease but could not identify the cause. The wave pattern was slightly irregular; sometimes that occurred for no obvious reasons. On other occasions…..

He looked to the horizon from where the waves originated. Yes, there was an irregularity almost at the limits of his view. He bided his time. It slowly became obvious that his fears were well grounded. Francesco and Maria were near the bow, re-baiting lines.

'Francesco, rogue wave, half a mile to starboard, I'm going about, then batten down.'

He put the tiller hard over and the bow swung to starboard to face the rogue wave that was sweeping towards them. Francesco glanced to starboard. The wave was very much larger than the rest.

'Leave the lines, Maria, stow the boathooks and toss anything that's loose into the covered area in the bow. We don't have long, I'll explain later.'

Maria sensed the urgency in both their voices and returned the boathooks to their rack. Sandals, a coat, a bucket and a satchel with bread, cheese and water were thrown into the bow. She noticed her father pulling loops of thick rope out from under the bulwark. She had not noticed them before; they had lain hidden by the lower edge of the rail.

Adam was trying to maintain the lugger on its new course while scooping up loose objects and placing them in a locker beneath the stern seat. She started to move back to help him.

'No, Maria, there won't be time for that. Stay with your father, he'll tell you what to do.'

She watched as Adam clipped a line to his belt and swiftly tied the other end to a metal ring on the stern. Her father put his arm around her shoulder and pointed ahead.

'It's a rogue wave; we have to deal with them occasionally. The boat will be thrown about a lot and we'll almost definitely take on some water. We'll lie side by side. See these two rope hand holds; you put your hands on both first and I will put mine on top of yours. You have to hold tight or we could be thrown out of the boat.'

He turned back to Adam. 'I reckon twenty or twenty five feet.'

'I agree, with the trough that's about fifty feet in total.'

'Maria, let's get in place. The first thing that happens is we'll drop into the trough in front of it, then the bow will bite into the wave and we'll take water as we shoot upwards. The boat will then fall away more abruptly than when we entered the first trough; these waves usually come alone but sometimes there maybe two or three. Adam will tell us when the danger is over and then we can

96

let go. He has to keep the bow to the wave. If we broach and have to face a second wave, even with our centre board we would likely capsize and be dismasted.'

Maria lay against the starboard hull with both hands holding the thick ropes. Her father's body held her against the hull and he wrapped his hands over hers, gripping firmly.

'It won't be long, Maria. Adam will count us down.'

Almost immediately they heard Adam calmly counting down from five. Despite her father's warnings, the speed of descent into the trough surprised Maria. She doubted she had ever moved so swiftly. They were lifted from the hull with only the ropes for support. Suddenly the sickening drop was over and the bow tilted up abruptly and their bodies were thrown back against the hull as the lugger was catapulted skywards. Water poured over the bow. She felt their small boat could not survive such an assault and that they must have shipped too much water. Abruptly the bow dropped again as they rushed into the trough behind the wave. All the water that had surged past them to the stern now rushed past them to the bow. She heard Adam's voice from the stern.

'Hang on, two smaller waves following, and then we're in the clear.'

The cycle was repeated twice more but the movements were mild compared to the main wave.

'That's it, Francesco, you can let go now, are you both unharmed?'

Francesco rubbed his hands. 'Probably a few bruises tomorrow, Adam.'

'What about you, Maria?'

'Much the same as my father, Uncle Adam.'

'Check for damage, Francesco. Can you start bailing, Maria, if we still have the bucket?'

Francesco completed his inspection. 'Three fishing lines have snapped and we've lost the hooks and weights. Mr Bates's wooden bow cover has held up very well and all the catches are secure. The blankets and pillows are soaked. We've lost one of the nets we tow with the fish that have been caught, even though we've been using a stouter rope. The mast, rigging and sails are all sound. Lunch will be a bit salty, but generally things are not too bad. We can release the reefs in the main sail, but we'll not get any speed on her until we shift this water.'

'Take the tiller, Maria; Francesco and I will bail first and rotate with you, so that in three hours we'll have steered once and bailed twice. We'll have some food when the first three hours are complete.'

He then turned to Francesco, with a laugh. 'Would you be kind enough to give me a compass bearing, so I may set course for home.'

Two three hour shifts baled the lugger dry. Maria stowed the undamaged fishing line and Francesco showed her how to repair the broken lines with replacement weights and hooks. They sat in a small circle in the stern and Maria distributed the remaining water and damp bread and cheese. The island was rising up before them and the freshening breeze was drying their clothes. The blankets and the pillows hung from the halliards.

'When we get back, they'll all have to be washed, Maria, to remove the salt but it's easier to deal with them when they're dry.'

The two fishermen exchanged glances and Francesco pointed to Adam. The Captain cleared his throat.

'Maria, when an episode with a rogue wave occurs, we never mention it back home to your mother; we don't want her to worry unnecessarily and we know, if we're careful, there's little risk. When you think about it, we've only snapped three lines and lost a few fish. I won't be mentioning it to Ruth and we'd be grateful if you would not mention it to your mother.'

Maria looked at her father. 'It's for the best, Maria, she'd only worry.'

She nodded. 'If that's what you both feel. I've never heard of rogue waves before, Uncle Adam.'

'They're not common, Maria. We might have to ride one out every year, I suppose. I was alerted this morning by some irregularity of the waves; the spacing was a bit abnormal and the heights varied more than usual. It is the sort of change that's easy to miss, but the pattern did not seem right. When this happens you have to keep scanning the horizon, particularly where the waves are coming from. Usually nothing happens, but sometimes you will spot a large rogue wave sweeping down on you. The boat will always handle it, if you can get the bow to the wave. If you don't react quickly enough and our boat is broadside to the wave, she would overturn and founder. Even if she righted herself, she would almost definitely be dismasted and that would also finish us if there were insufficient spars rigging and sails remaining to allow us to crawl home with a jury rigg. The person at the tiller has the prime responsibility to scan the horizon constantly for changes to sky or sea, but it's important for all of us to keep an eye on what is going on outside the boat.'

Maria wrapped the remaining cheese in a cloth and placed it back in the leather satchel.

'Why do we get rogue waves, Uncle Adam?'

'I don't think any one really knows, Maria. They've been mentioned in ships' logs for many years; some of them seem fanciful and some are probably just an excuse to claim on an over insured cargo. Some unscrupulous traders buy an old ship and fill it with ballast with no cargo. They need a corrupt captain and crew to scuttle the boat on the high seas and take to the lifeboats. They often claim to have been struck by a rogue wave. They then present a false cargo manifest to the insurers and claim for a cargo that was never lost. I was talking to Captain Pritchard about rogue waves when we had dinner on HMS Intrepid. He was saying the Royal Navy has knowledge of several waves, bigger than the one you saw today. Some well authenticated waves are thought to have been fifty feet or more. You have to double that with the trough that goes before and after the wave. I've never experienced anything like that.'

'What causes them?'

'It's uncertain. Captain Pritchard thinks they're probably caused by a big storm and spread out in an expanding circle. They only occur in vast open areas of the oceans, mainly in the Atlantic, but also the Pacific. He rode out one smallish one in the North Atlantic on a previous commission, but has experienced four bigger ones in the three years he has spent with the West Africa Squadron. He says some scientists in England think they're caused by underwater earthquakes. They are usually travelling in the same direction as the other waves, but that is not always the case.'

Francesco gave up trying to light a pipe of damp tobacco and took up the story.

'We had a rogue wave like that when I was sailing with your father. It was the first year I was his crew. You'll not remember much about him, Maria, but Adam's father was a very experienced sailor. At the time I didn't recognise it, but looking back he was a bit like Adam today; alert to an unknown danger. He had us on a tack that had the bow close hauled to the wind as he didn't like the irregularity of the waves, much like today. In fact a rogue wave was coming at us from the port beam. It seemed huge but it was probably similar to the one that struck us today. It might have caught out Mr Fletcher; he was scanning the waves ahead of us. Fortunately for us there was another fishing boat on our port side. They were also caught off-guard and capsized. We heard their cries when the wave was almost upon them and Adam's father only just had the time to swing the bow and tell me to hang on tight. We lost a lot of gear and bailed the boat as we slowly sailed to our upturned companions. There had been three crew and two were lost. We rescued the survivor and took the upturned boat in tow, but the weather was worsening and we had to cut her adrift and run for home with the sole survivor. We did much the same as today. Alfredo Gomez was exhausted so we put him on the tiller. Adam's father and I bailed for our lives, as the weather closed in around us. When I was exhausted, I took the tiller and Alfredo joined Mr Fletcher with a bucket. We crawled back to the beach as the storm overtook us. Alfredo never forgot our help and he gave us both a bottle of rum every Christmas until the day he died.'

Adam leaned forward and patted Maria on the head. 'You did well out there today. We always have to react quickly in a crisis; your father gave you an instruction and you didn't hesitate or ask why. That's important; swift, unquestioning actions are sometimes required. There's always plenty of time for explanations later.'

She smiled. 'I could hear the tension in your warning, although I didn't understand it, and then my father spoke in the same way. It was obvious that, whatever it was, we had to act fast. I don't think my body has ever been thrown about like that. At first it was like falling off a cliff and then we were pressed against the decking as we were thrown up into the sky, only to fall again.'

'Sometimes the settlement knows a rogue wave has occurred. If the direction is to the west they can enter the bay. That's why you've always been told to run to the high ground if the tide suddenly recedes too far down the beach. Just like today, it is the trough before the wave.'

The Sentinel rose up on the starboard bow and they entered the bay. Carmella stood on the beach with the trolley they used for the fish. As the boat reached the sand, Maria jumped into the water and her father passed her the half dry blankets and pillows. Carmella studied their tired faces and damp clothes.

'Let me guess, it was a wonderful day's fishing, everything went smoothly but you didn't catch many fish. You would like the blankets and pillows washed, even though I did them last week. Tell me about the rogue wave, Maria. Were you frightened?

Maria looked helplessly at the two fishermen. They shrugged sheepishly.

'It all happened very quickly, Mother. Uncle Adam got the bow to the wave and we didn't ship much water, but we did get thrown about a bit.'

'Has it put you off fishing?'

'No, Father, and Uncle Adam were very careful. I found it rather exciting.'

'That's what your father told your grandmother when he had his first rogue with Mr Adam's father. She resigned herself to him remaining a fisherman. It seems you've got your father's blood in your veins.'

Adam noticed Ruth and her brother walking swiftly across the beach. Carmella continued,

'It has not been a normal day here either. The settlement is in ferment. The Marines have barricaded themselves in their barracks and have refused to let anyone come in and inspect it. They only come out in groups of four, in full uniform with side arms.'

Adam was confused. 'Why would anyone want to inspect the barracks?'

'One of Matthew Draper's pigs is missing. He believes it has been killed by the Marines. All the settlement thinks he's right. There's talk of burning down the barracks' door.'

Ruth and Robert reached the group as Carmella finished her report. Robert took up the story.

'It's serious, Adam; the Marines are frightened and poorly led. All the farmers are furious. This could get out of hand and turn into a blood bath.'

CHAPTER EIGHT

They took their fish to the square and the small numbers were swiftly sold. The entrance to the barracks faced the meeting hall across the square. It had been built with defence in mind, in the days when there had been the threat of an attack by supporters of Napoléon. The windows were small with oak shutters that had a narrow slit for firearms. A single stout oak door was the sole means of access. Even the reduced number of marines, presently deployed, could defend it with ease. Two marines with rifles guarded the half open door. A small group of farmers and settlers stood nearby.

Adam had the feeling that one of the marines at the door was reporting their presence, which seemed to be confirmed when he stood aside to let Sergeant John Logan through, accompanied by four marines carrying rifles. They walked swiftly across the square to where the fishermen stood. The sergeant was carrying a sheet of paper and Adam noticed that one of the marines had a hammer. The sergeant addressed his remarks to Robert and Adam.

'You are respected people in this community. You have a duty to support the crown officers and maintain law and order. I will not have civil disturbance in my settlement. A pig has wandered off and probably fallen over a cliff, but we're blamed for its loss.'

Robert raised his hand. 'That's just the point, Sergeant. Pigs do not wander off; they stay close to their troughs. If you would just let one independent witness into the barrack for an inspection, and he confirms there is no pig present, the matter would be resolved. If any householder in the settlement were under suspicion, he would ask people into his home to prove his innocence.'

'That's out of the question. We're the law here and I'll not allow you to question those in authority. Spread the word I'm ordering a curfew and everyone must be off the streets by sunset and they are to remain in their houses until dawn. My men will be patrolling with weapons and torches. Anyone seen out after dark will be shot.'

He nailed the notice to the meeting hall door. 'Tell these men to go home. If my soldiers are provoked, they'll open fire. Make sure everyone knows about the curfew or you'll have blood on your hands.'

The marines returned to the barracks. Adam beckoned the farmers across the square. He looked at the sun, low in the western sky.

'I reckon we've perhaps an hour until his curfew. Perhaps the best way to defuse the situation is to suggest everyone complies with the curfew, but that we raise a complaint about Sergeant Logan and the general behaviour of the marines. Francesco and I could deliver it in Jamestown tomorrow. We need to ring the meeting hall bell to summon people to warn them of the curfew. There will be time, while they're gathering, to see if the settlers agree that we submit a complaint to the Governor General. Logan cannot complain if we ring the bell. He's told us to warn them.'

The settlement bell was used on Sunday mornings before the service, but apart from that, it was only used for emergencies. The sound carried to all the settlers in the small valley behind the beach and to several farms on the hilltops on either side. People streamed into the square and into the hall. Sergeant Logan, uncertain of the reason for the gathering, chose to line his men up in front of the barracks with their rifles and fixed bayonets. Adam and Robert led the meeting, accompanied by an indignant Matthew Draper who described the loss of the pig. He had found some blood in the sty and believed the pig may have been clubbed and carried away during the night. At least two people would have been needed because the pig weighed as much as an adult man. Matthew was careful in the use of his words. He did not believe the pig would roam. He did believe the marines frequently stole fruit and vegetables from the fields and he felt they were the likely culprits. Many heads nodded in agreement. Adam and Robert knew they did not have much time as the day was drawing to a close. They warned of the curfew and asked whether the settlers would wish to register a complaint with the Governor concerning Sergeant Logan and his section of marines. There was little need for discussion and the proposal was passed unanimously. Robert and Adam were invited to draft a letter to the Governor overnight and seek Edmond Davies's approval at dawn. Adam and Francesco were then to deliver it to the Governor's office in the morning and delay any fishing until later in the day. The settlers streamed out into the square and dispersed as the light faded.

Ruth, Robert and Adam drew up a letter of complaint after dinner and Robert slept in their lounge. He could see marines patrolling the cliff path intermittently throughout the night. The three settlers rose before dawn and made final adjustments to the document. They waited until the first rays of the sun fell upon the porch and then walked down to the school house in the settlement. The document was approved in its entirety, the teacher and her husband adding their signatures to the three that were already present.

Adam walked to the beach. Francesco stood with a group of inshore fisherman by the side of one of their boats.

'Is there a problem, Francesco?'

'Ricardo tells me he did not beach his boat here last night. It's far too close to the rocks. He always uses that metal ring over there. Someone has used the boat last night and with the curfew that can only be the marines.'

Adam smiled. 'Can we think of any reason why marines would wish to use a fishing boat last night?'

'To hide the evidence.' They chorused.

'I'll add that to our letter of complaint before we hand it in when we get to Jamestown.'

The lugger, a heavy boat for two fishermen to launch, was swiftly returned to the water, with the assistance of the other fishermen. They swung north out of the bay and, as soon as they had cleared Sugarloaf Point, tacked to starboard until Jamestown came to view. By an hour before noon they had moored the lugger and were walking to the Governor's mansion.

'Do you know much about the Governor, Adam?'

'What little I know is not very complimentary, I'm afraid. Captain Pickford has met him and found him opinionated and rude. I think the Reverend Wilkes finds him difficult to work with, but the chaplain is too forgiving a man to criticise him directly.'

When they reached the mansion, they asked to speak to his secretary. A thin man in a black suit appeared and took them to a small office. They told him their business and passed over the letter of complaint. The secretary read it slowly, his face impassive.

'Which one of you is Ceruso?'

Surprised by the question, Francesco raised his hand.

'Please wait here, gentlemen.'

Adam turned to Francesco, as the door closed behind the secretary.

'There's something wrong here, Francesco. Why did he ask about your identity specifically? You're not a signatory of the document.'

'I've got the feeling, Adam, that Sergeant Logan has got here before us, with his own version of events.'

Francesco's suspicions were swiftly confirmed. The secretary returned with four marines. The Governor will see you now.'

They were escorted to a larger office and the secretary indicated that they should stand several paces in front of a large, teak desk that dominated the room. Behind it sat the Governor; a portly man with an irritated expression on his face. The four marines positioned themselves behind the fishermen. Adam could see their letter of complaint lay on the Governor's desk with another smaller note by its side. The Governor slowly raised his eyes to Adam.

'Now tell me your side of the story.'

Adam explained the settlement's grievances; the marines were rude and poorly led, the settlement believed the marines had stolen food in the past, but did not have proof. They believed the pig had not wandered off and had been stolen, most likely by the marines. A request to search the barracks was not unreasonable, but this had been rejected, which many felt supported their suspicions. He criticised the need for a curfew last night and wondered, along with others in the settlement, if it had simply been a ruse to allow the evidence to be dumped at sea.

'Mr Fletcher, you live on an island that is a military outpost, far from civilisation. We wage wars from this island; at present it is against slavers but it will not be long before some country will wish to attack our trading routes and this island. This is not London or Devon; the needs of the Crown and the military come first. Sergeant Logan reports the settlement is rife with sedition and Ceruso is one of the ringleaders, creating discontent and showing disrespect to the officers of the Queen.'

Francesco started to move forward, but was immediately restrained by the marines behind him.

'That's not true, Sir. I am loyal to the Crown but do.......'

'Silence, man, and move back from the desk.'

Adam raised his hand as a request to speak. 'The charge against Mr Ceruso is not true and maliciously raised. Please speak with the Reverend Wilkes. He visited us recently to officiate at my wedding and he has some knowledge of the settlement. '

The Governor ignored Adam's plea. 'We received Sergeant Logan's request for reinforcement in the early hours of the morning. A detachment of marines left two hours ago under the command of Captain Todd. He'll assess the situation, quell any disturbance and then report back to me.'

The Governor turned to his secretary. 'Hold these men in custody until mid-afternoon. I don't want them getting back to the settlement before Todd, warning them of his arrival.'

He turned back to address the two fishermen. 'I will have order on this island, Fletcher, and your people had better understand they live under military rule.'

The marines escorted them to a small cell. They were not searched, but the door was locked and they could hear a marine patrolling in the corridor.

Adam sighed. 'That didn't go well for us, Francesco. Logan is a cunning man and he must have sent one of his marines off with a message at dusk or more likely when we were all in the meeting hall. I hope Captain Todd is a reasonable man, but I bet the evidence of the pig will have been removed before he gets there. There will be no lunch for us, I'm afraid.'

Adam's views were almost immediately proved wrong. Voices were raised in argument in the corridor and Adam heard Sarah's voice reprimanding the sentry.

'Albert, no one told you to starve these men. I know them, they're good people. Deny them food and I'm going to have to stop the supply of titbits from the kitchen that find their way to your mess table.'

The key turned in the lock and a red faced marine allowed Sarah in with a tray of food and water.

'I heard you were locked up, Mr Fletcher, and have sent a message to the Reverend Wilkes, but the Governor will not change his mind.'

She put the tray down on a small table. 'It's not much, some soup and cold meat, but I hope it helps to pass the time.'

They gratefully ate their lunch and settled down for the afternoon to pass.

In the early afternoon they heard the sentry come to attention. The door opened and Captain Benjamin Doyle walked in.

'This is a bit of a mess, Adam. As soon as I heard, I spoke to the Governor and explained the good work you both did when the Intrepid was in danger. He's a very difficult man to deal with once he's made up his mind. He has agreed to release you into my custody. If you agree to fish and not return to the settlement before six I'm happy to escort you to the quay now. Captain Todd is a good man and I think he'll calm things down.'

Adam gave him the assurances he required and explained that they had simply been the messengers carrying the settlement's justified grievances.

'I have no jurisdiction in that area, Adam. I understand the French are sabre rattling again; it's not likely to come to anything but, as you know, we have a long history of war with France and St Helena has a special resonance with the French because Napoléon is buried here. The Admiral and the Governor are very sensitive to unrest in areas of the island that might be used as a spring board for invasion. Prosperous Bay would be the obvious area of interest for any invasion. Logan's message struck a nerve with both of them and I would not be surprised if you found a frigate in your bay sometime soon.'

They walked to the quay and Adam shook the marine's hand. 'Thank you, Ben.'

'Tell your people to be careful, Adam. Logan has put you all in a very unsuitable position with the Governor. Treat Logan with care; gather evidence carefully. There are people in Jamestown who would speak up for you, but you must avoid trouble.'

The fishermen cleared the north of the island and sailed south on reduced canvas with all lines out at 15 fathoms. Late in the afternoon, with the sun low in the western sky, Adam brought the bow to starboard and Francesco retrieved the lines. The bay opened up in front of them. They could see marines on the beach with a mounted officer. Carmella greeted them.

'Did you deliver the message?'

'Yes, but it was not well received by the Governor. Sergeant Logan had got his lies in first. We were held in detention until Captain Doyle secured our release.'

'We thought that's what must have happened. That officer arrived with 30 men in the late morning and he's waiting to speak with you, Adam.'

'Why me?'

'He'll explain. He seems a fair person and his presence has calmed things down.'

Noting that they were discussing him, the officer rode over and dismounted.

'Captain Todd at your service.'

'Adam Fletcher at yours, sir. Carmella tells me you'd like to discuss matters with me.'

'I do, Mr Fletcher, I understand feelings are running very high in the settlement. They know that Sergeant Logan and his men are all in the barracks and my men are guarding the only access, the front door. No pig or parts can leave without being seen by my men. The settlement insists Mr Draper be allowed to inspect the barracks with me, but Sergeant Logan feels it would undermine his position if the man who accused the marines of theft is allowed to inspect their barracks. Mr Draper has been very reasonable about this dilemma and says he's happy to forego his inspection, but only if you join me as witness on behalf of the settlement.'

'Captain Todd, you're aware we were under curfew last night and one of the fishing boats was moved during the hours of darkness.'

'Yes, Mr Fletcher, I am.' The Captain raised his palms helplessly. 'I can't wind back the clock, but I think we both believe no pig will be found and that, quite reasonably, will not change anybody's mind about what is likely to have happened.'

'I will accompany you, but you're right that if we find no evidence of a pig, no one will be reassured. This is a loyal, law abiding settlement. It is the general view of the settlers that Sergeant Logan is the worst sergeant ever stationed here. The men are poorly led and he abuses his position as their leader. The best way to resolve this difficulty would be to replace him and this section of soldiers.'

'I hear what you say, Mr Fletcher, and privately I can tell you I understand your suggestion. It is not a situation I can control, but, if I get the chance to mould matters when I'm back in Jamestown, I'll try.'

They passed the marines at the barrack door. It was dim inside and it took Adam a couple of minutes to adjust to the limited light through the small windows. There were three sections to the barracks; a large open area at the door which had benches and tables and a metal stove. A rack of rifles stood by the door. There was no evidence of a pig or its remains. They entered a corridor with a single door to left and right. The door to the left opened up onto the kitchen with a cast iron stove. They inspected all the cupboards, pans and shelves and found no evidence of pork. The washrooms and latrines on the other side of the corridor also passed inspection. The final third of the barracks contained the bunk beds and lockers for the troops. A large cubicle by the door was reserved for Sergeant Logan. He smiled at Adam and indicated that Adam should enter.

'Please feel free to inspect, Mr Fletcher.'

Nothing abnormal was found. Captain Todd inspected every locker. There was no evidence the pig had been consumed in the barracks.

Adam shared the news with Robert, Matthew Draper and several farmers who had congregated in the square. The marine captain called for his horse.

'There's nothing more I can do here, gentleman. Mr Fletcher suggests a fresh deployment of marines with this section replaced. If that were to occur, would you consider it helpful?'

They nodded their approval and Matthew Draper added, 'and that includes Sergeant Logan.'

The captain nodded. 'It's not in my power, gentlemen, but I'll report your feelings back in Jamestown.'

The captain looked at his watch. 'It's too late to return to Jamestown tonight.'

He turned to his Sergeant who hovered close by. 'The men will stay in the barracks tonight and we'll leave at 08.00 tomorrow morning. Robert offered the captain accommodation for the night with feed for the horse. The captain walked up the hill with Adam and his brother-in-law. Ruth met them at the house and offered dinner. As the light faded, the horse was turned out to pasture and a convivial evening followed. The settlers hoped that Captain Todd would reassure Jamestown that they need have no worries about the settlement's loyalties.

Relations between the settlement and the marines remained tense. Sergeant Logan knew his section had overreached themselves stealing the pig, but had been surprised by the speed with which the settlement knew of its loss and where to apportion the blame. The result had been almost disastrous and had led to the one outcome he had always sought to avoid; critical comments about his section and his leadership being relayed to his superiors in Jamestown. Their ill-judged theft had almost created a riot without the benefits of the stolen pork – they had only managed two meals before carrying the remainder to the beach and dropping the weighted carcass in deep water. The curfew had been a brilliant way to avoid detection but he knew he would not be able to cover his tracks in that way again. He doubted Captain Todd had believed his story, but, in the absence of evidence to the contrary, he knew he would not be criticised. His section was ordered to tread carefully in the settlement and in future buy any provisions that were required. They must retain a position of authority and two man patrols would be increased for a while to emphasise their role within the community. His attempts to bed the Ceruso woman would have to wait. His desire for her was increased by the disdain which his comments had generated. There would be a way to break her; it was just a question of biding his time. He felt his handling of the theft of the pig had strengthened his authority within the barracks. The theft had not been his idea, but he should have taken more notice and realised fruit and vegetables were one thing, and even the occasional chicken would not be missed, but a pig was always going to be overly ambitious. He should have told them the pig was to be left alone; the trouble was that it had been Charlie Winter's idea and in recent months he'd had to be careful how he handled Charlie. They all enjoyed a game of cards and gambling for low stakes. Charlie rarely seemed to lose and John Logan owed him over fifty pounds. Charlie had been happy to allow the debt to grow until a few months ago, but was now pressing for payment. He was prepared to halve the debt, if the Sergeant could secure Charlie a promotion to Corporal. The balance of power was shifting in the barracks and John Logan did not like the change. Perhaps it was time to seek a transfer back to Jamestown or to one of the ships of the squadron. He had turned down the last two opportunities to return to Jamestown because of his designs on Carmella Ceruso. She would still be around in a couple of years.

Sergeant Logan sent out some night patrols, never fewer than two marines together. They reported that farmers were frequently seen in their orchards, if crops were ripe. The settlement saw his patrols as no more than loitering with intent to steal. It soon became apparent that what had been intended as an exercise to emphasise the marines' authority was having the reverse effect. The night patrols were discontinued.

A few weeks after the pig incident, Maria joined her parents in the square as the final fish were sold in the evening.

'I'm free tomorrow, Uncle Adam, could I come fishing with you?'

The wind blew in short gusts across the square, throwing up spirals of dust. Adam looked up at the sky. High clouds moved swiftly north and east. He looked at Francesco.

'What do you think?'

Francesco shook his head. 'Tomorrow would not be the best time, Maria. You're a good sailor, but it's going to be very choppy and I think we'll be thrown around a lot. Come down with your mother in the afternoon and help with the deliveries.'

The wind increased overnight, still coming in gusts. They pushed the boat out into the bay as the light in the eastern sky grew.

'A maximum reef to the main sail, Francesco. We'll have difficulty moving slowly enough to allow the lines to settle to the proper depth. I fancy a run south and east in the first instance without losing sight of the island. If we fish the area south of Saddle Point, we can always run down the wind back to the bay, should the weather get worse.'

A cool wind was blowing from the Antarctic and waterproofs offered only limited protection from the spray. The lugger bucked and rolled as Adam sought to keep a south east direction; fish were plentiful. They sat in the stern eating lunch as a larger wave broke over the bow and the lugger lurched over the crest.

'If the fish keep biting, Francesco, we'll be finished on this tack. Six more should be sufficient. We've had the best part of day and should be thinking of getting the catch to market.'

The island was receding from view and they were still two fish short of their quota.

'That will do, Francesco, I'm going about. When the sails are trimmed, start reeling in the lines slowly. We might still get a couple more.'

Adam chose his moment carefully, waiting for a patch of calmer water. The tiller was pushed hard over to starboard and the bow swung smartly across the face of the

116

wind. The sails were swiftly sheeted home and the lugger picked up pace on its final tack, running before the wind on course for Prosperous Bay. Francesco slowly wound in the lines with an additional fish for their catch. He looked over Adam's shoulder.

'There's a sail to the stern, skipper.'

They both studied the vessel approaching from the south.

'A frigate under a lot of canvass, Francesco. She looks in a hurry.'

They were being rapidly overtaken. As they watched the frigate, a cloud of smoke broke from her port side. Several seconds later they heard the sound of the canon.

CHAPTER NINE

'I wonder what that's all about. Are all the lines in, Francesco?'

'Yes. Perhaps we'd better heave to and see what he wants. I think it's the Intrepid, Adam.'

They hove to and the frigate swept towards them on their port side and then swung into the wind as the sailors reefed the sails. The frigate lost way and drifted down towards them. The lugger soon lay in the lee of the frigate and lines were thrown, which drew them to the accommodation ladder. Four sailors scampered down into the lugger with fenders and boat hooks to keep their boat free of the frigate.

'Captain Pickford's compliments, Mr Fletcher, could you attend him on the deck.'

They helped him time his jump onto the lower rungs of the accommodation ladder as the lugger rose and fell on the swell. Adam carefully climbed to the deck. Thomas Pickford stood at the entry port. He grasped Adam's hand. The breeze was stiffer than at sea level and they both braced themselves against the bulwark. Jacob stood close by with two boat cloaks and tankards of rum.

'I've a problem, Adam. I was setting off on patrol when one of the crew fell sick. I then came across HMS Swiftsure beating back to harbour. She had found three heavily armed slave ships which were trying to sail south of St Helena and on to the Caribbean. They know that our patrols are usually to the north. It's a new tactic to go south and travel in a convoy. Swiftsure has managed to slow them down by damaging their sails and rigging but has taken quite a mauling herself. I need to get down there to continue the attack until Swiftsure can raise reinforcements. If I can pass this sick man over to you, I can save valuable time and head south directly.'

Adam was surprised that one man's illness was dictating the ship's actions but agreed to carry the seaman to shore.

'It's not quite as simple as that. Perhaps you should get Francesco up to join us.'

Two more sailors went down to the lugger and Francesco joined them, gratefully accepting a boat cloak and some rum. Adam explained;

'They want us to take a seaman to shore, Francesco, so they can chase some slavers to the south of us.'

The captain steadied himself against the bulwark as a strong gust of wind tore across the deck and the frigate lurched over a larger wave.

'It's not a sailor, Adam, it's my first officer Jason Hewitt and he's not injured, he's sick.'

'With what?'

'That's the problem, we're not sure. A mail boat came into Jamestown from the West Indies earlier in the week. Jason went over to pick up our mail, but also to meet the first officer he knows from his previous posting in the Mediterranean. The friend was not very well when Jason saw him and then got a lot worse and was shipped to isolation on land. As we left, we heard the surgeon reporting that he might be developing yellow fever. Jason has gone down with similar symptoms. There are no secrets on this boat, gentlemen. All the crew knows we may have yellow fever on board; it's a killer and spreads rapidly. If it gets to the mess deck, we could lose most of the crew. I cannot take the crew to war with the slavers when they know we may have yellow fever aboard. If I can offload Jason, we reduce the risk and he has a better chance of survival in Jamestown. I'm sorry to involve you, but when the lookout saw a fishing boat so far out to sea on such a day I knew it must be you. Would you take him to the sanatorium in Jamestown?'

Adam looked over at Francesco who immediately nodded. 'Yes, Adam. Of course there's a risk, but if it gives Jason the best chance we should help.'

The captain looked over his shoulder to the darkening sky to the south.

'There's a protocol to these matters, Adam. When you get to Jamestown do not land – heave to close to the quay and summon the superintendent from the infirmary. They will tell you where to land him. Jacob, get the first officer on deck. I suggest you lay him just forward of the mast, not in your sleeping accommodation. Jason knows you'll try to keep your distance, he'll have a flask of water with him.'

Jason Hewitt was carried out onto the deck in a canvas sling, which was rigged to a line and pulley on the yardarm. His face was flushed, with sweat standing out on his forehead. Francesco returned to the boat to prepare the area where the first officer would lie.

'Take care of him, Adam, I have a great affection for my first officer.'

'We will, Thomas. Good hunting.'

They shook hands at the entry port and Adam returned to the lugger, jumping the final part as his boat rose up to meet him. Jason lay wrapped in a blanket on the canvas sling. A tarpaulin was passed down and wrapped around him. The sailors used the boat hooks to push the lugger's bow away from the frigate's side. They held the stern close to the accommodation ladder until the bow was at right angles to the frigate. There were hasty goodbyes as they leapt onto the ladder and Adam and Francesco pushed the lugger free. The sails began to fill and the lugger cleared the lee of the frigate into the full force of the wind. They resumed their previous course for Prosperous Bay. The frigate swiftly gained way and responded to the rudder, the bow swung to the south with the sails close hauled to the wind.

'I think we'd better get closer to land, Francesco, before we tack north to Jamestown.'

They ran before the wind in the same direction as the waves; even on reduced canvas the boat was travelling fast. Spray flew over the stern and both fishermen were cold and wet. Francesco finally voiced the, as yet, unspoken concern.

'Are we going to be able to beat around the north of the island in this?'

'In the normal course of events we'd not even consider it. What's in Jason's best interests?'

'Not for all three of us to be lost at sea.'

'We don't have a doctor in Prosperous Bay. Carrying Jason to Jamestown overland in this weather would probably kill him.'

The wind shrieked through the rigging and the crest of a large wave broke over the stern of the boat. Francesco started bailing.

'It has to be Prosperous Bay, Francesco. Somehow we have to nurse him there. We'll run for cover in the bay and then decide what to do.'

They cleared Bay Point and entered calmer waters.

'We'll have to follow Captain Pickford's suggestions, Adam. We can't bring the boat to the beach. If we anchor in a couple of feet of water someone can come close enough to be told of our situation.'

'Yes and perhaps further along the beach to the south, Francesco. We can't take him to a house in the village, he'll have to come to my house; it's sufficiently isolated and we can nurse him there until the diagnosis is known. Someone will have to get Ruth down to the beach so I can talk to her. We'll not be able to carry him through the village.'

121

'We could suspend the canvas sling from the boom and take him up the path to the cliff top at the southern end of the bay, away from the settlement. It's a long way round, but no one will want us to take the more direct route between the houses.'

They could see Carmella wrapped in a hooded cloak on the beach. They anchored close to the shore and beckoned her to the boat. She left her cloak on a beached boat and waded out to them.

'Don't come too close, Carmella.'

They explained their problem and the tentative solution. Adam could see Maria trotting across the beach towards them.

'Get Maria to fetch Ruth and then perhaps she can sell the fish. They were all caught and put in the nets before we even saw the frigate. I think we'd just better start with the view that treating Jason in isolation is simply a precaution. It's not as if we know he has yellow fever.'

Carmella nodded. 'I wondered if perhaps you should stay with us, Adam, for a few days until we find out the cause. If the settlement gets nervous no-one will want to buy fish from us. I can supply Ruth with anything she needs, just placing them on the porch and keeping my distance.'

Maria ran to the cliff top and returned with Ruth.

'I'm sorry, Ruth, I didn't feel I could let Captain Pickford down. We had planned to take Jason to Jamestown but the weather has made that impossible. There are serious risks for you if it is yellow fever.'

She put Adam at his ease. 'If I had been there, I'd have done the same as you, Adam. I sat next to him at dinner on the Intrepid; he's a good man and deserves the best chance. There's no other way to deal with the matter. I'll make a bed up in the living room and he can be nursed in isolation if Carmella supplies us with provisions. We've all the water we need.'

Adam started to release the boom. 'So it's agreed, we'll moor the lugger fore and aft here. Maria, please sell the catch for us; we may be able to join you later. Carmella, will you go with Ruth and prepare the living room for our arrival. Put some clothes in a bag for me and put them on the porch. You'll have plenty of time before we reach the house. I don't know how yellow fever spreads, but I presume Francesco and I should get him into the cot and withdraw outside immediately. If the weather eases we can fish to the north tomorrow and Francesco can sell some of the catch in Jamestown while I get advice from the doctor at the infirmary.'

The sling was attached to the boom and the first lieutenant was gently lifted over the side with a fisherman at each end of the spar. They moved slowly south across the beach to a small, infrequently used path that led up to the cliff top, stopping to catch their breath on several occasions before they gained the high ground and, eventually, Adam's cottage. Carmella stood at a distance carrying a bag of Adam's clothes. At the sight of the fishermen, Ruth kissed Carmella on the cheek.

'Carmella, promise me you'll keep at a distance once Jason is in the house.'

'It'll not be easy, Ruth, but I know it has to be that way. We'll get into a routine. I'll come three times a day and get you whatever you require. If you start to feel unwell, promise me you'll tell me.'

'I will, my friend; take care of Adam, I know he'll worry about the risk he has exposed me to. I'm not afraid; I nursed my mother and my father. We'll all do our best for Jason.'

They hugged again and then Ruth returned to the porch. The fishermen laid Jason gently on the ground. The ladies held the ends of the boom above the first lieutenant as the ropes that held the canvas were removed. They picked up the corners of the canvas and carried him to the cot which Ruth had laid out in the corner of the living room.

'He's soaked, Ruth.'

'It doesn't matter, just lay him on the cot and then withdraw. I'll take care of the rest.'

'I'll come by every morning and every evening, Ruth.' He held her in his arms and kissed her.

'I'll look forward to seeing you; go quickly and leave me to my patient.'

She mopped his brow; his skin was hot and moist to the touch. 'Jason, it's Ruth, Adam's wife. You're staying with us until you're better.'

His eyes were clear and he nodded, but seemed unable to speak.

'When you're in a dry bed, I'll bring you some warm milk and then you must rest.'

She took off his sodden clothes and washed and dried him before removing the canvas sling. The linen beneath him had remained dry and she covered him with a sheet. She looked for spots which might give a clue as to the diagnosis. She knew that the spots of smallpox tended to involve the face and the limbs and those of chicken pox, the torso. What had her mother told her about yellow fever, did the patient go yellow? There didn't seem to be any evidence of that with Jason. She warmed some milk and held him forward so that he could sip from the mug. He could only swallow with difficulty, but they both persevered until the mug was empty. She laid his head back on the pillow. He was exhausted and lay with his eyes closed, beads of sweat running back onto the pillow and sheet. She soothed him and held a cool cloth to his forehead. He developed a rigor, shivering, despite his high temperature. Ruth heard Carmella call softly from outside.

'How is he?'

'Barely conscious and burning up. Ask Adam to find out everything he can about yellow fever. I need to know what to look for. Tell him Jason has no spots at present; he does not look yellow, which I hope is a good sign.'

'I think it's the eyes that go yellow, Ruth, but I'll get Adam to check.'

'How's the settlement taking it?'

'We've not mentioned yellow fever. People are concerned and many offered to help, but they understand it's better if only one person comes out here to supply you. There's no panic and Maria had sold almost all the fish when we got back to the square. She was bargaining with that marine that buys their food, Charlie Winters. I think he hoped he'd get a bargain in our absence, but Maria was not having any nonsense from him and we simply stood behind her and watched her complete the sale. He had the good grace to admit the fish looked good and that it was a fair price. We were very proud of her. Bring out a couple of pots and I'll pour some broth into one for both of you and some fish soup in the other for you. Dorothy Lloyd gave me the loaf and Lucy Davies promised me a lamb stew for you tomorrow. Try to get some rest tonight, Ruth, I'll be back at dawn.'

When Ruth returned to the cot Jason was unconscious, his limbs twitched with involuntary movements as if he was having a nightmare. He muttered low incomprehensible words. She placed a portion of broth on the marble slab in the pantry for Jason to have in the morning and ate her dinner at the table. She would light the stove in the morning and wash his clothes. At Carmella's suggestion, they had placed Jason's cot so that Ruth could see him as she lay in bed, if the door was open. She placed a lamp behind his pillow and trimmed the wick so that there was only sufficient light to keep him under review. She was unsure whether it would have any benefit but hoped that, if she had a cold shower regularly, it might reduce the risk of catching Jason's illness. It was impossible to care for him at a distance.

Refreshed by the shower, she turned her bedside lamp low and tried to rest. Sleep would not come to her. Jason tossed restlessly in his cot, occasionally shouting out in terror or confusion. After a couple of hours Ruth put a shawl around her shoulders and sat by him, holding his hand and telling him a story about the settlement. The conversation seemed to calm him and she continued to talk in a soothing voice, telling him about her parents and their lives on the farm. He did not seem to be so hot, but remained confused and irrational. She found it easy to talk to him about herself, confident that the effect was simply a soothing sound to supplement holding his hand.

'I envy you, Jason, and your sex which allows you to travel the world under the command of a kind and courageous captain. You've lived in England and visited London and the major ports in England and the Mediterranean. Your life is hard and demanding, but you work with an able crew and can take courage from those around you; all working to a common purpose to defeat the enemy and survive on a dangerous ocean. The abolition of slavery is a principle worth defending. I'm sure there are occasions when you have to decide, in an instant, a matter of critical importance. I have confidence that you'd be a man who'd choose correctly. I've only had to make one such decision in my life and I chose badly. I hoped it was something I could repair with time, but now I begin to doubt that'll be the case. Opportunities don't always repeat themselves and we must accept the consequences of the choices we make, even if the challenge comes to us unexpectedly. When I was ignorant of the world at large I had no cause to feel restless, but now I feel unsettled about my life in a small village on a minute, remote island in a vast ocean. Perhaps it was the dinner on the Intrepid which created those feelings; I enjoyed your company and hearing about life in your world. I still have the rose you gave me that night. However, Jason, in the matter of duty I know I am your equal. Tonight and for the days that follow we work together to save your life. I have my own loyal crew to support me and with God's will you'll soon be restored and I'll return to being a support to Adam, the Cerusos and the settlement. I think there will be times, perhaps in the evenings in years to come, when I will sit out on the porch looking down on the ocean, wondering how you, Captain Pickford and the loyal crew of the Intrepid are faring.'

She wrung out the cloth and mopped his brow. He was cooler and calmer. She sat quietly holding his hand. He remained calm. Gently she slipped her hand from his and raised herself from the chair. Almost immediately his restlessness returned. She kissed his forehead.

'Don't worry, Jason, I'll stay with you.'

She sat back in the chair and clasped his hand, resuming her soothing monologue.

Ruth woke with the dawn and could hear Carmella calling her from outside. Jason's breathing was irregular and the high temperature had returned. He remained unconscious and she was still holding his hand. Her neck, back and arms ached and she could only rise slowly from the chair. Carmella stood beyond the porch rail.

'I'm sorry, Ruth, you look awful.'

'I sat with him all night, Carmella, to try to keep him calm. I fell asleep in the chair and have just woken up. I ache all over and feel terrible. Perhaps a cold shower will help. Is Adam coming up?'

'Yes, in a few minutes.'

'Give me the food swiftly and turn him back. Say I've gone to bed to rest. I'd rather he didn't see me looking like this. I'll look forward to his news this evening when he's been to Jamestown.'

Ruth showered and dressed and washed Jason's clothes. He did not regain consciousness, but his temperature seemed lower, when she laid the back of her hand upon his brow. She had some lunch and managed to sleep for a couple of hours before being woken by the sound of Jason shouting orders to reef the sails. She returned to the chair by his cot. His temperature was rising again and his breathing sounded different, as if his throat was partly blocked. She tried to coax some water through his lips, but he only coughed and gagged and she was afraid she was doing more harm than good. She made some tea and sat by him reading from her bible. He seemed to find her voice comforting and lay quiet. Carmella called her and she went out onto the porch, shading her eyes against the setting sun.

Adam and Francesco had carried a bench up from the settlement and they placed it several paces from the verandah. Ruth had already tied a red ribbon across the entrance to the verandah to stop visitors getting closer. Carmella carried two metal containers.

'How is he, Ruth?'

'He's still unconscious and delirious. He shouts out occasionally; I think he's at sea in a storm. His temperature was lower this morning but it's rising again now.'

'If you get your containers, Ruth, I can pour soup into one and Lucy's lamb and potato stew into the other. We thought we'd have our dinner with you.'

They sat several paces apart, supping mugs of soup.

'Carmella said you sat with him all night, Ruth.'

128

'Yes, Adam, he was delirious and got very agitated. I fell asleep in the chair and woke up very stiff this morning. I did get a chance to rest early this afternoon. He was cooler and calmer then, but he's not regained consciousness. He seems to get worse in the evenings and that's when his temperature rises. How did you get on in Jamestown?'

'The medical superintendent was helpful. Jason's friend is also delirious. They think it is yellow jack, that's yellow fever. I don't think we've ever had the disease in the settlement. The Navy knows the condition all too well; in the past it has decimated our men in the West Indies. He told me it can also be caught in Africa and our sailors have sometimes caught the disease from slaves being transported to the New World. Some slave ships have lost almost their entire cargo of captives by the time they've made the crossing. The superintendent thinks the gross overcrowding is the reason why so many slaves die, although no one knows how the disease is spread. He suggests you keep the house as well ventilated as possible, although he doesn't know if that'll make any difference. He cannot spare anyone to send here and he thinks Jason's best chance of survival is to remain here being nursed.

'When I took his wet clothes off, Adam, I looked for signs of spots, thinking it might be chicken pox or small pox, but I didn't find anything.'

'The superintendent says keep him cool and calm. If he regains consciousness give him water and clear broth. He hopes the fever will settle. Every day in a coma without water and broth brings him closer to death. Some young men can survive several days like this, but most die after three to five days in delirium. If he's still alive in two days I'll go back to report Jason's progress and learn of the fate of his friend.'

'Is there no other form of treatment that might help, Adam? His throat seems partly blocked and before he lost

129

consciousness he looked as though he had some difficulty swallowing.'

I'll pass that on to the superintendent. Are you short of anything?'

'Candles, Adam. Apart from that, I have what I need.'

They heard Jason cry out in alarm.

'I'd better go. It's been nice to have supper with you.'

'We'll do the same tomorrow, Ruth.'

Carmella mimed a kiss. 'Try and get some rest, Ruth, you have to remain strong.'

Ruth returned to Jason's cot and felt his brow; the fever was back in full force. She sat forward on the chair to hold his hand more easily and began to read.

Jason's fever became worse as the evening turned into night. He was agitated and drenched with sweat and only her hand gripping his seemed to anchor him in calmer waters. Ruth was exhausted and knew she could not cope with another night in the chair. It would be highly irregular but she would need to bring his cot to the side of her bed so that she could offer comfort, but still get some rest. No-one would be able to see from the front door and the main window would have to remain closed and curtained. There were two high windows above the bed, which could be left open with a good flow of air across to the door.

Jason was not a tall man, but he was well built and she found the combined weight of the officer and the cot almost too much as she slowly dragged them over the flagstone floor. Eventually she had the cot by her side of the bed. No one must know of this temporary expedient, with her patient in such close proximity. She could feel the cool draught from the windows above her and hoped, if the disease was transmitted through the air, that the ventilation would prove adequate.

She showered again and put on a fresh nightdress. The beds were of similar height and she lay on her side and picked up Jason's hand. She spoke soothingly to him, talking about earlier events in her life; her hopes and her worries. The effect, as previously, calmed him and she fell asleep with her hand firmly in his grasp. He did not cry out and the night passed in silence.

CHAPTER TEN

Ruth woke in the pre-dawn light and slowly stretched out on the bed, taking care not to disturb Jason's grasp of her hand.   His breathing was slow and sounded more obstructed. She gently disengaged her hand and showered and dressed in preparation for Carmella's visit. She was sitting on the verandah when Carmella arrived with Adam.

'He slept well, but he still feels hot. I've not tried to wake him for fear he remains delirious. I think his throat must be affected, it definitely sounds as though it is partly obstructed. I managed to sleep for most of the night and feel a lot better.'

'Here's fresh bread and broth, Ruth, and Matthew Draper's housekeeper has promised me a rabbit stew for the evening.'

Adam dropped a bunch of candles onto the table where Ruth's metal pot stood, now full of broth from Carmella's jug.

'We'll fish off to the east today, Ruth, and just supply the settlement.   I won't come up tomorrow morning. Francesco and I will start early and fish off the North Cape so we can get to Jamestown in the early afternoon. I hope I'll be able to find out more from the superintendent for our discussion in the evening. Let me know tonight if you learn anything more about his condition today and I'll pass it on to the superintendent when we meet.'

'Some oil for the lamps would be useful, Adam. I've one near his bed set on low overnight, so I can observe him from a distance without disturbing him.'

She could feel the colour rising in her cheeks at the deception. She could not look her husband and her friend in the eye and deflected attention by picking up the supplies and taking them indoors.   She poured a glass of water and returned to the verandah. Adam seemed in no hurry to leave.

'Do you feel well, Ruth? You look a little flushed this morning.'

'I don't think I'm sickening with anything. I was very tired yesterday, but I got a good night's sleep and I think today will be better. Jason seems to get worse in the evenings and the early parts of the night. I know he's young but he cannot survive high fevers night after night if he's having no water. Perhaps I might be able to coax him to drink, if he regains consciousness today. Thank you for the supplies, I'd better attend to him and perhaps I'll have more positive news to report this evening.'

The day passed slowly. Jason lay quiet and unconscious in his cot in the morning and Ruth took the opportunity to perform all her household chores. When these were done and she'd had some soup and bread for lunch she tried to wake Jason and get him to drink some water. He could not be roused and the attempt produced a period of agitation that only settled with the help of a prolonged monologue by Ruth on the birds and the animals she had seen on St Helena. When he was quiet she lay down on the bed next to him and held his hand. She slept into the late afternoon and woke to his restless movements. His temperature had risen again and his breathing was getting more strained. No man could live like this for long.

Carmella's visit was cut short by Jason's delirious cries from within.

'I'll have to go, Carmella. I feel so helpless, there's so little I can do. I think I'm going to lose him.'

Carmella started to move forward to comfort her friend. 'No, Carmella, please keep your distance.'

'You'll not lose him, Ruth. I know he'll be receiving all the love and care you can provide. If he dies, we'll all have lost him to the disease or to a higher authority. You're tired, make sure you eat and drink and try to remain strong.'

Ruth left the rabbit stew on the stove to keep warm and took bread and a mug of broth to the cot. Holding Jason's hand and reading the Bible did not calm him. The fever raged and Jason was, once again, living a nightmare on the quarter deck of a warship shouting orders and gibberish. What little reserves that remained to him were burning away in his delirium. In the early hours of the morning he became quieter; it seemed more through exhaustion than recovery. His brow was cooler, the fever was less.

Remembering Carmella's advice, Ruth forced herself to eat a bowl of the rabbit stew and felt the better for it. She showered, donned her nightdress and slipped between the sheets alongside his cot. Was the breathing less obstructed? Yes it sounded better, but then she realised the change was not necessarily an improvement. Jason's breathing was very shallow. She studied his torso in the limited light from the oil lamp. She had turned the sheet down to his waist in the hope of reducing his temperature. Was his chest rising and falling at all? She raised herself on an elbow to study him more closely. Had he died unattended whilst she ate the rabbit stew? No, there were movements there but very slight ones. This must be the beginning of the end. His ravaged body had nothing more to give. She drew his hand across to her and kissed his palm.

'Please live, Jason, please live.'

Exhausted, she fell asleep clutching the sailor's hand.

Ruth woke at dawn. Memories of the previous evening flooded back to her. She did not dare open her eyes. Jason's hand was still in hers. She could not hear the sound of breathing and knew his mouth could not be more than two feet from her. His hand felt warm, she had been clutching it to her chest. She had learnt to take a pulse at the wrist when her parents had been dying and she knew that it was not always easy to feel. Cautiously she advanced a finger to the area, but could feel nothing.

'Please, God, he has not died whilst I slept.' She opened her eyes. His position was unchanged, his mouth half open with dried spittle at the edges. He was breathing, but it was so shallow as to be barely noticeable. She kissed his hand and laid it gently by his side.

When Carmella arrived, Ruth was already showered and dressed.

'He had a terrible evening and most of the night, Carmella. He was delirious and agitated, burning up reserves he could ill afford to lose. He's calmer now, but I fear it is the prelude to death. I dare not try to get him to drink, for fear it'll be the final straw.'

'The men left about an hour ago, Ruth, and hope to be back by mid-afternoon. Perhaps the superintendent may have some better news for Adam. It's a fish soup today for you and more broth for both of you if Jason wakes up. I'm making a fruit pie from Robert's orchard. I'll bring it up this afternoon, when the men return.'

The day passed slowly. Ruth moved quietly around the house, washing clothes and linen. She did not disturb Jason who remained comatose on the edge of existence. After lunch she lay on the bed next to him and picked up his hand. He did not register the change. She kissed his hand and traced the creases of his palm with her fingers. She slid her slim fingers between his and held his hand to her chest.

'You're not alone, Jason. Stay with us, stay with me.'

She woke abruptly at the sound of Carmella coming up the path. Jason was unchanged. She slipped from the bed and walked out onto the verandah, squinting into the sunshine. Carmella sat on the bench with the two fishermen behind her.

'How is he, Ruth?'

'Unchanged from this morning, Carmella. He's barely breathing and I've not dared to try to rouse him. I fear his battle is nearly over. Did the superintendent have anything new to say?'

Adam cleared his throat. 'Yes, Jason's friend did not have yellow fever. The superintendent thinks it's a disease a French doctor described a few years ago, diphtheria. It spreads through close contact and for many people the disease is fatal. There is no special treatment beyond the care you're already providing. The Naval policy for diphtheria is that he remains in isolation for two weeks from the time the symptoms developed.'

'Is Jason's friend showing signs of progress?'

Francesco twisted his cap in his hands and looked at the ground. Carmella looked at Ruth with tears in her eyes. Adam cleared his throat again and spoke gravely.

'I'm sorry, Ruth, he never regained consciousness and died two hours before I arrived this morning.'

Carmella made to move towards the verandah. 'No, Carmella, I'll see this through to the end alone. There's no point in adding to the risks. I feel tired, but I'm not unwell. If he lives, we remain in isolation for the two weeks.'

'That is right, then you can both mingle freely and, if he's well enough, we can take him to Jamestown. The house has to be cleaned with a thin solution of quick lime. That was the advice of the French doctors.'

'And if he dies?'

'We would not be able to use the settlement graveyard. Francesco and I would dig a grave overlooking the ocean.

You would wrap him in linen and put him on the canvas sling. We'd bring the boom back up and carry him to his grave. We would sprinkle quick lime powder in the grave before it is closed. You would still have to remain in isolation for the full two weeks.'

'I see. Perhaps if you'd leave me now I'll have some rest in case the agitation returns with the evening; I doubt he'll have the strength, but it would be better to be rested.'

'I'll bring food at dusk, Ruth.'

'Thank you, Carmella.'

Ruth walked into the bedroom. Jason remained unconscious, his chest movements barely perceptible. She brought a bowl of water and gently washed him, enjoying the intimacy that the action allowed. Ruth could feel the contours of his body through the thin cloth and was reluctant to bring her task to completion. Emboldened by the contact, she kicked off her shoes and lay on the bed stroking his naked body with her fingers. She held his hand and fell into an untroubled sleep.

Carmella had to call out several times before Ruth appeared at the door.

'Is there any change?'

'No, but it can't go on much longer. Normally by now his temperature is beginning to climb, but I think he's too reduced by the disease, even to respond to it. I feel so helpless and he's such a fine young man with his whole life ahead of him, were it not for this dreadful disease.'

Carmella poured a thick fish soup into one of Ruth's containers and some broth in the second. She lowered a linen bag onto the table with a loaf and the apple pie.

'Are you eating, Ruth?'

'I am, I'll have some of this as soon as I get inside. Prepare yourself and the men for the worst, Carmella. I can't see Jason surviving the night.'

It was dark by the time Ruth prepared herself for the night vigil. She trimmed the oil lamp and had a shower. There was no breeze and the room felt warm. The stone floor was cool beneath her feet. She walked naked to the chest of drawers for a fresh nightgown, revelling in the feeling of air against her naked body. She half opened the drawer and then changed her mind. Jason was on the point of leaving this world; he would do so with dignity and loved by one who cared for him. She slowly slid the drawer closed and went to his cot. There was no fever but still the shallow breathing. He did not stir. It was easy to use his sheet to draw him onto her bed. Ruth lay on her side and held him in her arms, sharing his pillow. She kissed his cheek and whispered in his ear.

'Jason Hewitt, you must not die. A lot of people want you to live. Your captain, Thomas Pickford, left you in our care because he loves you and trusts us to make you well. The doctors say there is no treatment for the disease you have, beyond care and love. Believe me you have both in abundance. I fear you're at the boundary of existence and I pray there's still time for you to row back to our world. There is so much that is beautiful yet to be experienced. If any strength remains in you, come back to us, come back to me. If your course is already run, know that you will die in my arms surrounded by my love. If there is a God watching over us, forgive me my actions; they are borne out of love for this man. Please spare him; he has much goodness to share with the world.'

Ruth raised herself up on her elbow and kissed his forehead, then his closed eyes, and finally his lips. She wrapped her arms around him and rested her forehead against his cheek.

'Live, Jason, please live for me and all those who love you.'

The first signs of light through the curtains warned Ruth that the night had passed. She remembered closing the nightshirt drawer and all that followed. Her eyes were closed and she could not feel her left arm. She knew the sheet only covered her ankles and that her naked body was still touching Jason. Her right hand held his and was lying on his stomach. Her head had slipped down onto the side of his chest during the night. There was no movement or sounds of breathing. She experienced an overwhelming feeling of sadness, and then anxiety, as she became aware that she was being watched. Cautiously she opened her eyes. The light was still dim, but their position in the bed would be obvious to any onlooker. The curtains at the window were in place and she turned her head to the door – empty. Confused, she lowered her gaze to Jason's muscular stomach. Her fingers were extended, entwined with Jason's left hand as they rested on his stomach. She was surprised to find he had moved his right hand on top of hers. Ruth was hampered by her left arm remaining trapped under Jason's back as she raised her gaze to his face. The eyes she had kissed in farewell the previous night were open but unblinking. She could feel her own eyes filling with tears. She kissed his cheek.

'I hope you regained consciousness before you died, Jason, and knew you were surrounded by love.'

His eyelids slowly closed and then opened again.

CHAPTER ELEVEN

Hardly daring to believe what she had witnessed, Ruth gently pulled her arm out from under Jason's back. She had neither use nor feeling below the elbow. She slid off the bed, moved the cot and then sat on the edge of the bed by Jason. His brow was cool. Jason's eyes had not followed her, but remained open, staring straight ahead.

'Can you hear me, Jason? If you can, blink twice.'

At first she thought he had not heard her instruction, and was about to repeat the request when he complied. The movements were very slow and deliberate. His lips were cracked and his tongue was heavily furred. He was alive, but barely so, and clearly the battle was not over yet.

'I'll get you water, Jason. You must drink, even if it exhausts you.'

Ruth ran naked to the kitchen, her left arm swinging uselessly by her side, her fingers tingling and painful as the circulation returned. Cursing her useless limb, she pushed all the pillows behind Jason's head and back and knelt next to him on the bed. Drinking the first mug of water seemed to take an age but Ruth had the satisfaction of seeing his tongue moisten and move more freely. She was half way through the second mug when she heard Carmella call from beyond the verandah. Ruth donned her robe and ran barefoot to greet her friend.

'He's alive, Carmella, and his temperature has settled, at least for the present. He is conscious, but still on the very edge of existence. I can't stay; I want him to have as much fluid as possible for fear he lapses into a coma again. I thought water first and broth later.'

'Go to him, Ruth, I'll bring warm broth at noon.'

Jason finished the third mug of water by mid-morning. The feeling and power to Ruth's arm was restored. Jason was barely conscious; she removed the extra pillows.

'Rest now, Jason, I'll wake you later when Carmella has brought warm broth.'

He closed his eyes and slept.

By sunset he had consumed several mugs of water and two of broth. His temperature had not risen but his breathing remained light and laboured. She planned further broth for her patient later, if he seemed strong enough to cope.

Ruth sat on the verandah drinking wine. Robert and Adam lay on the ground. Francesco and Carmella sat on the bench. Robert was opening a second bottle.

'Jason's asleep at present. I'll wake him after you've gone and try and get more nourishment into him.'

'Has he spoken yet?'

'No, there is still something wrong with his throat and his breathing sounds obstructed. I don't know if he cannot speak or he's just too exhausted to try. It would be heart breaking to lose him now, but he is still very close to death.'

Noting that Ruth's glass was empty, Robert advanced to the table at the edge of the verandah where all transactions occurred. He paused with the bottle above her glass.

'Should Jason's nurse be drinking on duty, Adam?'

'Your sister has done well, Robert, she deserves the refill and more besides.'

'If I weren't in isolation, Robert, I'd make you pay for that. You know Adam has a place for you on his boat if you misbehave.'

Adam laughed. 'I think we can do better than that, Ruth. If you were to restore Jason to Captain Pickford, I'd imagine he'd be happy to press-gang your disrespectful brother and carry him off to sea.'

'An excellent idea, Adam; the notion of Robert in irons, bouncing around the South Atlantic in a gale is very appealing after all the years I've had of mockery and disrespect.'

'Captain Pickford would probably give us a few guineas for a good lookout in the cross trees, Ruth. The mast top swings about a lot more than at deck level. Robert is always telling us how sharp eyed he is. Mainmast lookout would be just the place for your brother.'

'That's enough, Adam. Your wife can have as much wine as she likes. When we had dinner on the Intrepid, I felt slightly seasick even at anchor in the bay.'

They talked on into the dusk. Adam left, promising to report the change to the superintendent in Jamestown the following day and see if there was any additional advice on Jason's care.

Ruth walked back into the house. She knew she was now living two lives and closing the front door took her from one to the other. She found the move to her new life exhilarating and she doubted that was caused solely by the wine. She sat by Jason on the bed; a young man still close to death. She held his hand, feeling more full of life than she could ever remember.

'If only I could pass half these feelings to you, Jason, the remaining half would be plenty enough for me.'

Jason managed two mugs of broth and one of water before collapsing back onto the bed. Ruth washed and dried him, reassured that his tongue now looked more normal. She showered and dried herself slowly, delaying the decision that had preyed on her mind all afternoon. Jason was conscious, and propriety required she should at least return him to his cot, even if it remained next to her

142

bed. She should also wear a nightgown. But the voice of her new life rebelled. Jason remained close to death and if, pray God, he survived he would likely have no memory of these times or, if he did remember, might consider them a hallucination. Ruth walked to the bed and lay down beside the first officer. She wove her fingers between his and rested them on his stomach. He did not wake but she felt the pressure of her touch momentarily reciprocated.

'Survive this night, Jason, and we'll build on today's progress.'

The friends gathered again at sunset in front of the verandah. Ruth had slept well and the day had gone smoothly with Jason taking more broth than water. She held her glass to be filled by Adam and told them how Jason was progressing.

'He's asleep now, but he's definitely made good progress. He's had some more water and broth and I've more confidence that he's turned the corner. However, sometimes when I raise his head to take some fluid, he seems about to faint.'

'Has he spoken?'

'No, and I think it may be quite a while before he does. His tongue is now moist, but his throat must be inflamed. Even fluids cause him pain as he swallows.'

'That fits in with what the superintendent was telling me today. Diphtheria does cause inflammation to the throat. Many of the people who die with the disease do so because they cannot breathe.'

'He's hardly breathing at all, Adam. It's very shallow and his throat still seems partly obstructed.'

'Is he getting worse?'

'No, but he's not improving. His temperature has returned to normal and the delirium has passed, but I don't suppose we can relax until I can report his breathing is getting easier. Is there anything else I could do to improve his chances, Adam?''

'No, just build up the fluids and the nourishment.'

Carmella glanced at the fish pie she had brought. 'It's obviously going to be quite a while before he can cope with this sort of food. I'll discuss it with our friends; we need nourishing food but in liquid form.'

Ruth laughed. 'Just remember there are two of us here in isolation. The fish pie looks delicious.'

'Do you still keep an eye on him at night, Ruth?'

Adam's question threw Ruth off balance. She diverted attention by offering her glass for a refill. She knew the colour was rising in her cheeks but hoped the rosy glow of the setting sun would mask her embarrassment.

'Now that the delirium has passed, I check him last thing at night, before I turn in, and then first thing in the morning. If we've turned the corner, Adam, how many days in isolation remain?'

It must feel like a lifetime already, Ruth, but I think it's only six days and five nights that have passed. You'll have to put up with this for another eight days I'm afraid.'

The conversation then moved to other matters; there had been a new argument between the settlers and the marines. Ruth was content to be a bystander to the conversation, sipping her wine and watching the thin cloud moving across Diana's Peak. Her second life, beyond the closed door, must terminate in eight days. She could not in good conscience keep his cot in her bedroom for much longer. She smiled inwardly; the position of the cot was hardly a moral issue when Jason was not sleeping there, but in her marital bed. How would she behave tonight? Would she be naked or wearing her night dress? Would Jason be in the bed or in the cot? The sun touched the top of Diana's peak and the light began to fade. She swirled the wine in her glass and watched rivulets run back down to the surface. She felt she knew what the decision was likely to be.

Ruth waved Adam and her friends goodbye and walked back through the front door. The sensation of moving to a different life was stronger than before and was coupled with a youthful excitement, which she could not remember experiencing in the past. 'Ruth Fletcher, what has become of you, where is this going?'

Ruth knew that she was cautious by nature and preferred situations where she had an element of control. However, her feelings for Jason were so intoxicating that she found her usual need to control was subordinated by a desire to experience new emotions, whatever the cost. She kept Jason in her bed, revelling in the contact of their uncovered bodies. She wove her fingers between his and laid her hand on his stomach. On this occasion, Jason slowly moved his free hand to cover them.

The first officer's recovery was slow. The following night Ruth wore a night dress and also drew Jason back onto his cot by her side. Halfway through the second week he sat on the side of his bed for a short time and stood up two days later. Ruth helped him shower and shave and reluctantly drew his cot back into the living room. Adam cut a stave and, with Ruth's help, Jason took his first, tentative steps. He still did not speak. His obstructed breathing seemed to be slightly easier but he was subject to paroxysms of painful coughing which left him exhausted. Adam and his friends came up on the evening of the twelfth day and Ruth surprised them by bringing Jason to the front door. He raised his hand in silent greeting. Ruth spoke on his behalf.

'Jason still cannot speak, but he wrote me a note today. He wanted to come to the door tonight to thank you for your kindness. He hopes he'll be able to communicate his thanks verbally soon. '

She looked up at the pale, drawn face.

'Do you think that is perhaps enough for tonight, Jason?'

He nodded. Ruth walked him back to his cot and helped him to lie back. She kissed him on the cheek and squeezed his hand. 'Well done, rest a while. I'll be back shortly and perhaps you'll take some more food. Carmella has a rabbit stew with some small fragments of meat and potato.'

She walked back on to the verandah and closed the door behind her. Carmella spoke for them all.

'How much weight has he lost, Ruth? He looks like a ghost.'

Ruth smiled. 'I should have prepared you. In truth, he's so much better than he was, but I know he has a long way to go. We haven't talked about it, Adam, but I would worry if we tried to move him to Jamestown when the two weeks of isolation are complete.'

'I agree, Ruth, he really cannot go anywhere soon; he needs to strengthen here. I doubt you could even take him for a walk along the cliff path for a week or so. His duties at sea are arduous and I'm sure Captain Pickford will want him to be restored to full health before his return to the frigate. The superintendent advised that, if Jason recovered, he'd be better not to convalesce in Jamestown Infirmary, as he'd be exposed to other diseases in his weakened state and might succumb.'

To Ruth's consternation, Robert offered to host Jason for the latter stages of the convalescence, but Adam seemed content with the current arrangements.

Two days later, the isolation was lifted and Ruth ceremoniously removed the red ribbon across the entrance to the porch with Jason standing behind her. There were several ladies in attendance with buckets and clothes. The thin solution of lime was mixed and all the surfaces of the house were wiped down while Jason sat on a chair, overlooking the sea. He tugged Ruth's arm and pointed to the east. She put her arm on his shoulder and scanned the horizon.

'I can't see anything, Jason.'

He smiled and mimed the shape of a boat. Within the hour, they could see a frigate on course for Prosperous Bay. Carmella put down her bucket.

'It's the Intrepid, Ruth. Would you like me to go to the beach and bring up Captain Pickford? He may not know that Adam was unable to take Jason to Jamestown.'

The Intrepid was battle scarred. The mizzen mast had been shot away below the topsail and there was only a single jib above a foreshortened bowsprit. The bulwarks were scarred and in places missing. Ruth and Jason watched Thomas Pickford descend the accommodation ladder and cross to the beach in the gig. Carmella pointed up at them and Ruth waved. They crossed the beach, making for the path through the settlement. The captain's concerns were evident as soon as he caught sight of his first officer. Ruth stood by her patient.

'Welcome, Thomas, I hope you don't mind if Jason doesn't stand. He's been sitting out longer than he ever has so far, because the ladies have been cleaning the house. Our period of isolation finished today. Jason did not have yellow fever, rather a disease called diphtheria. The weather was too bad to get him to Jamestown after you transferred him. We've nursed him here; he's been very ill, but is slowly on the mend. I'm afraid he's not yet been able to speak because his throat has been inflamed, but he writes me notes and feels it's getting better.'

'You're both out of isolation, Ruth?'

'Yes.'

The Captain dropped on one knee and took Jason's hand. 'It's good to see you alive, Jason, although it seems you've quite a way to go before we could call you well.'

Jason pointed to the Intrepid and the sailors who were taking the opportunity to make some repairs.

'Yes, Jason, we took a bit of a hammering and lost Jenkins and Sykes, but we kept the three slavers tied down until Swiftsure and Fearless appeared. One slaver caught fire and sank. The other two were captured and are on their way to Rupert's Bay.'

Carmella brought a chair and Thomas Pickford sat with Jason recounting the battle. Carmella smiled.

'He really cares for his first officer.'

'Yes, they're like father and son.'

Lucy Davies appeared and said the house was now cleaned and ready to be occupied. They helped Jason back to his cot. Ruth took Thomas Pickford back to the verandah and talked about their plans for Jason.

'Ruth, I'm in total agreement, this is the best place for him at present. He's with friends. I'll revisit you in a couple of weeks, but I wonder if that'll not be long enough.'

'He was very close to death for days, Thomas.'

'I'm so pleased I saw Adam's lugger on the ocean that day. I don't doubt Jason would have died if he'd been cared for elsewhere. I need to return to Jamestown today to start more major repairs. I know you'll take care of Jason.'

It soon became obvious that Ruth would now have to share her patient more widely as the ladies of the settlement fussed over him. With Carmella's help, she regained authority and, after tea in the kitchen, the ladies of the settlement returned to their homes leaving Carmella and Ruth to clear up the mugs and plates. They heard the sound of men's voices outside and then a knock at the door.

'I hope we're not going to be overwhelmed with visitors, Carmella. Jason is asleep; they'll have to see him some other time.'

Assuming an uncompromising look, she opened the door.

'Second lieutenant, George Rutherford, at your service, Mrs Fletcher. I had the pleasure of meeting you at the Captain's dinner. Compliments of Captain Pickford, might I bring in some gifts in appreciation of your kindness in caring for Mr Hewitt.'

A row of seamen stood behind him on the path. She opened the door more widely and they trooped past touching their forelocks and smiling broadly. George Rutherford identified the gifts as they passed her.

'Some wine, Miss Ruth, a leg of salted ham, a keg of port, a brass lamp and a selection of knives for the kitchen. Albert has several coils of rope that could be useful for the lugger; they are surplus to our needs.'

The last man in the line carried no gift. He held a slate and some chalk.

'I think you may have met Mr Bates, our ship's carpenter. The Captain wondered if you felt you needed any furniture constructed for your house, as a late wedding present.'

Carmella chuckled at Ruth's confusion, as the sailors trooped through to the kitchen with their gifts. Carmella turned to the ship's carpenter.

'There can only be one answer to that question, Mr Bates. Perhaps your men would like some refreshment, Mr Rutherford, after their arduous climb from the settlement. Miss Ruth will need time to gather her thoughts.'

Ruth regained her composure. 'Of course; how thoughtless of me. Do you think it would be appropriate,

Mr Rutherford, if they sample some of the barrel you've brought?'

'As you wish, Miss Ruth.'

The seaman moved towards the barrel. 'Holdfast. Bring me the mugs, Miss Ruth, and I'll give them a naval portion.'

Jason had now woken and the second lieutenant and the sailors paid their respects. Mr Bates sat in the kitchen with Ruth and Carmella.

'Whatever we make will be in seasoned oak. There would be room in the sitting room for a sideboard on that wall. We could do a matching wardrobe and blanket chest for the bedroom, if you have the space. I can't improve on your table and chairs; they're very well made.'

Ruth was overwhelmed by Captain Pickford's kindness and approved of all their suggestions, but hesitated to make a choice. Carmella steered the discussion to a more practical conclusion.

'Perhaps Mr Bates can measure up wall space in the bedroom and sitting room and use his judgement, Ruth.'

The carpenter, realising the choice would likely rest with him, left to take the measurements. When these were complete, the sailors gathered on the verandah.

'Thank you, Mr Rutherford, and please thank the Captain on my behalf.'

Ruth sat with Jason on the cliff top in the late afternoon. As soon as the gig had been swung aboard, the frigate weighed anchor and set course for Jamestown.

Ruth's double life had collapsed when she had removed the ribbon on the verandah. The extent of the change only became apparent when Adam returned to the marital bed. He was hungry for pleasure and she did not feel she could refuse him. She responded to his touch lamely and then found it was easier if she imagined it was Jason who was sharing his love with her.

150

'Dear, God, what have I done? Am I to spend the rest of my days loving another man rather than my husband?' She felt fortunate she still had Jason to herself during the day. Recovery remained painfully slow. By the time Captain Pickford returned two weeks later, Jason could speak quietly. He walked the cliff path with Ruth each day and they were beginning to increase the distance gradually. Despite Ruth's complaints, he pushed himself to the limit and each night retired to bed exhausted. The frigate was fully repaired with no evidence of the previous damage. The captain sat on a chair on the cliff top, sipping a glass of wine. Jason drank water.

They watched the longboat return from the frigate and saw some furniture being carried through the surf. The Captain chuckled.

'Daniel Bates offers his apologies, Ruth, for the lack of progress with your furniture. His Captain kept distracting him with repairs to the frigate. Nevertheless, he has some objects for you which will be with us shortly.'

Two matching oak bedside tables and a sideboard for the living room wound their way up the hill from the settlement.

'They're beautiful, Mr Bates.'

'Thank you, Miss Ruth. Is Mr Hewitt better?'

'Yes, he can speak now. Come and meet him.'

She stood back as the three sailors talked on the cliff top with, as a backdrop, their home swinging at anchor in the bay. The camaraderie was obvious.

'I'm a lot better, Daniel. Thank the team for their work. Ruth Fletcher saved my life; I have no doubt of that.'

Captain Pickford called Ruth over. 'Ruth, I expect to be returning here in two to three weeks. Would you be happy to continue looking after Jason?'

'We would, Captain. He can still only manage to walk short distances on the flat and I'm sure it will take more time for his body to strengthen.'

Jason raised his hand and spoke in a low voice. 'I plan to double my distance on the cliff top, Captain, and then start doing sections of the path down to the settlement. When I feel I can cope with those, I'll start running on the sand on the beach and swimming.'

Thomas Pickford turned to Ruth. 'Keep an eye on him, Ruth. Make sure he doesn't overdo it.'

'I'll try, Thomas, but he pushes himself far harder than I think is wise.'

'Build it up slowly, Jason.'

'Yes, Sir.'

'Am I entitled to remind him of your order, Captain?'

'You are.'

For Ruth the days passed all too quickly. They walked the cliff top for a few more days and then the descent into the village. She sat on the cliff top when he started running on the beach and then swimming in the bay. Adam continued to rise early and was rarely home before sunset. Ruth knew her time with Jason could not continue much longer and dreaded the thought of the frigate's next appearance in the bay.

They finished breakfast on a day Ruth knew must be close to the end.

'More running on the beach today, Jason?'

'No, Ruth, I'm content with my fitness for the moment. I wondered if you'd walk with me along the cliff path to the lookout at Bay Point.'

'You're not hankering after your first sight of the Intrepid are you?'

'My feelings are very mixed, Ruth. I am drawn back to my ship, but my time here has been very special and will not be forgotten.'

'I shall enjoy walking with you.'

They walked along the cliff path enjoying a gentle on-shore breeze. The sea was calm and the lugger, which she sometimes could see, was fishing beyond the horizon. She longed to hold Jason's hand but knew that was not appropriate.

'You were very ill, Jason, when Adam and Francesco brought you to the house, slung from the boom. What are your memories of those times?'

'I remember the lugger and feeling very hot, then cold, and the climb up to the cliff top swinging from side to side; like being in a hammock during a storm. I recall you undressing me and the fever as I lay in my cot. I remember dreaming I was in a storm and the Intrepid was close to foundering. You were by my side at the wheel and told me all would be well. The storm raged around us but I knew we'd survive. We were alone on the boat. I turned to you and realised we were both naked. You held me and the storm abated. At first I thought the dream had changed and that we had gone to my cabin and were in bed, but I gradually realised that could not be the case. I was frightened of dying and felt death stalked the shadows in the corners of the room. You put your arms around me like a protective cloak and talked to me about so many different things and of your hopes and aspirations. I think you told me about your parents and the birds and animals you've seen on the island. I knew the shadows were closing in. I felt I was being drawn down a stone staircase to a boat on a dark sea. Voices in the shadows said I was not to worry about the journey and that all would be well. My fear settled and I saw there was a man standing in the boat and he beckoned me; I felt calm and ready to join him. But you were standing with me on the top step; you held me close to you and told me I must stay with you and that you loved me. The battles with the shadows seemed endless. I felt tired and detached from the result but gradually your will triumphed over the boatman. Slowly the boat and the steps faded from view and I knew I was lying in your arms. There was darkness but a different form of shadows that did not threaten or want to take me on a journey. You placed your hand with mine upon my stomach and it seemed to anchor me in calm water. I wanted to hold you but I did not have the power to respond. Over time, I think some power did come back and I managed to move my hand to cover yours, but I'm not sure if it's what I did or what I wished to do.'

'You did move your hand to cover mine.'

'I hoped I had. It was the start of my recovery. I felt I was slowly regaining control of my body.'

Ruth was overcome with surprise and embarrassment.

'You remember everything, Jason. I had no idea; what must you think of me?'

He stopped and turned to face her and stroked her cheek. 'Perhaps I should delay telling you until we get to the lookout point.

CHAPTER TWELVE

They walked on in silence but Ruth did not feel the atmosphere was uncomfortable; they were two people at ease, who had been bonded by extreme events. She realised his recollections had been a lot more intimate than she had appreciated. The revelation, whilst a shock was, on consideration, a benefit. She had been obliged to hide her feelings, because she thought she had been the sole witness. A declaration of her love for him would not now be necessary. She was pleased he had shared the earlier experiences, although Jason's recollection was in part clouded by fever and confusion.

The cliff path curved out towards the sea and rose through a gentle gradient. She could see the disused observation post in the distance with the metal brazier on a pole that had acted as a beacon, when Britain had been at war with France. It would not be long before she learnt how Jason felt about her. Most likely her love for him would be kindly and caringly rebuffed; a married woman, plain, ill-educated and who knew little of the world; she would be unlikely to attract the interest of a young first officer making his way in the world. The path became steep near the end and was uneven. He offered her his hand and they climbed together. The gradient eased and there was no longer need for support but he continued to hold her hand. They skirted the beacon and walked across the grass-covered promontory to the edge of the cliffs. They could hear the surf breaking on the rocks below. Jason scanned the horizon with particular interest to the north, looking beyond the Sentinel.

'No sails today, Ruth. They'll not come today.'

He led her to the observation post. It was built of stone and roofed in oak. It was a single room with no windows to the back wall. There was a window to each side, and one on each side of the entrance at the front. The windows and the door had long since been removed and reused in other houses. The floor, once beaten earth, was now covered with low grass and moss. An oak bench had been firmly fixed to the back wall and remained in serviceable condition. They stood by one of the front windows looking out to sea. His arm was around her waist and she felt comforted by his proximity. He turned towards her and lifted her up to his height. He kissed her gently on the forehead and then on her closed eyes and finally her lips. The kiss was light and tentative, seeking a response. She placed her arms around his neck, running her fingers through his hair. Her lips parted and the passion grew within them. He swung her up and carried her to the bench, without taking his lips from hers. She lay back across his thighs, held in his powerful embrace. His right hand gently explored her contours through her thin skirt; their lips parted but he kept his face close to hers.

'When I was very ill and could not move, you slept with your hand in mine. I found it very reassuring that I was not alone. I wanted to rest my hand on your stomach and hoped I would live long enough to do so. Although I was close to death, your naked body excited me and I hoped I would regain my strength and return your love. May I loosen your skirt and rest my hand on your stomach as you did on mine?'

Ruth nodded her approval. She lay back with her eyes closed and felt the cord at her waist loosen. He slid his hand onto her stomach, both sighing with the release of pent up pleasure. Passion was growing within them and he pressed more firmly. She arched her back. They stood up and she undid the drawstring on his breaches as he undressed her. Naked, they lay on their discarded clothes and the thin grass.

Jason paused. 'Are you sure, Ruth?'

'Yes, Jason. I know you'll sail away tomorrow or the next day and I may never see you again, but I want to share your love. I want all of you.'

Ruth lay back enjoying all the sensations she hoped she would have experienced, if her foolish instinctive remark had not killed off Adam's love in the days before their wedding. Jason was gentle and caring; they were both consumed by a passion which was only slowly spent. He rose and checked the path. No-one was in sight and their privacy was guaranteed. He lay back down and held her in much the same way she had held him in the recent past. They spoke infrequently, enjoying their newfound intimacy. The shadow of the beacon slowly lengthened, marching across the grass and reminding them that the time must come when they should dress and return to another life. When they had been in quarantine their private world had been the house, now it would be the observation hut. She laid her head against his neck.

'You know, Jason, this cannot lead to anything. I gave an oath to Adam to stand by him for life. I knew when I agreed to marry him that he was an honourable man and a good friend. I was not sure, in such a small community, if it was sensible to expect more and I hoped that love would grow with the passage of time. I think I may have missed the chance for love to grow; it was a momentary error, but I suspect it has had long term consequences. Captain Pickford and your officers would not see this as an appropriate relationship; their first officer stealing the wife of the man who helped to save their ship. He gave over his house and asked his wife to nurse you back from almost certain death.'

Jason was silent for a while and then nodded his agreement. 'You're right. I would be ruined. I would have to leave the ship and probably the Navy.'

'Does that mean what we feel is wrong?'

'No, Ruth. How we feel is right, but not for the people we are. I would like to develop our love till the moment I am recalled. I doubt I'll ever have a similar relationship in the future. You may feel it's futile, but I want to experience it and lock it in my memory.'

'Yes, Jason, I'm afraid that's the best we can do and I would not have it any other way.'

They dressed and slowly walked back along the path, holding hands on the steeper parts. When they reached the level area of the path she forced herself to release his hand. Her instinct was to walk arm in arm and register all the happiness and exhilaration that welled up inside her, but she knew that such emotions can easily be read from afar. Jason sensed her difficulty and kept his distance.

She knew a reputation is easily lost in a small community, but felt she would know if her name and Jason's were being linked in the settlement. The first two weeks, when they had been in quarantine, was beyond suspicion and her decision to volunteer to care for him was considered heroic. The days that followed had not given cause for gossip. Jason was obviously still extremely weak but she knew that the last two weeks, when he had been restored to full health, could prove the most hazardous period. The position of the house favoured privacy as it lay at the top of a hill beyond the edge of the settlement, on a path that only extended to the observation point. Some cultivation was carried out in the thin strip of flat land inland of the path, but the soil was poor and activity was restricted mainly to grazing which rarely required the attention of the farmers. For the last two Sundays, Jason had attended church with them. Ruth always sat between Robert and Adam, enjoying being flanked by two tall, young men. She made sure Jason's attendance did not change those arrangements so he sat next to Robert at the end of the pew.

As they approached the house, the lugger came into view from behind the Sentinel.

'We should go down to the beach, Ruth.'

They walked on and joined an angry Carmella on the beach with the wooden trolley they used to exhibit the catch.

'Let me guess, Carmella, more trouble with Sergeant Logan.'

'That's right. He should be reprimanded and demoted for his behaviour. He thinks he owns the settlement. Please don't tell Francesco, he's getting increasingly angry with the sergeant's behaviour.'

'In that case, Carmella, you'd better compose yourself or Francesco will realise there have been further problems. Is there nothing you can do to help, Jason?'

'I could speak to Captain Pickford when I'm back on ship, Ruth, but the naval officers have no jurisdiction over the marines, especially the land based ones. The Captain was amazed at the Governor's assessment of the previous incident. The Governor considers the whole island, in effect, to be a military installation. To him, the normal rights of civilians do not apply here.'

The fishermen had found a good shoal of fish early in the day. They had been to Jamestown in the early afternoon and sold the bulk of the catch, including some to the Intrepid. Captain Pickford was pleased to hear Jason was restored to full health; he hoped to complete taking on stores within two days and then would sail south to pick up his first officer.

Ruth hoped she was hiding her dismay, and experienced some sadness when Jason appeared to receive the news with enthusiasm. She chided herself for her selfish thoughts. He could not be criticised; a young officer returning to his life at sea. She should expect no other response.

They all helped drag the boat onto the sand and walked back to the square. The remaining fish were selling well when Private Winter walked over from the barracks in the company of Sergeant Logan. The atmosphere immediately became tense.

'You want to watch that wife of yours, Ceruso, it'll not be long before she's visiting the barracks and she'll not be selling fish.'

Francesco exploded. 'I've warned you before, Sergeant, interfere with me or mine and you'll end up fed to the fish. That goes for the rest of your rabble too. You're all a disgrace to your uniform.'

Jason intervened. 'Sergeant, hold your tongue and show some respect to the settlers.'

The Sergeant paused. 'With respect, Mr Hewitt, you've no jurisdiction here. A lot of them are scum and need firm handling.'

The marines withdrew and the two families shared the remaining fish between them.

If Adam was aware of any changes in relationships, he did not show it. Ruth lay beside him that night hearing his regular breathing, but knowing the man she had fallen in love with slept only a few feet further away. Perhaps they would have only two more days together.

For the next three days Ruth and Jason stood on the verandah in the morning watching the lugger sail into the rising sun and then took the cliff path to the observation point. Ruth packed a lunch and they remained there till early afternoon. They never spoke of their impending separation, but simply rejoiced in each other's company, sharing minds and bodies. They had finished lunch on the third day and Ruth lay naked on a rug; Jason walked over

160

to the window that overlooked the cliff path, to see if any settlers were in sight. He did not return swiftly to her side. She stiffened and turned to check. He was leaning on the sill, looking to the north and shading his eyes.

'Sails?'

'Perhaps.'

He returned to lie by her side and they made love, for what they knew would be the final time. They started gently, both savouring the moment, but it swiftly erupted into a desperate passion, with the knowledge of their impending loss. He held her quietly as the gentle breeze cooled their skin; a breeze that also brought the Intrepid, and their separation, more swiftly. Jason returned to the window.

'Is it as you thought?'

'Yes, it's the Intrepid. We should dress.'

He lifted her gently to her feet and held her in his arms and they shared a long and lingering kiss. Jason took out a gold locket and chain from his waistcoat pocket.

'Ruth, I'd like you to have this. My mother gave it to me before I left for the South Atlantic. He flicked it open to reveal a miniature portrait of himself in the lid, and one of his mother in the back. He lifted out the picture of his mother and carefully wrapped it in a small linen pouch. She studied his portrait.

'It's a very good likeness of you, Jason. I think you know it'll never be far from my heart.'

He undid the clasp and she turned round so that he could place it around her neck. She then turned and buried her head in his chest and sobbed.

'It's such a beautiful gift and I've nothing to give you.'

He held her tightly and gently rocked her until the sobbing stopped. 'I cannot agree with you, Ruth, you have given me my life and now your love.'

They dressed and walked back in silence to the house. Jason's belongings were already in a kit bag. The frigate was entering Prosperous Bay. They shared one final swift embrace and then walked out into the sunshine and down to the beach. The longboat was already moving towards them, the oars moving rhythmically. Several sailors were standing in the boat, which also included cargo. The gig followed on close behind with Captain Pickford seated in the stern. The boats grounded their bows on the sand simultaneously. Jason saluted his captain.

'Ready for duty, Captain.'

'You look good, Jason.'

The Captain smiled at Ruth. 'It's a tribute to the care you gave him, Mrs Fletcher.'

She smiled back wanly. 'It's been a pleasure.'

Mr Bates joined them. 'Can my men carry this furniture up to your house, Mrs Fletcher?'

'How very kind of you, Mr Bates, thank you.

The Captain and Jason flanked Ruth as they walked ahead of the sailors. Ruth was happy to let the Captain update Jason on recent events and their orders. The sailors placed an oak wardrobe and blanket chest in the bedroom which matched the design of their previous gifts.

'They're beautiful, Mr Bates, I know Adam will wish to thank you personally, if not today then sometime in the future.'

'Give him our best wishes, Mrs Fletcher. There is talk of postings elsewhere for some officers and perhaps the Intrepid. Adam may not find us in the harbour at Jamestown on his next visit.'

The Captain's steward, who had accompanied them up the hill, passed Jason an object wrapped in cloth which Jason untied.

'Ruth, I asked Captain Pickford to get this for me as a present for you in gratitude for everything you've done for me.'

For Ruth the word 'everything' hung in the air. He held out a brass, naval, oil lamp of a pleasing design.

'That's for your bedside table.'

'Thank you, Jason. Yes, that would be an excellent place for it. I shall cherish the lamp and it will remind me of you,' and, swiftly regaining her composure, 'and your brave Captain and crew.'

Captain Pickford looked at his watch. 'The wind is light and failing, Mrs Fletcher; if you'll excuse us we must leave swiftly to regain the ocean breeze.'

'Would you mind, Captain, if I remained up here to watch you leave.'

'Of course.'

She shook his hand. 'Farewell, Captain, and to you, Mr Bates. Goodbye, Mr Hewitt, I'm pleased we were able to be of service to you.'

He shook her hand and the sailors returned to the beach. She stood on the verandah as the boats were lifted aboard. She saw the men swarm up into the rigging and heard the now familiar chant and the sound of the capstan, counting down the seconds she would have sight of Jason Hewitt. The anchor rose and the sails were unfurled and filled languidly. Slowly the frigate gained way and swung out towards the ocean. She could see Jason by the stern rail, looking up at her, as the ship gathered pace and the sails stiffened in the ocean breeze. She watched until she could see the frigate no longer, tears coursing down her face.

When she walked back into the kitchen she found a letter from Jason propped up against her new lamp.

You could not blame a rose,
but it started when we met.
A form of magnetism perhaps,
even to the attraction of opposites.
A natural force beyond governance,
which could not be created,
and would not be suppressed.
Thank you for your love,
through those perilous days.
A chapter closed, but never forgotten.

CHAPTER THIRTEEN

The days passed slowly for Ruth, as she tried to come to terms with her loss and hide the cause of her sadness. She knew it was a risk but chose to wear Jason's locket almost all the time; it was not always visible and did not appear to raise comment in the settlement. She introduced Adam to the locket with caution; it had been a most generous gift and she was taken with its delicacy and beauty. Theft was uncommon in the settlement and few houses had locks to the doors. However there had been one or two losses of small objects recently which were swiftly blamed on the marines. The locket was a small object of high value and therefore at risk of loss. Ruth reasoned that it was safest when worn around her neck. She also justified the choice by stating that she would be mortified if the Intrepid returned and she did not have the locket to wear. It seemed wise to take it off in bed at night and she chose to hang it on the brass knob on Jason's lamp that was used to adjust the height of the wick. When Adam slipped away to fish in the hour before dawn, she would ask him to open the curtains as he left. Later she would open the locket and watch the first rays of the sun strike the lamp and illuminate the officer she had come to love.

Ruth had lost weight during Jason's illness and convalescence and Carmella took her low mood to have arisen as a delayed reaction to the stressful time she had experienced. William Mott, whose son had wished to crew for Adam, was dying of consumption and the ladies were organising a rota to assist his wife, Elizabeth, with his care. They were unanimous in their view that Ruth had done enough, and it would be wrong to expose her to the risk of catching the disease in her current, weakened state. Ruth felt tired and unsettled; her normal routine, which she had enjoyed before Jason arrived in her sitting room, no longer satisfied her. Their vegetable patch, which she normally tended for several hours each day, had become unkempt and she did not have the heart to restore it to order. She knew her restlessness would have to be borne but that did not make the process any easier.

However, within a week of the Intrepid clearing the bay, the routine of the settlement was shattered. The Fletchers were the first to be involved in events. It was mid-week and they had retired early, as Adam would be leaving for the boat before dawn. In the early hours of the morning, they heard the sound of voices calling Charlie Winter's name. They put on robes, picked up lamps, and went out onto the cliff path; four marines stood with lit torches. Charlie Winter and Sergeant Logan had been on night patrol. They had split duties and the sergeant was to patrol the village with Private Winter on a wider sweep from the cliff path, back behind the village and on to the high ground near Sentinel Point. Charlie Winter had not returned and was now two hours overdue. The remaining marines were searching the village. The Fletchers returned to bed, but within an hour the alarm bell in the village was ringing and they hurriedly dressed. They could see some lanterns two fields away, in an area where Matthew Draper farmed. The fields closest to the village were more fertile and could sustain a crop of vegetables. They were joined by Sergeant Logan accompanied by Lucy and Edmond Davies. The Davies family represented the closest the settlement had to a doctor as Edmond Davies and his wife had worked as volunteers in a missionary hospital in South Africa before moving to St Helena.

'Is Charlie Winter injured?'

Sergeant Logan turned on Adam angrily. 'What do you know about this, Fletcher? How do you know it involves

166

Charlie? You'll swing for this - and don't pretend you think it is an injury. He's dead, murdered.'

'No wild accusations, Sergeant. If you have called out Edmond and Elizabeth at this time of night it has to be for a medical reason and we know Charlie Winter is overdue returning, your search party told us who was missing an hour ago. My wife was witness to their conversation. '

All five walked onto the field where there were potatoes ready to be lifted. Charlie lay face down with a short trowel in his right hand and a small sack in the left that looked partly filled with vegetables. He was pinned to the ground with a four pronged pitch fork, which had been driven through his back up to the hilt. Matthew Draper joined them from the far side of the field.

'I'm sorry this man is dead, Sergeant, but what possible interpretation can you put on this beyond he was killed stealing my potatoes.'

'It's a set-up and you know it.' The sergeant snarled. 'And that makes you a prime suspect as the owner of the scene of the crime. Have you got witnesses to prove you have not been out tonight? And I do not mean that tart you call a housekeeper.'

Lucy Davies interjected. 'That's the second false accusation that you've raised tonight, Sergeant. Are your sister and her husband still with you, Matthew?'

'Thank God they are, Lucy. Isobel went to bed at ten, but I sat up drinking with Albert. We were preparing to turn in when I heard the alarm bell.'

Edmond Davies held his lamp close to Charlie Winter's body. 'There's nothing we can do, Lucy, he's dead and it can only be murder. You could not fall on a pitch fork to create such an injury.'

He knelt beside the body and peered closely at the back of the victim's head.

'That's interesting, Sergeant, there is a cut and some bruising to the back of the head. It's only about an inch across. Perhaps he was struck by a hammer or something similar, rendered unconscious and then killed with the pitch fork.'

Several other settlers joined the group, including Francesco Ceruso.

'What happened, Adam?'

'It's Charlie Winter. He has been murdered. Sergeant Logan considers the sack and trowel is a set-up. Matthew sees it differently. Is Carmella with Maria?'

'No, I've just sent Maria to stay with the neighbours. Carmella is helping at the Motts tonight; William is close to death.'

Sergeant Logan stood quietly on the edge of the crowd. Four marines arrived with a stretcher and Charlie was lifted on, face down, and carried back to the barracks. The sergeant followed them.

'It'll be like the previous time, Francesco, he'll send his corporal to Jamestown tomorrow and we must expect troops in large numbers by the early afternoon.'

'I presume we're fishing as normal?'

'I don't see why not; if they want to ask questions, as I am sure they will, we'll be back by mid-afternoon. Get whatever rest you can, Francesco, and I'll see you by the boat at six.'

Sergeant Logan did send his corporal to Jamestown at first light, reporting the death. He addressed the rest of his section:

'We need a major presence in the village until more men come from the home barracks. I want two of you on the beach and two on the cliff path, two more on the track to Jamestown and the remainder to patrol the settlement. If anyone wants to leave, get their name and their reason for leaving. Don't stop them, just get their details. Report back at noon.'

As soon as the barracks were empty, the sergeant bolted the door and went to Charlie Winter's body. He took the key from the chain that Charlie always wore around his neck, and opened the private's locker. There were few personal effects; the sergeant did not expect to find much; he did not have many himself. He found a small leather bag wrapped up in a shirt. He emptied the contents onto the mess table; a gold ring, perhaps Charlie's mother's wedding ring and a leather purse containing 46 sovereigns. The amount provoked a surprised exclamation from the sergeant. 'Charlie, you were even better at cards than I thought.' As expected, there was also a note book where Charlie had annotated the sums he was owed by the other marines in the section. In the main they owed a couple of sovereigns, except Sergeant Logan whose debt was 47 sovereigns. 'Not any more, Charlie, that debt is about to go up in smoke'. He walked over to the stove and opened the front. The wood glowed as he tossed in the book and watched the fire consume the evidence. He glanced at the door to confirm that he was alone. 'Let's keep this in round numbers, Charlie, I'll leave you ten sovereigns. The boys know you must have quite a bit stashed away. You'll not need the rest.' He counted out ten sovereigns and put the coins back in Charlie's purse along with the gold ring and three letters from his family from the distant past. He locked the remaining money in his own locker and dampened down the stove. Charlie's locker key was returned to the chain around his neck.

When his section of marines returned at noon, Sergeant Logan again removed the key from around Charlie's neck and opened his locker, as if for the first time. He opened the small bag and poured the ten sovereigns onto the table, feigning surprise.

'I knew he was good at cards, but I'm surprised to see he'd won ten sovereigns.'

He then went through the motions of searching for a notebook or any record of other debts.

'If any of you owed him money, it seems he must have carried it in his head and he's left no record. The absence of a record wipes the slate clean for all of you. We'll wrap up his belongings in a kit bag and return it to the barracks. Joel, just countersign this receipt, confirming the contents of his locker.'

John Logan noted his remarks were greeted by a variety of emotions: pleasure by the simpletons who realised they were released from their debts; cynicism and disbelief by the remainder, including Joel Hooper who, nevertheless, initialled the sergeant's receipt.

Four sections of marines arrived in the mid afternoon with a Captain James Cecil in command. His left arm was supported in a sling. He strode into the barracks.

'A word with you in private, Sergeant.'

They spoke in the kitchen for several minutes and then returned to the square.

'Sergeant Logan, you and your men are to pack and leave for the barracks in Jamestown within the hour. Take Private Winter's body and his personal effects.'

'No-one has tried to leave the settlement this morning, Sir, beyond Adam Fletcher's lugger, but he and his Italian crewman normally leave before sunrise.'

'Francesco Ceruso?'

'Yes.'

'What time do they return?'

'About an hour from now, Sir.'

The Captain turned to his Sergeant. 'Get a picket on the path out of the settlement and another to the beach. The rest are to clean up the barracks, it's a disgrace. Let me know when that boat returns. I should meet those two, even if it is their routine to leave so early.

Ruth sat with Carmella on an upturned boat waiting to unload the catch. Lucy Davies joined them.

'It's weird, Ruth, the soldiers are very polite. The officer has a tight hold on discipline. No one is being asked any questions about where they were last night. They just seem to be waiting for something to happen. The only people asking questions are the residents, no one seems able to come forward with a name. We know Logan's men stole food and other things, but I can't see any of the settlers resorting to murder. I always thought Charlie Winter was one of the better ones, for what it's worth.'

They saw the sail of the lugger, far out at sea, and within the hour the bow drove into the sand and Francesco leapt down and tied the boat to the metal ring on the rock. Captain Cecil walked over.

'Which one of you is Adam Fletcher?'

'I am.'

'How many fish do you have?'

'They're here.'

'We'll take several for the marines. Settle with him, Sergeant, and take them to the barracks.'

The payment was made and the marines removed their part of the catch. Ruth, Lucy, Carmella and the two fishermen stood in a group. Adam broke the silence.

'I'm thinking this conversation is not yet complete, Captain?'

'No, Sir, it is not.' He turned to Francesco.

'You, I presume, are Francesco Ceruso?'

'I am.'

'My orders are to have you taken to Jamestown tonight.'

'For what reason?' exclaimed Carmella.

'In truth, I do not know. It is felt you can help with the enquiry. If it reassures you, Madam, I was not sent to arrest your husband, simply to organise his immediate transfer to the capital.'

'May I change clothes?'

'Swiftly.' The officer glanced at Francesco's bare feet, 'Shoes would be useful.'

'Sergeant, send Corporal Jones and four privates, not with back packs but with rifles. A couple of lanterns will be required, as they'll not be there before nightfall.'

'Now that you're back, Mr Fletcher, I would like all adults summoned to the community hall. I want to make some announcements.'

The bell was rung and the adults of the community gathered. Captain Cecil strode to the lectern used on Sundays for the sermon, accompanied by his sergeant. Several marines lined the walls.

'Thank you for coming. As you know, a marine was murdered last night and I'm tasked with getting to the bottom of it. It's been obvious to me, since I arrived, that there is a bad atmosphere here between the military and this community. I consider myself a fair man and I do not assume that the residents are the cause of those bad relations. I have some developments to report to you; Sergeant Logan and his section left for Jamestown in the early afternoon. They will be interviewed on arrival. It's unlikely that they'll be returning here in the foreseeable future. I was sent here with two instructions; to seek out the truth and to transfer Mr Ceruso to Jamestown. It is felt he has information which may help with the enquiry. I do not know what that information might be. As I speak, he's leaving with some of my men.

This afternoon I wish to interview several people. If I call out your name, please go and stand by one of my marines, only one person to each marine. When the list is complete, the remainder can disperse. In closing I should say that I'm not part of the land-based administration here; I was injured in a battle with several pirate slavers off Africa two months ago and was brought to Jamestown Infirmary. My recovery is almost complete and that is why the Governor has sent me. I come from a service that expects civilians to respect my men and to trust them. My men will expect respect but know it has to earned, as does your trust. If you have justified complaints, come to me with them, my men know what I expect of them.

As to the names; Mrs Ceruso, Mr & Mrs Fletcher, Robert Morgan, Mr & Mrs Davies, Matthew Draper, the Lloyd sisters. No, ladies, please go to separate marines. The rest of you may go. I will wish to interview others tomorrow. Please meet here again at 11 o'clock.'

Most of the group to be questioned was still standing within earshot. Edmond Davies whispered.

'Shall we meet at our house for dinner, when the interviews are complete?'

They nodded in agreement and walked to their separate stations in the room.

Matthew Draper was the last to arrive at the Davieses. Carmella had been interviewed first. Maria was sleeping with the Davies children and Carmella would also spend the night there. Ruth had gone back with Adam and brought a fruit pie and a bottle of rum. Emma Lloyd had developed severe palpitations and retired to bed; her sister Dorothy sent their apologies. Ruth spoke first.

'I liked him, Adam, he was courteous and straight forward. I told him I thought Sergeant Logan was a poor leader of men, lecherous, arrogant and ill disciplined. His attentions to Carmella were disgracefully unwarranted and not reciprocated.'

Adam responded. 'I think he'll have got that from every one of us, Ruth. I mentioned how he constantly goaded Francesco, but despite all the provocation, Francesco's anger never extended beyond words.'

Edmond Davies poured another shot of rum. 'He asked us about alibis and Lucy and I could support each other. It was fortunate your sister stayed over, Matthew.'

'I've never been more grateful for their company; a death on my land whilst stealing my crop and, as it turns out, my pitch fork used as the murder weapon. That would have had me as the main suspect without a doubt. We keep the pitchfork and some tools in a shed between the fields, it's not locked, and anyone could gain access.'

'What about you, Robert?'

'It's curious, I have no alibi. I turned in early and didn't hear the settlement bell. Matthew came over to check on me before walking back to his house. He said you'd all dispersed and that Adam and Francesco were still planning to fish, so I didn't disturb you. The captain noted I had no alibi, but did not make an issue of it. Perhaps I'll be called back tomorrow.'

Edmond Davies turned to Carmella. 'Did he give you any reason why Francesco was sent to Jamestown?'

'No, but he tried to reassure me it was not necessarily for bad reasons. I don't think he was being devious, I really felt he didn't know. Francesco does not think he can help at all and doesn't know why he's been singled out.'

'It's unfortunate you were staying over at the Motts on a night when alibis were required, Carmella, but Maria was at home and that should not be a problem.'

'Carmella, perhaps Maria could crew for me tomorrow, and why don't you come along? If we start early, we can travel under reduced canvas to Jamestown, trailing some line and picking up a few fish. We can then walk to the

Governor's office and see if Francesco is able to join us for the return trip.'

'Thank you, Adam; I'd like to do that.'

The group broke up, promising to share any information that became available and reassuring Carmella that it could not be too long before Francesco was returned to them.

Carmella met them on the beach at dawn. Ruth, conscious of the fishermen's previous problems at the Governor's office had asked to join them. There was room for Adam and the two wives on the stern seat. Maria moved swiftly around the boat stowing the mooring rope, trimming sails and setting out the baited hooks and line. Ruth whispered to Carmella.

'She really is at home out here.'

'It's true, Ruth, she seems to come alive on the water.'

Adam moved the tiller to starboard for a slightly wider clearance of the Sentinel and Maria noted the subtle change in course. Unbidden, she adjusted the jib and main sail to accommodate the new direction.

'It's not just a case of her being at home out here, Carmella, she is a natural seaman like her father. Most of the orders that would normally be required on a boat under sail are never given here. Francesco and Maria note the change and perform the action instinctively. Maria is already one of the best I've ever worked with. Do you remember early on when she experienced that rogue wave? I told her then never to get too absorbed with inboard matters and always to keep an eye on the horizon. She's never forgotten that. If you watch her, every few seconds she'll check outboard.'

'It's not what Francesco and I planned for her, Adam, but there is no denying her ability.'

By mid-morning they were moored in Jamestown. Adam sold their modest catch to a local fisherman and they walked up to the Governor's residence. There was a more military atmosphere evident; two light canons, normally used by horse artillery, flanked the main door with two fully armed sentries.

'Perhaps we should ask for the Reverend Wilkes, Adam, he'll probably be able to let us know what's going on?'

'I think that would be wise, Ruth. I'd prefer to avoid another interview with the Governor.'

A servant took them through to the Reverend's office. 'He'll join you shortly.'

Within seconds the Pastor bustled through the door in a state of agitation.

'Sit, please sit.'

As Adam framed the question in his mind, he feared the response he might receive.

'Reverend, we've come to pick up Francesco Ceruso, if his interview here is complete?'

The Pastor addressed his nervous remarks to Carmella. 'Carmella, I'm sorry to say you cannot. Mr Ceruso is now in custody for the murder of the marine.'

'That's impossible. He cannot have been involved; he was at home with my daughter.'

'So I understand but, nevertheless, it's the decision of the Governor. I don't know all the details, but ….'

The door opened and a junior officer entered. 'Are you the fisherman from Prosperous Bay?'

'Yes, this is Mrs Ceruso.'

'So I understand. The Governor would like to see all of you.'

They were ushered into the Governor's office.

'Fletcher, isn't it?'

'Yes, Sir, this is my wife and Mr Ceruso's wife and daughter.'

'Your husband is in custody, Mrs Ceruso, for the murder of Private Winter.'

'But that is impossible, Sir.'

'No doubt the possibility, or impossibility, will become evident in Court.'

'But surely, Sir, Captain Cecil's investigations are still going on in Prosperous Bay.'

'Superseded by fresh evidence.'

'What fresh evidence?'

'All will be revealed in Court; an eye witness. I have already organised for Mr Ceruso's representation in Court.'

Adam intervened. 'Do you have a date in mind, Sir?'

'Tomorrow.'

'That won't allow time for any defence to be prepared.'

'It's timely justice, Fletcher, which we seek for the murder of one of my men. The people of Prosperous Bay need to learn that there will be no insubordination under my command. You are dismissed. The trial will start at 10 o'clock tomorrow in the meeting hall here in the residence.'

Adam persisted. 'Do we have a judge on the island, Sir?'

'I'm the ultimate representative here, Fletcher.'

As they walked over to the door, the Governor called after them. 'One final matter, Mrs Ceruso.'

They turned. 'How old is your daughter?'

'I'm twelve, Sir.'

'Thank you, child.'

Adam gave vent to his dismay and anger. 'I don't know what we or Prosperous Bay have done to deserve this treatment.'

Ruth hugged Carmella and Maria. 'Is there anything we can do, Adam?'

'Yes. Carmella, you should stay here and work with the Reverend Wilkes. See if you can get to see Francesco and glean whatever information you can. Ruth, can you organise accommodation for us and for your brother Robert, Matthew Draper and the Daviesess. If there's not enough room, the men can sleep anywhere. I'll sail back to Prosperous Bay and try to get them here for the start of the trial. I wonder if the Governor wants this trial over before the settlement even realises it is taking place. It's time this island had a representative council to insist civilians are treated democratically. Don't worry, Maria, I can manage the boat on my own. I'd rather you spent the time trying to see your father.'

Adam grounded the boat on the sand at Prosperous Bay in the mid afternoon. He walked straight to the marine barracks seeking a meeting with Captain Cecil.

'Good evening, Mr Fletcher.'

'Not so good, Captain. Are you aware that Francesco Ceruso is under arrest in Jamestown for murder?'

'No, Sir, I was not, nor was I aware that was the Governor's intention when he sent me here to make enquiries.'

'The trial starts at 10 o'clock tomorrow with the Governor presiding.'

'But surely.... I'm surprised, Mr Fletcher.'

'About what, Captain?'

'Frankly, in confidence, I am surprised about everything concerning this matter; the judgement applied, the timing and the process. Your settlement is portrayed in Jamestown as a pit of vipers. Now that I'm here I see no evidence for that. What is your plan, Mr Fletcher?'

'To gather our influential friends here and to sail back to Jamestown overnight.'

'Do you have any concerns about Mr Ceruso's conduct in this matter?

'None whatsoever, Captain. He was ceaselessly provoked by Sergeant Logan and in the end certainly used violent language to protect his family from abuse, but I would stake my own life on his innocence.'

'I've not met a single resident who feels differently. If it will assist you, I will ride to your brother-in-law's house and that of Mr Draper to speed your return.'

'I would be grateful, Captain, and would that your influence had been present previously.'

Adam walked on to the Davies's and within the hour all his friends were aboard the lugger. Captain Cecil wished them a safe journey.

'I'm afraid it'll be cold on the water overnight, Lucy, but I hope Ruth will have accommodation for you on our arrival. I'll sail by compass readings, but, for safety's sake in the dark, we'll need to swing more to the east than would be required in daylight. I've never tried to enter Jamestown at night and therefore plan to dock at first light. I know you hate the ocean, Robert, but I know Carmella and Ruth will be grateful for your presence.'

'Sea sickness is of no consequence, Adam. We all have to be there for Francesco and his family.'

Adam's friends settled down to sleep, leaving the fisherman at the tiller with the compass illuminated by an oil lamp. The sky was clear with a million stars flickering above them and only the thinnest sliver of moon to compete with their brilliance. The sea was calm and Adam experienced an overwhelming feeling of tranquillity and freedom. He did not feel he had ever been so detached and demoralised by the injustices of humanity. He knew the following day would most likely give rise to more anger and bitterness, and contrasted it with the contentment that came from sailing his lugger upon a vast ocean, under such a majestic sky.

Adam approached land cautiously in the hour before dawn and was relieved to find that his navigation had brought them to the west of Sugarloaf Point. They entered Jamestown harbour in the pre-dawn light. Ruth had left a message with the harbour watch and they made their way swiftly into town and were reunited with their friends.

'They allowed us only ten minutes with Francesco; he has no idea why he's been accused nor does he know what evidence has given rise to the charge.'

'Does he know who is representing him?'

'Yes, a junior officer from a frigate which is undergoing repairs.'

'Who is prosecuting the charge?

'His Captain.'

Matthew Draper raised his eyes to the ceiling. 'Well that's not equitable for a start.'

Robert turned to his sister. 'Why naval officers, Ruth?'

'That's the biggest surprise of all. It seems it will take the form of a court martial, even though Francesco is a civilian.'

Carmella turned to the men with tears in her eyes. 'Everything about this is wrong; I'm going to lose my husband for a crime he did not commit.'

No one felt able to contradict or reassure her.

It was getting close to the hour. Silently they put on their coats and walked up to the Governor's residence.

CHAPTER FOURTEEN

The Reverend Wilkes sat with them on the back row of the court room. Francesco was handcuffed to a chair with two marines in attendance. The Governor sat behind a desk, two officers seated behind him. A board on an easel displayed a crude map of Prosperous Bay and the site of the murder. A naval captain, one Adam did not recognise, read out the charge of murder. Francesco was asked how he pleaded.

'Not guilty to the charge.'

The prosecutor described the bad relations between the settlers and the military. He recounted the events two days previously and pointed out the area Charlie Winter was due to patrol. He read a statement Sergeant Logan had submitted to the Governor. The sergeant had been completing his patrol when he saw Francesco Ceruso running down the path leading into the settlement from the field where they had found the murdered marine. He had been in no doubt as to the identity of the man he had seen. The sighting had occurred close to midnight. Mr Ceruso had subsequently denied he had been out that night, but he had been seen running from the scene of the crime. He had lied when questioned under oath and the judge should find him guilty.

The first officer rose to his feet.

'Where is Sergeant Logan? I wish to question him about his statement.'

The Governor leaned forward. 'That's not possible, nor is it necessary. Sergeant Logan and his section were transferred to the settlement at Thompson's Bay yesterday and he is not available to be questioned.'

The first officer tried to object but was overruled. During this exchange the door at the back of the court opened and Captain Cecil walked in, taking off his cloak and riding gloves. Francesco was called to the stand. The handcuffs were removed and he was escorted to the witness box. The first officer asked him for his account of the evening of the murder. Francesco stated he had not left his house until the settlement bell had been rung. Maria had gone to bed at about 9 o'clock but had not fallen asleep until later. The captain, for the prosecution, asked if there had been violent conflicts with the marines previously. Francesco admitted he had threatened Sergeant Logan with violence in the past if the sergeant molested his wife or his daughter. They had never come to blows.

'Mr Ceruso, the evidence is conflicting; in the interest of clarity what time did you leave your house on the night Charlie Winter was murdered?'

'I did not leave the house, Sir, until I heard the settlement bell. I then took my daughter next door to our neighbour. I spoke to my wife briefly at the Mott's front door before walking up the path to the scene of the murder; several settlers and marines were present.'

'You know Sergeant Logan testified you had previously run back into the settlement. How could he have come to that conclusion?'

'Possibly mistaken identity but, more likely, a malicious lie.'

'Why would he feel the need to do that?'

'For many months he has made inappropriate suggestions to my wife and has been angered by her refusal to submit to his wishes.'

'You played no part in Charlie Winter's murder?'

'I am under oath, Sir. I did not.'

'Thank you, Mr Ceruso. Please return to your seat. I have no further questions for the prosecution, Governor.'

The first officer representing Francesco turned to Adam with a helpless look on his face.

'Your honour, I'd like to call Adam Fletcher to the stand.'

Adam moved forward to the small table that represented the witness box and took the oath. He knew he could not rely on the junior officer to ask him the right questions and decided on a statement to cover most of the points his friends thought should be made.

'Your honour, I do not believe Francesco Ceruso killed Charlie Winter. I have no faith in Sergeant Logan's testimony. The court should be aware that Sergeant Logan accused me of the murder until he realised my wife could vouch for me and then again he accused Matthew Draper of the crime until it became apparent he also had an alibi. At no stage, when we were at the scene of the crime, did he mention seeing Francesco running back into the settlement, even when Francesco walked up to us in the field, along with other settlers. For many months the sergeant has harassed Mrs Ceruso in a disgraceful manner and all the settlers will testify that she never gave him cause for encouragement. It is true Francesco did, on occasion, threaten the sergeant verbally, in an attempt to protect his family. The sergeant was universally despised in the village and his section had a poor reputation, but I do not know of anyone who would wish to kill Charlie Winter.'

The Governor sat stony faced and did not feel the need to make notes. Adam moved on swiftly for fear of being silenced.

'I know his daughter, Maria, was with him in the house that night and can vouch for his presence. Unfortunately Francesco's wife, Carmella, was not there; she was nursing a neighbour dying of consumption.'

The Governor shook his head. 'The court cannot rely on the statement of a child, Mr Fletcher; her evidence is inadmissible. It therefore follows that Mr Ceruso has no alibi.'

The first officer looked pleadingly at Adam for additional evidence in support of Francesco's innocence. Adam did not think he had anything more to add.

The Governor turned to the captain. 'Any questions to the witness, Captain?'

The officer rose, he looked troubled, perhaps at the Governor's decision concerning Maria.

'There is just one thing, Mr Fletcher. Is it possible that, on the night of the murder, Sergeant Logan could have known Francesco Ceruso had no adult alibi?'

Adam paused and thought back to the night in the field. He remembered his short conversation with Francesco when he asked if Carmella was with Maria. *'No, I have just sent Maria to stay with the neighbours, Carmella is helping at the Motts tonight; he is close to death'.* He remembered Sergeant Logan standing at the back of the crowd in the semi darkness, a witness to his conversation.

'I'm afraid he will have done and, to my eternal regret, I was the one who inadvertently informed him. When we left the field, Sergeant Logan would have known that a man he hated and whose wife he coveted had no adult alibi.'

Captain Cecil raised his hand and, noting the Governor was ignoring his request, stood up. The Governor could no longer overlook the officer.

'Captain Cecil, you wish to speak?'

'I do, your honour. I have to say I'm surprised by the speed of events in this matter. I have not completed my enquiries in Prosperous Bay and would have expected anyone accused of the crime to be tried when all the facts are available. I note you are evaluating the evidence as in a court martial, although Mr Ceruso is a civilian. Is this perhaps simply a preliminary review to assess if Mr Ceruso should remain in custody until a later trial, at a time when Sergeant Logan could defend his testimony?'

184

'It is not, Sir. The murder of a marine is a military matter and St Helena is a military outpost. All inhabitants remain under martial law. Swift action will give a firm message to the settlers in Prosperous Bay. You've not been on the island long enough, Captain; we've had problems previously with that settlement.'

'All my enquiries to date, Governor, do not support the view that the settlers are seditious.'

'There are additional witnesses to be called, Captain. I suggest we move on and let you return to your investigations, if you feel more work needs to be done.'

Captain Cecil nodded curtly to the Governor and left the court.

The Reverend Wilkes was called to the witness box. Yes, he had been present at the Fletchers' wedding celebrations when there had been an altercation between Sergeant Logan and Francesco Ceruso. The fisherman had made some threats, but he could not remember the details.

'Were they addressed to Sergeant Logan or the marines in general?'

'I'm afraid I cannot remember. They might have been a threat to the marines in general; I could not exclude the possibility, Captain.'

Matthew Draper, Edmond Davies and Robert Morgan spoke on Francesco's behalf, but none could contradict the evidence submitted by Sergeant Logan. Edmond, speaking last, returned to the seat next to Adam.

'This is awful, Adam; it seems there is nothing we can do.'

The Governor looked at his watch. 'Gentleman, we will recess for twenty minutes to allow the prosecution and defence to prepare their summing up. I'll then deliver my verdict.'

The captain and first officer walked out together. Lucy took Maria to get some water whilst the friends gathered around Carmella. All tension had gone from her features, now replaced by resignation and despair.

'They've executed him already. I cannot believe I'm living through this. I know it is a nightmare that will never end.'

The Reverend Wilkes gestured to Adam and the pair detached themselves from the group and walked out into the sunshine.

'Prepare Carmella and yourself for the worst you can imagine. When the verdict is given, take care of Carmella and Maria but bring them to my room, all of you. I will try to ensure Francesco is allowed to attend briefly.'

They returned for the summing up. The naval captain spoke first. 'There is one witness who identified Francesco Ceruso returning to the settlement around midnight from the scene of the crime. The witness is a man in authority and, if his evidence is to be believed, it makes Francesco Ceruso a liar under oath. Doubt has been cast on the integrity and motives of the sole witness so it will be for others to decide if the sergeant's testimony is truthful. One of her majesty's soldiers has been murdered and, if the court considered Francesco Ceruso responsible, a sentence of death would be appropriate.'

The captain turned to his first officer. 'However, I'd be remiss in my duty if I did not tell you that my first officer and I have discussed these matters together in the short time available to us to compose our closing statements. I know he shares Captain Cecil's concerns about the speed with which the trial has been convened, the process of the trial by court martial and the absence of the principle prosecution witness for cross examination. I would wish to put on record that I share his concerns. The death of a soldier is a grave matter, but so is the provision of justice for a civilian on this island.'

Emboldened by his captain's speech, the first officer spoke articulately in defence of Francesco Ceruso. In his view, there was still time to bring Sergeant Logan to testify. He knew of no precedent where the rules of a court martial were applied to a civilian and he questioned the status of St Helena as a purely naval outpost.

'I'm worried that the concerns my captain and I have raised will give rise to a miscarriage of justice. I believe there is at present insufficient evidence to convict Francesco Ceruso. A conviction would be unsafe and he should be acquitted of the charge.'

'Thank you, gentleman, there will be a short recess while I consider my verdict.

Ruth and Lucy stood with Carmella and Maria. The men stood in a small group close by. Matthew Draper whispered under his breath. 'Bigoted tyrant; he's no need for a recess. He's made up his mind already. The whole thing is a charade.'

Adam replied in a low voice. 'Whatever happens here, and we all fear the worst, such rank injustice must never be allowed to recur. The settlers need to set up a civil council to represent their interests; delegates from Jamestown and outlying areas. We are not part of a military establishment, we have civilian rights.'

They returned to the court room to hear the verdict. The walls were now lined with marines. All stood as the Governor re-entered the room.

'Francesco Ceruso, I find you guilty of the charge of murder concerning the death of Marine Winter. There was known to be bad blood between you and the marines and there is damning evidence of your return to the village from the scene of the crime about the time of the murder. I sentence you to death by hanging. The sentence will be carried out at dawn tomorrow.

I note the land you own in Prosperous Bay was granted to your grandfather in recognition of twenty years' service in her majesty's navy. In my judgement your action of murdering Marine Winter forfeits your right to ownership of the land so the plot and any habitation will return to Crown ownership. Your family must vacate the plot by the end of the month. I make one additional order in this matter. I will not have a martyr remaining in the settlement fomenting unrest; your wife must leave the settlement and live elsewhere on the island.'

He addressed the court in general. 'I want a line drawn under this. The settlement needs to make a fresh start. The marine detachment in Prosperous Bay will be doubled in strength until I'm satisfied that law and order is restored. The court is adjourned.'

The friends shielded Carmella and Maria as the courtroom slowly cleared. Francesco was escorted from the room. Maria clung to Carmella, tears streaming down her cheeks. Carmella's expression was unchanged; a sad detachment, as her predictions had been confirmed.

Adam turned to his friends. 'The Reverend Wilkes wants us to come to his office, all of us. Perhaps he'll be in a position to help.'

They guided the distressed family the short distance to the pastor's office. He greeted them at the door.

'Please be seated, I hope I've provided enough chairs. I spoke to Adam during the recess as I had some inkling of the verdict. The Governor has very strong views about religion and has previously voiced his criticism of the Crown gifting land to any settlers who are not English and protestant; for him, an Italian name is immediately suspect, even though Francesco's grandfather served 20 years in her majesty's navy, with distinction, as a sailing master; that apparently counts for nothing. I remonstrated with the Governor last night stating that if he revokes the land grant, which he is entitled to do, he makes Mrs Ceruso destitute. He would not be deflected from his plan, I'm afraid, and, as you know, has insisted that Carmella is also expelled from the settlement. I spoke to Sarah in the kitchens here and they have need of an additional servant in the laundry. The appointment is under the control of Sarah and the superintendent of government house. They have great sympathy for your situation and the job is yours for the asking. The offer comes with accommodation and a modest wage. However, there would be one difficulty; Maria could not live with you.'

Ruth's heart went out to the friend she had known and grown to love over recent years. All the confidence and decisiveness that Ruth had respected in Carmella was gone, obliterated by the magnitude of the events. It seemed likely that decisions would have to be made on Carmella's behalf. Ruth turned to Adam. As she started to speak she was gratified to find he was nodding an endorsement to her remarks.

'Maria must come and live with us. We can continue with the previous arrangements where Lucy takes care of her continuing education and Maria fishes with Adam.'

'As my partner, Maria, you'll be taking on your father's position. I promise we'll come up to Jamestown at least twice a week to sell the fish. You can come up and visit your mother. Will it be possible, Pastor?'

'I'm sure Sarah would agree, Adam.'

Ruth turned to Carmella. 'My friend, we'll take care of Maria as if she were our own. I promise you I will love her as I would a sister. '

Carmella scanned the strained faces around her. Lucy offered her support. 'You know we'll play our part, Carmella. Maria will have good people around her and Adam will ensure she'll get to see you regularly.'

The pastor rose to his feet. 'Is it agreed then, Carmella?'

She nodded her approval. 'When will I start?'

'You do not need to leave the settlement until the end of the month; I'll tell Sarah that you'll arrive then. I've spoken to the captain of the marines and he has agreed that Francesco can be brought here to meet with you for a short while. I hope to be back with him swiftly.'

Ruth watched Carmella brace herself for the final meeting with her husband. Carmella realised she could not offer her husband anything but a confident view of the future. Her friends knew they must support her in this charade. Francesco must die knowing all will be well with his family. They turned as the door opened and Francesco joined them.

The captain saluted. 'There are two men outside the window and there will be more in the corridor. I am content to wait outside; I'm sure you'd prefer some privacy.'

Maria flew into her father's arms and buried her head in his chest. Carmella was transformed. She walked over smiling and put her arms around the pair of them. Francesco's eyes swept the room.

'My friends, it's as I'd feared. I promise you I was not Charlie Winter's murderer and Sergeant Logan's testimony is untrue.'

Edmond shook his head. 'Don't waste your time with such remarks, Francesco. There is no one here who ever believed otherwise, nor is there anyone in the settlement who feels differently.'

Francesco continued to hold his family close to him, talking to his friends over Carmella's shoulder.

'I still can't believe I've been convicted of murder, or the manner in which it has occurred. However, the captain has told me we don't have much time and it's the future we must discuss. I had not expected my land grant to be revoked or that Carmella and Maria would be expelled from the settlement.'

Carmella disengaged herself from his embrace. 'The Reverend Wilkes has been very helpful, Francesco, he's got me employment here in Jamestown. Ruth and Adam have agreed to look after Maria, and Lucy will continue her education. She'll come up to see me frequently when Adam is selling fish.'

Ruth had to admire the performance. A minimum of detail, everything was organised, there would be nothing to worry about. Adam walked over to Francesco. 'My good friend, Maria will be my new partner. I'll care for her as I did for you and you did for me, as we always must when we risk our lives on the open sea. It'll be as it was before; Lucy will continue to look after Maria's education.'

Francesco's brow furrowed. 'Partner, Adam, that'll not be popular with some of the settlement. Daniel Mott would hope he might be considered, and his father's illness will create some sympathy amongst the English settlers.'

'William died two days ago, Francesco. I'm sure you're right it will produce some unhappiness if your replacement is not English and male; however today must be a time for promises and reassurances as to the future. I promise you Maria will be my partner until she wishes otherwise. I want her with me not only because she's your daughter, but also because she is the best. Daniel Mott would never perform to Maria's level; he has no instinct for the work. I choose Maria because, together, we stand the best chance of coping with all the dangers of ocean fishing.'

Ruth joined them. 'Francesco, Maria will live with us, and Adam will ensure she can visit Carmella frequently. I've already given my promises to Carmella; I'll treat Maria as I would a sister. I promise always to take care of her interests – our two families have been close and now they are one.'

Francesco removed the chain and medallion from around his neck. He studied the worn and faded image of

Horatio Nelson's features on one side with affection. The other face bore a simple legend:

HMS GOLIATH
FIRST OF AUGUST 1798
ABOUKIR BAY

He turned to his daughter.

'Wear this with pride as I have done. The Governor treats us as second class citizens, but the Ceruso family have no need to feel inferior to anyone on the Island. My grandfather rarely talked about it but I know that, although he was wounded, he stayed at his post at the wheel throughout the engagement. It is a story you should pass on to your children. It was an epic battle. The English fleet under Nelson found the French moored in a defensive line across the bay at dusk. They surprised the French by attacking immediately. Goliath was the first battleship to engage the enemy. Captain Foley noticed that the 'Le Guerrier' had left a gap of a cable's length between the vessel and its mooring buoy. He asked your great grandfather if he could thread the Goliath through the gap so that they could attack the French from inside the defences. With Captain Foley by his side, and the sun setting, he brought Goliath through the narrow gap and a furious battle followed throughout the night. By dawn the French fleet had been annihilated, only two of their battle ships escaped with eleven destroyed or captured. Nelson presented your great grandfather with this medallion and complimented him on his superb seamanship and bravery. Always remember your great grandfather fought with distinction for his adopted country. You are a Ceruso; we have no need to feel inferior to any man, least of all the Governor.'

He kissed the medal and closed the chain around Maria's neck.

'Thank you, father, it will always be with me.'

Ruth and Adam spoke quietly with Francesco for a short time; private remarks at a life's end. They left the room and slowly the number of friends outside the door grew as everyone left to allow Francesco and Carmella some time alone. Maria joined them and was comforted by the ladies. A few minutes later, Carmella opened the door. She looked composed.

'Thank you for your consideration, Captain. My husband is ready to return to his cell.' She walked out of the residence, holding her daughter's hand without a backward glance.

They all walked back to their lodgings, not wishing to return to Prosperous Bay until the sentence had been carried out. A message arrived from the Reverend Wilkes; the execution would take place at 7am in the barrack's square. It would not be open to the public. Francesco had asked if Adam and Ruth would escort Carmella to the barracks while the others took care of Maria at the lodgings.

Edmond Davies and Matthew Draper spent the evening visiting the more influential members of the local community to discuss setting up a citizen's council to represent the interests of the civilians on the island. They found there was widespread indignation in Jamestown at the manner in which the civilians had been treated and great sympathy for Francesco Ceruso.

Sleep did not come easily to the group and all were awake long before dawn. Maria expressed the wish to be looking out to sea, at the time of her father's death, so the group left early to climb a local promontory. Adam, Ruth and Carmella walked to the barracks through deserted streets.

They were met at the gate by a sergeant of marines and escorted to the square. Francesco and the Reverend Wilkes walked out of the barracks and approached the gallows. Oak steps led up to a platform where a single noose hung in the still air. The major of marines beckoned Adam.

'Mr Fletcher, I suggest the three of you stand here, with you at the back of the two ladies. When I signal to you ensure the two ladies turn away. Do not let them turn back until all is finished. I will try to have Mr Ceruso lowered to the ground as soon as the doctor feels the sentence has been carried out. I think the Governor feels Mr Ceruso should be buried here, but he's not said so formally and I'm ready to release his body to you, if that is Mrs Ceruso's wish.'

They stood where the major had indicated. Francesco received a final blessing from the Reverend Wilkes. Then he paused at the bottom of the steps and looked for a final time at his wife and friends. He turned and climbed to the upper platform and reached out for the black bag to cover his head. Again he paused, surveying the sky in the dawn light, as he had done so often in the past, looking for clues as to how the day would unfold. He placed the bag over his head and allowed the noose to settle on his neck. Adam drew both women round into an embrace and they buried their heads against his chest. They all heard the sound of the bolts drawn from the trap door and the sharp groan of a rope abruptly under load.

'Wait, Carmella, not yet.'

Francesco's passing was mercifully swift; his body was lowered to the cobbles and the hospital superintendent confirmed death.

The major walked over. 'Mrs Ceruso, I can release your husband's body. If you wish him to be buried in Prosperous Bay, my men will take his body to Mr Fletcher's boat.'

She nodded her approval.

'In a moment we'll fire the signal gun to announce the execution has taken place; my condolences, Madam.'

The Reverend Wilkes joined them. 'Would you like me to officiate at the funeral, Carmella?'

'Thank you, Pastor; I know Francesco would have approved of that.'

Four marines carried Francesco at shoulder height on a stretcher. His body had been wrapped and tied in a blanket. A sergeant and a detail of marines led the procession down to the harbour through streets that remained deserted, as if the community were ashamed of the Governor's actions. Maria and their friends joined them on the quay. No one felt the need to speak. The marines stowed Francesco in the covered section in the bow and withdrew. Adam and Maria reverted to their sailing roles and the lugger moved slowly out into the main channel on a light breeze. There was only one frigate in the harbour whose sailors had bought fish on several occasions. The rail was lined with sailors, standing in silence with their heads bowed. As the lugger cleared the stern of the frigate, they recognised the captain and first officer from the trial. They raised their hands in silent salute.

CHAPTER FIFTEEN

The breeze stiffened as they left the inlet. Adam sat alone in the stern. His face was ashen, having been the only witness to the moment of death - Francesco's fall, abruptly arrested as his neck snapped straight. The slow pendulum of body movement, with the legs twitching, both gradually subsiding. Maria had found an old pair of Francesco's trousers in the bow and exchanged them for her skirt, so she could move around the boat more freely. The ladies and the Reverend Wilkes sat near the bow with the men seated just aft to the main mast. No orders were given as the captain and his new partner guided the lugger to a different tack. It was as if Francesco was still his partner, on his final journey, but in the form of his daughter. The bow lifted to the waves as they sailed north to clear Sugarloaf Point. All the familiar sights and smells Francesco had known so well. There were shadows on the western side of the Sugarloaf as the sun rose in the eastern sky.

When Adam gauged he had travelled sufficiently far north, he looked over to Maria who stood by the mast. There was a new maturity in her expression; a child catapulted into adulthood by the previous three days. She raised an eyebrow and looked to starboard. It was as if neither wanted to break the silence. He nodded and adjusted the tiller. The boat settled on a starboard tack as the lugger started to cross Flagstaff Bay. Adam knew the lives of all those on the boat had been changed by Francesco's death. However, over and above the general loss, he was aware that three of them were bound by a deeper grief. Francesco's widow and his daughter would carry the heaviest burden but Adam had also lost his partner. It had been a relationship of complete trust. Losing his friend in such a brutal manner had left his senses numbed. Thank God the others had not seen the final moments. He doubted Carmella and Ruth would ever forget the screech of the bolts as the trap door was released and the sickening groan as the rope tightened.

They sailed on in silence across the bay and then cleared Barnlong Point, gaining sea room in the ocean to the east. Eventually he turned his gaze to Maria. She was watching him, seated with her back to the mast. She looked worried, and he sensed that he was the object of her concern. Adam had no doubt he looked haggard. He could only respect her strength; she had just lost her father yet she was concerned about his grief. Three days ago she was a child, but now she was an adult and his partner, to be trusted and respected. He offered her a bleak smile and nodded to the starboard side again. The Sentinel came into view as they ran south towards the bay.

A rider must have been despatched to the settlement since a marine lieutenant and six troopers were on the beach to greet them. Willing hands drew the boat up onto the beach. The soldiers carried a stretcher. The lieutenant saluted Adam and turned his attention to the Reverend Wilkes.

'Welcome Padre, I was told you were on board. A grave has been dug in the cemetery in anticipation of your arrival.'

The pastor turned to the widow. 'May I suggest, Mrs Ceruso, that your husband is taken to your house, so that the ladies can prepare him for burial. I suggest we gather in the meeting hall in about an hour.'

She nodded her approval and Francesco was carried to the settlement. The lieutenant took Adam aside. 'Mr Fletcher, several of my men would like to attend the service; not as a unit, but on a personal basis.'

'I'm sure that would be appreciated, Lieutenant.'

Francesco was laid to rest before the sun had set. His grave was next to his father and his grandfather's; the sailing master who had served with distinction on a seventy gun ship of the line at the battle of the Nile. Ruth and Adam escorted Carmella and Maria back to their house.

'When do I start as your partner, Adam?'

He was surprised by the abruptness and familiarity of the question, but smiled inwardly. Carmella started to intervene, to apologise on her daughter's behalf.

Adam laughed. 'I take no offence, Carmella. Why shouldn't a partner call me by my first name. As to when we fish, I'll be happy to start tomorrow but will leave the choice to you.'

Mother and daughter exchanged glances. Carmella shrugged. 'Why not tomorrow, Adam?'

'We'll leave at dawn, Maria. Just local fishing tomorrow, I think. I don't have the heart to return to Jamestown so swiftly.'

Husband and wife walked slowly up the hill to their house.

'I have no food, Adam.'

'I doubt either of us has an appetite.'

He poured two liberal measures of rum into mugs and they sat out on the porch overlooking the sea as the light faded. They retired to bed, as the final glow over Diana's Peak dimmed, and fell into an exhausted sleep.

Adam woke refreshed in the pre-dawn light. He dressed swiftly and gently opened the curtains as Ruth had requested. As he walked through the square on the way to the beach he noticed several settlers standing close to the recently widowed Elizabeth Mott and her son, Daniel. The young man stood by his mother with his hands in his pockets, staring at the ground. She called out to Adam.

'Mr Fletcher, we were all very sorry to hear of Mr Ceruso's death; a man much admired by the community. However, now that he is no longer here you'll need a new sailing partner. My husband and I have always been hopeful that you would look favourably on Daniel. I'm sure he would learn quickly and serve you well.'

Adam had known this was a subject that would need to be faced, but was unprepared for the speed with which it had occurred.

'I'm sorry, Elizabeth, I will be unable to offer Daniel work. I promised Francesco at the time of his death that I would have Maria as my sailing partner.'

Mrs Mott's expression darkened, with a look of confusion. Adam knew it was likely to be followed by anger.

'Surely, Mr Fletcher, she's only a child and the work is not seemly for a girl.'

'I'm sorry, Elizabeth, she has sailed with me quite frequently in recent months; she has learnt the trade and enjoys the work. Lucy Davies promised Francesco she would continue her education in the evenings. I know this must sound unusual but they are deathbed promises and I could not go back on them. As you probably know, Carmella must leave the settlement by the end of the month; Maria will come and live with us.'

'What does Mrs Fletcher think about that arrangement?'

'She suggested it, Mrs Mott. The Fletchers and the Cerusos have been closely linked for more than thirty years and the events of the last week have changed the lives of our families forever. Ruth and I made promises to Francesco and Carmella, obligations we're happy to accept. I'm sorry I can't help Daniel.'

The other settlers, also of English descent, watched in silence but Adam doubted that would remain the case when he walked on to his boat. Mother and son stood between Adam and the beach. He walked round them and could sense the depth of hostility from the onlookers.

Maria slipped into her father's role without difficulty. Adam enjoyed explaining the nuances of ocean sailing and fishing and she was soon in a position to sail the lugger singlehanded, if necessary. They escorted Carmella to Jamestown at the end of the month and saw her established in her small bedroom in the eves of an annexe of the Governor's mansion. Maria moved in with Adam and Ruth. Their kitchen was spacious and they had been able to partition off a separate bedroom, using wooden boards with a curtained entrance. They swiftly settled into a new routine and Ruth did not find it difficult to keep her promise to Francesco and Carmella. She enjoyed the young girl's company and her enthusiasm for life. It was as if she had gained a younger sister.

Harmony prevailed in their home and on the lugger, but Adam and Ruth were soon aware that their promises to Francesco and Carmella had caused resentment. Adam realised that, with hindsight, the split had occurred along predictable lines. Their English friends understood Adam's choice and the Fletchers' obligations to the Carusos. Those who were not of English stock also approved of the choice; Adam, and his father before him, had always had the respect of settlers from other nationalities and freed slaves, because of their choice of the Cerusos as sailing partners. However those English families who were not close friends were strongly opposed to Maria's employment. Daniel Mott, who had so recently lost his father, should have been preferred. The wives of the disaffected group were swift to question Adam's motives for working in isolation at sea with a young girl on the threshold of womanhood. Adam noticed subtle alterations to his fish sales; some English families no longer bought his fish. Overall sales were maintained by increased sales to other nationalities. Adam and Ruth realised their decision had split the settlement, but were not able or willing to resolve the conflict.

Four days after the trial, Captain Cecil returned to the Governor's house to present his report. After a considerable delay, he was admitted to the Governor's office.

'Well, Captain, what can I do for you?'

'I've come to provide you with my report on the marine's murder.'

'Not really necessary now, Captain. Francesco Ceruso has been convicted and executed. I presumed you had completed your enquiries when the verdict was announced.'

'You sent me from the court, Governor, to continue my enquiries. I left Jamestown directly and did not hear of the execution until two days later.'

'What more did you discover when you returned to Prosperous Bay?'

'I didn't return to Prosperous Bay, I did not feel that would advance the issue. It seemed to me the crucial witness was in Thompson's Bay. The first officer, representing Francesco Ceruso, gave me a copy of Sergeant Logan's statement as I left. I was curious to meet this marine, whose evidence could not be questioned.'

The Governor shifted uncomfortably in his chair.

'Sir, you have exceeded your orders.'

'No, Governor, I have not. My brief was to collect evidence concerning the murder; you did not restrict the enquiries to Prosperous Bay.'

'What conclusions did you reach?'

'I arrived in Thompson's Bay unannounced and caught him unawares. I sent him away from his men and interviewed each one, having advised them of the seriousness of the situation. They provided a lot of background information. The sergeant did make very improper remarks to Mrs Ceruso and in recent times to her young daughter. The marines felt Mr Ceruso's remonstrations were reasonable. The sergeant is a poor disciplinarian and corrupt. He gambles and he loses. It seems Charlie Winter was a shrewd card player and all of them owed him money; the men did not know the figures but most thought the sergeant was heavily in debt to Charlie Winter. Since Charlie's death, Sergeant Logan has apparently 'come into money'. I find that interesting. I interviewed the sergeant twice; on the first occasion I talked him through the events of the murder. I did not reveal to him that I had a copy of his statement in my saddlebag. I left him in isolation again while I compared the two statements. There were several, very obvious inconsistencies, which he was unable to explain with any credibility when we met again. If he had been cross examined by the first office in court, his evidence would have been found to be unconvincing. It is my conclusion, Governor, you have almost definitely executed the wrong man. The sergeant sent Charlie Winter to steal some vegetables, as frequently occurred; on this occasion he struck Charlie on the back of his head and, while he was unconscious, killed him with a pitch fork. By doing so, he relieved himself of his debts, stole the marine's money and removed the husband of a wife that he coveted.'

'How dare you question my judgement and authority? I will break you for this, Captain.'

'Do not threaten me, Governor; you do not have the jurisdiction. My convalescence is now complete. I take the next Indiaman back to London where new orders will await me. Here is your copy of my report, the original goes with me to London. We'll let others decide on your conduct of this case. You would do well to remember we are no longer at war with France. That should be obvious to you of all people – Napoléon is buried on this island. The man you executed was a civilian and you did not safeguard his rights. Good day, Sir.''

Adam and Maria visited Carmella frequently, sometimes with Ruth. All the strength and vibrancy they had known from the past had deserted her. Sarah said she performed her duties faultlessly, but spent her free time reclusively. She was never seen to smile or laugh and looked gaunt and pale. Several months after the trial, she developed a cough. The hospital superintendent suspected consumption. Permission was given for her to return to Prosperous Bay. Ruth nursed her in their living room. The trip from Jamestown in the lugger had been cold and wet and Carmella developed pneumonia and within two weeks was dead. She was buried next to her husband before the anniversary of his execution.

A representative council was set up in the months that followed. Adam and Edmond represented Prosperous Bay. The island had lost confidence in the Governor and many knew Captain Cecil had submitted a report which was critical of his actions. Five months after the trial, Sergeant Logan was transferred back to Jamestown and reduced to the ranks. A month later, the Governor was recalled and replaced; no reason was given for either decision.

Two years later, relations with France were considered to be sufficiently cordial to allow the release of Napoléon's body. A French frigate 'La Belle Poule' moored in Jamestown harbour and the Emperor's remains were returned to France.

The battle with the slavers reached a new intensity and the West Africa Squadron was reinforced.

CHAPTER SIXTEEN

ST HELENA 1844

Ruth sat in a rocking chair on the back porch watching the lugger return in the afternoon light. She had been in a pensive mood, no doubt provoked by their sixth wedding anniversary. The marriage had not, so far, been blessed with children. At first this had not been a concern, but it had now become a sadness that was growing in her heart; the thought she might never have a child. Maria had grown into a beautiful young woman; slim and with long, dark hair like her mother. Her complexion was overly dark for some social circles; the inevitable consequence of her antecedents and life outdoors on the ocean. Ruth and Maria had become like sisters, enjoying each other's company.

Until recently, the fishing had remained plentiful and the proceeds of their work now came to one family. However, over the previous year an increasing number of fish were found to be blighted; they had lost their sheen, with ragged scales. These could not be sold and had to be thrown back into the ocean. Ruth now often joined them when there was a trip to Jamestown; the ladies would shop while Adam sold the catch. They were happy times marred only by Elizabeth Mott's grievance which continued to fester. Ruth and Maria were never criticised to their face, but they were both resigned to the belief that Maria's employment would never be accepted by some of the English community. There was to be a meeting of the representative council later in the week in Jamestown and Maria and the Fletchers had booked two nights' accommodation. Edmond and Lucy Davies would sail with them.

The council meeting took up most of the day and the ladies enjoyed exploring the island capital. Residents looked back to the days of the East India Company with nostalgia, since it had been a time of plenty. The more recent years of British rule had been stringent, but the island was now providing a base where captured slave ships could be brought. The boats were burnt and the captives returned to Africa or taken, as freemen, to the West Indies.

Ruth gently rubbed Jason's locket between her fingers and thumb; it was a habit she had fallen into shortly after receiving it. The smooth gold surface was broken by small indentations created by the profile of a dolphin etched onto the surface. She wondered where Jason's duty had now taken him. When parting they had agreed that exchanging letters would not be prudent. Mail deliveries in Prosperous Bay were rare and regular exchanges would inevitably be noted. The decision had been for the best, but she regretted its effect. She rose and returned to the kitchen to prepare the vegetables for supper. The sun sank lower in the sky throwing shafts of light across the kitchen floor. The colour slowly turned from yellow to gold and then a deepening red as sunset approached. She heard the sound of laughter coming from the path. There had obviously been a race which Adam was losing badly. When Maria reached the porch, she threw up her hands as if reaching the tape. She turned and hugged Adam.

'I win, Adam. You said I could be Captain tomorrow if I beat you.'

'Yes, but I had to carry all these heavy fish and make sure they were not damaged.'

He passed the fish over to Ruth who went through the motions of testing their weight. She smiled.

'There are only three of them, Adam. It can only have been a modest handicap. You can't go back on your word.'

Adam threw up his hands. 'You two, you always stick together. Alright, Maria, perhaps we'll avoid races up the hill in the future; you're too fast for me.'

Laughing, the trio walked through to the kitchen. It was a pleasant time of the day. Maria showered first and then helped Ruth in the kitchen with the evening meal. They usually drank watered down rum.

'What time did you arrange with Edmond and Lucy, Adam?'

'I wondered if there might be an early morning mist; I said 8 o'clock by the boat.'

Maria laughed. 'I like these visits with the Davieses; we get a nice lie in.'

They stayed up later than they normally would. Ruth sat back and watched as Maria recounted a situation when she had been sailing the lugger and Adam had nearly fallen out of the boat. Adam feigned outrage at her mockery. It was not just a case of two sisters; Maria had a brother and a sister. Ruth was surprised that matters had turned out so well with Maria, considering the appalling trauma of the loss of her father and her mother only a few months later.

The weather for the trip to Jamestown was ideal; a warm, gentle breeze with almost no swell, even when they were at the extreme of their northern tack, before swinging west across Sugarloaf Point. The ladies sat near the base of the mast. Adam and Edmond shared the stern seat.

'The inshore fishermen are suffering, Adam. They'd hoped the New Year would see fish blight clear up as a fresh generation of fish was born. The blight this year is just as bad as last year and no one wants to buy such diseased looking fish.'

Adam surveyed the horizon. 'They'll be tempted to sail out further today, Edmond; they know they stand a better chance of normal fish further out even though their boats are not built to cope with anything other than mild weather. Whatever causes the blight seems mainly restricted to the shallower waters nearer the island. Even Maria and I have had to throw out quite a few offshore fish and the number is slowly rising. I've not spoken to Ruth about it yet or Maria, but I think we'll have to sail further east and north to improve the catch. It will mean staying out overnight two or three times a week. I plan to try it in the next couple of weeks; it should allow us to sell more fish in Jamestown before bringing the residue back to Prosperous Bay.'

'Adam, you know that you have my full support in the choice of Maria as a fishing partner. Lucy and I witnessed the promises you made to a dying friend, but Maria has grown into a beautiful woman. You know there is still bitterness amongst some concerning your choice. Nights out at sea; just you and Maria, will cause a lot of talk amongst the women. You must be aware of that?'

'I am, Edmond. I've not set out to be confrontational and once I had made my promise to Francesco there was nothing I could do to appease Mrs Mott and her son. As a family, we have simply had to accept the resentment from some in the settlement. This new problem is much the same, people will not buy diseased fish and we must sail further out. I'm sure the women will talk and I wish there were some other way to resolve the problem.'

The group was in no hurry and Maria had set out lines as soon as they were well clear of land. Ruth and Lucy watched as half of the catch of fish, with dull and ulcerated skin, were thrown back. Maria sat down next to them.

'It's hopeless, Lucy. Normally I would not set the lines until we were twice as far from the island and even then a fair number of the catch is diseased.'

By early afternoon, the boat was moored in Jamestown. Adam and Maria sold their catch to Sarah, who knew the representative council was meeting the next day and had guessed Adam would likely appear with a catch to sell. A kitchen maid carried the fish back to the Governor's residence and Sarah and the fishermen sat at a table outside a harbour tavern.

'The fish on offer most days, Adam, is awful.'

'I know, Sarah, we're being driven further and further out to catch fish free of the blight.'

Maria frowned and shivered. 'Are you alright, Maria?'

'Yes, Adam. I felt a cold draught.' She pulled her shawl closer around her shoulders.

A man stood in the shadows several feet inside the tavern. Unshaven and unkempt, he swayed gently on his feet. The man had been successful once, but was now embittered and angry at his loss of position in the world. The arrogant officer, Captain Cecil, and his own treacherous squad, had stolen his hard won stripes and reduced him to the ranks. They had known enough to demote him, but not enough to charge him with murder. He had not found it easy to return to the ranks and had difficulty showing respect to corporals and sergeants. The Marines had discharged him from service earlier in the year; part time work in the harbour kept him from total destitution.

She had to be the Ceruso child; she looked the image of her mother. He had hunted for Carmella in Jamestown when he returned from Thompson's Bay, but no one knew what had become of her. He studied Maria's features as she turned towards him whilst replying to a question from the Governor's cook. He smiled; perhaps the day was not so bad after all.

'Another tot, Ned, I have the money.'

The council meeting went well and the ladies spent the day shopping and at ease. They dined late, with plans to sail back to the settlement in mid-morning. However, at dawn there was knock on Edmond's door. Ruth stood there fully dressed.

'Apologies, Edmond, Adam does not like the weather. He feels we should leave immediately and get back before matters get worse. Would you mind leaving without breakfast?'

Edmond laughed. 'It sounds as though I might not keep it down, even if I ate it. We'll be with you shortly.'

Within half an hour, Maria was raising the mainsail and they were clearing the harbour.

'I should tell you, Adam, that my stomach is rumbling and, as a lay person, I can see no difference in the weather compared with two days ago.'

Adam laughed. 'Edmond, I may be wrong and, if so, I apologise for depriving you of your breakfast.'

Lucy lightly poked her husband's stomach. 'It'll do him no harm, Adam.'

Ruth turned to Maria. 'What do you feel about the weather, Maria?'

'To an extent, I agree with Edmond; I can see no change from two days ago.' She scanned the northern horizon and took in the clouds moving slowly to the east.

'It may look the same, but something's changed. I think Adam is probably right, although I would not have had sufficient confidence to haul everyone out of bed early.'

They continued on their northern tack, clearing the land to the east. Ruth sat watching Maria and her husband. Everything was in order within the boat and their attention was fully focused on the surrounding ocean. Both were alert, their awareness heightened for any clues nature might provide. The wind began to rise and the sails were reefed. The calm surface of the sea became choppy; it felt colder and Ruth and the Davieses were grateful when Adam suggested they made themselves comfortable in the covered section of the bow. The Davieses chose to rest but Ruth preferred to sit by the entrance watching Adam and Maria sail their boat to the safety of Prosperous Bay.

Adam chose to stand by the tiller, seeking a slightly better view of the surrounding ocean. Maria opened a locker and brought out two canvas ponchos with short lengths of cord for belts. She donned hers and took over the tiller as Adam braced his legs widely apart and struggled into the rough canvas. Within minutes Ruth could see why Maria had produced the garments, as spray began to fly over the stern from some of the larger waves. It was obvious the two knew each other's minds and trusted each other's judgements. Maria ran lightly forward and crouched close to Ruth.

'It won't be long before the final tack and the run south should be swift. How are the Davieses?'

'Not too good.'

'An hour should see us back in calm waters and the beach.'

The lugger lurched onto its final tack south, leaning over further in the strengthening, westerly wind. Maria sat with her back to the mast, watching Adam as he stood by the tiller. His attention seemed drawn to the ocean off the port bow, in the east. Unbidden, Maria joined him in the stern. He pointed to an area on the port side. Ruth watched them stand together as Adam spoke with his mouth close to Maria's ear. Whatever he thought he had seen, it was only visible intermittently and Maria did not seem able to confirm the sighting. She tied a rope around her waist and Adam secured the other end to the boat. With Adam's help she climbed onto the stern seat, then onto the stern counter clutching the backstay and rose up on her toes for maximum height. Adam sat down with one hand on the tiller and the other tensioning the rope around Maria's waist. At first it seemed to Ruth to be a false alarm, but Maria continued her vigil. Suddenly she half raised her hand, as if to point, and then stopped and frowned. A couple of minutes later it was obvious a definite sighting had been made. The fishermen moved swiftly; the sighting was changed to a compass bearing and they reduced sail, and swung to port, running before the wind. Once they were established on the new course, Maria joined Ruth.

'I'm sorry, Ruth, Adam has noticed something further out to sea. It took me a while to spot it, but it looks like wreckage of some sort and we'll have to check it out. Hopefully it'll be a quick circle around it and on into the bay.'

Ruth and Maria stood grasping the hardwood roof as the object slowly came into view.

'It's an upturned boat, Ruth; it has no keel. Dear God, I think it's the Sea Witch. They'd be crazy to be fishing this far out of the bay. '

Adam beckoned them both to the stern and took off his tarpaulin poncho, passing it over to Ruth.

'Put this on, Ruth, it should keep some of the spray off you. I'm going to come up to the wreckage so it lies on our port beam, the left side of the boat. You will need to steer her because I'll be amidships with Maria with the boat hooks. You will need to bring us to the wreckage so that we are almost touching it on the port beam as we pass. Watch for my signal. As we pass, I want you to push the tiller away from you, hard to starboard. The boat should come up into the wind and then just try to keep her in that position for long enough for Maria to get the sails down. Hopefully we'll have hooked onto the wreckage by then.'

Maria moved to the middle of the boat, releasing two boat hooks from clips under the coaming. Ruth settled into the stern seat, leaning out to check on the position of the wreckage. Adam's hand was on top of hers, subtly adjusting the pressure on the tiller to maintain their course to the portside of the wreckage. A wave slammed into the stern counter, showering both of them with spray.

'The boat is with you now, Ruth, watch out for my signal.'

Another wave soaked them both with cold water from the distant Antarctic regions. She shivered and pushed sodden hair from her face.

'I'm ready, Adam.'

He went to the centre of the boat and Maria handed him a boat hook. Ruth tested the tiller, making simple adjustments to appreciate how sensitive it was to minor alterations. She kept the wreckage as close as she dared to the left side of the bow. Another wave soaked her, but she felt a surge of exhilaration piloting the lugger in such a rough sea. She looked to stern. The sky was black and what looked like sheets of rain obscured the land. Then the whole western sky lit up with lightning, instantly replaced by darkness. It was frightening, but also exciting to be at the mercy of the elements with only skill and ingenuity to protect them. The wreckage was almost upon them. The upturned stern was facing them and she could read Sea Witch on the counter. The mast and the sail lay on the far side of the boat. Adam signalled and she pushed the tiller away from her as Maria and Adam tried to secure a firm hold. The bow swung into the wind and the boat lost way, the sails flapping. With cries of triumph both fishermen hooked onto the wreckage and Maria instantly passed her boat hook to Adam, as he braced his legs to keep the boats in contact. Edmond and Lucy Davies watched from the bow, as Maria lowered the mainsail. Adam started to shout a request to Edmond but it was lost in a peel of thunder accompanied by the first drops of rain. He beckoned them to the centre of the boat.

'We will have to try to lift this side of the boat. When we were coming upon the wreckage I thought I saw a foot protruding from this edge. I hope Silas has been rescued but I fear he may have died out here alone.'

They passed a rope around a rowlock protruding from the Sea Witch's coaming and elevated the side sufficiently to allow the interior to be inspected. Silas Tate floated into view. Adam leaned outboard and passed a rope around his torso and drew him aboard as Edmond and Maria held the coaming above the water.

Ruth sighed. 'Another widow for Prosperous Bay.'

Ruth knelt to get a better view inside the Sea Witch. Her eye was caught by a bright flash of colour in the water. Dear God, the long blond hair of Daniel Mott. 'Adam, Daniel Mott is also in there.'

A prolonged roll of thunder rendered conversation impractical, but no additional words needed to be said. They all knew that what was already a catastrophe had taken on an additional significance. They drew him gently out from under the boat and Adam passed a rope around his body and lifted him without difficulty into the lugger. They laid the bodies before the mast and covered them with a blanket. Adam released them from the Sea Witch and the lugger drifted downwind and swung to port on a heavily reefed jib which Maria had hoisted. A reefed mainsail followed and they settled on a tack into the darkness in the west. The Davieses retired to the bow while Maria returned to her station by the mast. Ruth sat with Adam at the stern. Neither spoke for a while. Squalls of heavy rain drenched them, but Ruth did not feel the need to seek shelter. They were all soaked and she preferred to be exposed to the elements rather than crouch within the cramped cover in the bow.

'This will not go away, Adam.'

'I know. Silas was mad to sail out this far. He was never a skilful sailor and has no real experience of the ocean.'

'I never even realised Daniel Mott crewed for him.'

'I don't think he does, or did. Of all the days to sail with Silas, it had to be the day when Silas gambled on deep sea fishing.'

A break in the sheets of rain allowed them sight of the Sentinel and Adam adjusted the tiller. The seas were getting less steep as they entered the lee of the land and the Davieses ventured out of the bow compartment, as they reached the bay. Several settlers and the marine sergeant had come down to the beach as the lugger cleared the Sentinel. As they approached the beach, the sergeant hailed them.

'Welcome back, Mr Fletcher. Have you had any sight of the Sea Witch; she's overdue and with the weather changing for the worse....'

Adam could see Mary Tate by the sergeant's side. 'I'm afraid we have, Sergeant, I'm sorry, Mary, the Sea Witch has foundered. We found them about an hour ago; I'm afraid your husband and Daniel Mott are dead. We've brought them home for burial.'

A crowd gathered swiftly as the boat was drawn up onto the sand. Silas's body had already been lifted from the boat and passed to his grieving family. Adam raised the body of Daniel Mott and brought it to the edge of the lugger. The crowd parted to allow Elizabeth Mott through.

'Don't you dare touch my son, Adam Fletcher; you're a murderer. If you had done your duty as an Englishman, my boy would still be alive.'

Edmond Davies, already on the beach, hurried forward to relieve Adam of the body of the young man. Ruth could see that many were in agreement with the widow's sentiments. Maria busied herself with stowing the sails. The sergeant intervened.

'Let's not have any trouble please. Take the bodies to the settlement and leave the Fletchers to complete their work here.'

The crowd dispersed, leaving the Fletchers and the Davieses and Maria on the beach. Their work complete, the five walked into the settlement. Lucy kissed Adam when they reached the Davies's door.

'Why don't you come for dinner tonight? It'll be something fairly light as I doubt Edmond will feel able to cope with more.'

Adam looked up, as another squall of rain lashed the houses, and then at Ruth.

'There'll be no fishing tomorrow, and it would be insensitive in any event.'

Ruth replied on their behalf. 'That would be kind of you, Lucy, we'll see you later.'

The trio walked slowly back up the hill, knowing their position in the settlement was even more isolated than before.

Ruth, Adam and Maria chose to stand at the back of the congregation during the funeral of the two fishermen. As they were leaving the church Mary Tate thanked Adam for bringing her husband's body home. She seemed embarrassed by Elizabeth Mott's vitriolic denunciation on the beach but the Fletcher's relationship with many of the English stock in the settlement was greatly weakened.

Adam discussed the problems of the fish blight with Ruth, when they returned from the funeral. She had seen the appearance of the fish Maria had been throwing back, and the frequency with which it had been occurring. The bow compartment of the lugger had been partitioned with a curtain from the time of Francesco's death, to ensure an element of privacy. Ruth knew that a change in fishing methods would be required. They settled on two nights at sea each week, weather permitting. It would be a Monday and a Thursday night with daytime fishing on the

Wednesday and Saturday. On Tuesdays and Fridays they would hope to sell the bulk of their fish in Jamestown and bring the remainder back to Prosperous Bay. Sarah would know there would be fish available in the early afternoon on Tuesdays and Fridays for the Governor's kitchen. They would have fish to sell in the settlement on the other days.

'Please speak candidly, Ruth, are you happy with Maria and me staying out two nights each week?'

'I'm not unhappy with the situation, Adam, because I know how it's arisen. We gave Francesco a promise and I've never had cause to regret the choice we made. The fish Maria showed me last week could not be offered for sale and you'll have to fish further out. I love Maria as a sister; we both know there'll be more talk and people will consider it scandalous. I'm resigned to the mock indignation and snide remarks that are bound to occur, but you, or perhaps we, should ensure Maria realises this is not simply a fishing matter and that there are wider implications.'

The discussion with Maria the following night was brief. She did not see it was anything more than a fishing matter, and thought it was no business of discontented people. Adam raised the importance of a young lady's reputation, but Maria felt the people whose judgement mattered to her would know her for who she was and the rest could go hang themselves. Ruth doubted further discussion would alter Maria's view and the trio resolved to start the new plan the following week.

The response was much as Adam and Ruth had anticipated. They caught fish of better quality that were much sought after in Jamestown and in Prosperous Bay. Some of the settlers might smirk and raise an eyebrow, but they still queued to buy the fish. Adam involved Mary Tate in the selling of the fish in the settlement square. She helped Maria with her deliveries to houses and there was always a fish for her to take home. She enjoyed the status that came from still having a role in the life of the settlement.

The nights at sea did provoke a change in Ruth. Several weeks into the new arrangement, on a Monday morning, she stood in her nightdress watching the lugger clear the bay. She knew she would be alone with her thoughts that evening. She was more sensitive to the relationship between Maria and Adam when they were back home in the evening. They were close, but they had always been close and, when sailing they shared a telepathic rapport, which was obvious to all. There was a casual familiarity which could only come through profound respect. She found she was stroking Jason Hewitt's locket more frequently. She smiled at the irony of the situation, exhibiting some worry about her husband's fidelity when she had been consumed by her love for the young naval officer. Deep in her heart she knew Jason Hewitt would always be the love of her life. She chuckled. 'Ruth Fletcher, you can hardly complain at the cards that fate has dealt you. You love and respect your husband and Maria; there is nothing to be done.

The overnight arrangements in the boat were in fact a deal more casual than Adam and Maria had implied. They had been out overnight occasionally in the past, in response to foul weather, or more commonly when becalmed. There was a curtain which split the bow into two halves to allow privacy but they did not change into sleeping attire and Maria, who had a dislike of small spaces, preferred the curtain reefed up to the roof. They had often lain under their own blankets talking into the night. They now fished for longer on Mondays and Thursdays into the late afternoon. Adam bought a small stove which was held on a bracket by the curtained entrance to their accommodation. Ruth provided simple meals which could be heated at the end of the day. They would set out a sea anchor which brought the bows into the wind, and settle down to warm stew and a loaf of bread, washed down with water and grog. The sunsets were often spectacular and St Helena was rarely in view. If the night was warm, they sometimes took their bedding out of the bow and lay on their backs under the sky. Adam taught Maria the names of the stars and how they could be used for navigation.

As the months passed, Adam felt the settlement was adjusting to their night-time absences a little better. The settlers were getting larger amounts of better quality fish and his involvement of Mary Tate was considered to be kind and thoughtful. There had been one or two storms which Adam had not predicted, when they had been far out to sea, but in their skilful hands the lugger had coped without difficulty.

Adam was sitting in the stern one Monday afternoon, cruising slowly west with all lines out, when he sensed there was a change to the weather. Maria was sitting on the floor of the boat reading a book that Lucy had loaned her. It would be half an hour before the fishing lines were checked. She had come to them a wiry, young girl and had now matured into womanhood. Her hair was tied back showing her neck to good effect. Her brown eyes scanned the text, her brow occasionally furrowed. She became aware of his attention and looked up.

'Something the matter, Adam? Are you worried about the weather?'

'Do you feel it, do you also feel the change?'

'Yes, a bit, but what is it that I'm feeling?'

'I don't know, Maria. Captain Pickford says it's the air pressure which alters before the weather changes and the best sailing masters can sense it a few hours in advance. When you've finished your chapter, wind in the lines and we'll sail closer to the island. If we are in its lee, we should be spared the worst of it.'

By the time Maria had finished her chapter, the sky was darkening in the west and the wind was freshening. She returned Lucy's book to the canvas bag which hung from a hook in the bow. By the time the fishing lines were stowed, they were running through a rising sea and the air temperature had dropped by several degrees. They donned their ponchos and Maria joined Adam on the stern seat.

'Another half hour on this tack, Maria, then we'll lay out the sea anchor and ride it out.'

A boat hook, imperfectly held in its clips at the side of the boat, broke free and fell to the deck. Maria moved forward.

'I'll sort that, Adam.'

She bent down to retrieve the boat hook and a gust of wind blew up her poncho to reveal her tanned back and her buttocks outlined against her taut trousers. Adam was distracted by the `inspection of her body and failed to note an isolated wave coming from the port side. Maria was facing to starboard and was holding the boat hook with both hands, close to the side of the boat. The lugger tipped abruptly to starboard; Maria dropped the boat hook and desperately reached out for the coaming but her hands and the wood were wet. In a second, to Adam's horror, she was gone with only the boat hook clattering to the deck, as witness to her passing.

Adam cursed his stupidity and grabbed an almost empty water cask they had been using and threw it after her. He could see her head was above the water and she was swimming to the cask. Almost immediately the large waves obscured her from view. Visibility was dropping and the light fading, in part because of the storm, but in any event he knew it would soon be dark. He swung the tiller to port and the bow swung onto a new tack to gain sea room before he started the search.

How could he have let this happen? It was fundamental to their partnership that each looked after the other. If Maria was working to starboard, Adam must protect her from danger on the port side. He had failed her totally and she was lost in a wild and darkening sea. She had trusted him and he had allowed himself to be distracted by her beauty. He knew his love for her was not entirely platonic and was devastated by the thought he might be responsible for her death.

When Adam had gained enough distance to the north he tacked again to run down on where she might lie. The wind was driving the boat too fast and he could not see any sign of the poncho or the cask; only dark waves on a near bottomless sea.

CHAPTER SEVENTEEN

It was dark and, an hour previously, Adam had given up all hope of finding Maria alive. He had been obliged to waste valuable time reefing the sails to slow down the boat for the search. He had hoisted lamps at bow and stern but they shed little light over the water and he knew he would not see Maria unless she was within a few feet of the side of the boat. He realised it was useless to continue, but he could not rest, even if it only meant he might recover her body for burial in the settlement.

He gripped the tiller with despair in his heart. Did he really want to return to the settlement, to admit his incompetence and loss? Better perhaps to simply set course south to the great Antarctic wastes until starvation, thirst and the cold released him from his torment. It had taken her death for him to realise the importance she'd had in his life. He now appreciated the depth of his affection – no, more than that, love.

The wind and the waves had eased and the vast, black, silent ocean beyond the range of the lamps emphasised his isolation. The lugger was now moving slowly through the water. He sat down on the stern seat with his head in his hands.

Adam's contemplation of the Antarctic ice fields was interrupted by a knocking noise, coming from the port bow. Hardly daring to trust his ears, he seized the stern lamp and moved carefully up the port side of the boat. He cursed the poor illumination and then saw the water cask slowly moving down the side of the boat. It was partly obscured by Maria's long black hair. She lay face down in the water, but had held the cask at the level of her neck so

222

that the small barrel was almost completely submerged, leaving her face a couple of inches from the water. Her neck was turned so that she was facing the boat. Her eyes were closed, with no evidence of life. He grasped the cask and with difficulty forced her stiff hands loose. He lifted her cold, rigid body from the ocean as the cask continued its journey to the stern.

Adam laid her on the deck and took the sails down swiftly. He then set the sea anchor to hold the bow into the wind for the remainder of the night. He laid out the blankets in the bow; his on top of Maria's and then returned to the body of his companion with a towel. He stripped her and dried her and then cast his own clothes aside. He carried her into the bow and laid her stone-cold body on the blankets. Adam drew her to him and wrapped the blankets closely around them, in the hope that some of his body heat might bring her back to life. He cradled her head on his shoulder ensuring most of his body was in contact with hers. He could not feel her pulse and there was no sign of breathing. He drew her up so that her face was at the same level as his and kissed her, trying to breathe warm air into her lungs.

'I'm sorry I failed you, Maria. You're back with me now and I'll not lose you again. Sleep in my arms. I wished I'd realised how much I wanted to be with you like this. It is only now I realise how much I love you. Rest with me, Maria, and tomorrow we'll sail for the frozen south together. It will not be long before our spirits are reunited.' He tightened his embrace and fell into an exhausted sleep.

Late into the night Adam awoke. Their positions were unchanged. He had given heat to her body but there was no sign of life. It was as if she were sleeping; perhaps this nightmare would pass and they would wake up to another normal day. He kissed her and he felt her stir. Her arms tightened around his neck and she responded to his kiss.

Neither spoke as Adam kissed her and stroked her with passion, overwhelmed with joy at her survival. She drew him on top of her and any momentary caution Adam might have had was lost in her passionate responses. They came together with a gasp of pleasure and the terrors of the evening melted in the heat of wild and desperate coupling.

They lay side by side exhausted, with their lips close together and breathing in each other's air. She stroked his cheek.

'You came for me.'

'Of course.'

'I don't remember being rescued.'

'I think you were close to death.'

'I swam to the cask as you taught me to do when I was 12. The water was very cold. I thought I saw your mast once or twice but nothing definite. When the light faded, I knew I couldn't survive. A great sadness came over me, only partly because I knew I was dying. My sorrow was as much to do with the end of the Ceruso family. How harsh our fate would have been; my father killed for a crime he did not commit and my mother dying from a broken heart. She had no will to live after Father was executed and consumption overwhelmed her. And sadness also, Adam, that I never told you how much I loved you. I know it's not right to say so and it is disloyal to Ruth, who has been so kind to me, but over the last year my love for you has changed. I'm glad you now know the depth of my feelings; perhaps you'll send me away?'

'I couldn't do that, Maria when I've only just found you. The changes in your feelings for me over the last year are similar to those I have been experiencing. I didn't realise until tonight, when I was searching the ocean, how much those feelings had changed and how strong they've become. Perhaps we should rest now and talk again at dawn about how we will deal with our love.'

She snuggled up closer and they slept in each other's arms.

They woke mid-morning, the sea was calm with a light breeze. She kissed Adam's stomach and he knew she would be aware of how much he was aroused. Emboldened by his response, she sat astride him as he lay with his arms behind his head.

'So, Captain Fletcher, I'm deeply in love with you; will you send me away, or perhaps make me walk the plank?'

'Do not mention such things, even in humour, Maria; not after last night.'

He groaned with pleasure as she adjusted her position.

'Or will you love me as I love you?'

He drew her towards him and the question was answered. Not the reckless love making of the previous night but a more cautious and thoughtful union.

By late morning they had put the boat to rights and were sailing slowly towards Jamestown with the fishing lines out. They sat in the stern eating bread and fruit, washed down with water.

'Will you tell Ruth, Adam?'

'Not at present, we need to think; perhaps we both need to consider how we would wish the future to be. We've both had a love slowly growing for the last year, which exploded into life last night. The genie is out of the bottle and I doubt we could get him back in, even if we wanted to. We have employment which takes us away in total privacy twice a week for almost all of two days. I'm married to a woman I care for and respect and I would not want to hurt her. Today I think we should concentrate on fishing and quietly think things over. It'll not be long until

Thursday and, when we are back out on the ocean, we can share our thoughts about what we should do.'

She nodded and they ate their meal in a companionable silence. The remainder of the day went well. The normal routines were now accompanied by small affirmations of love; a head stroked or an arm around the waist when sitting at the tiller. They watched the island of St Helena rise up from the sea. Adam stood behind her with his arms about her waist, rocking gently with the movement of the boat.

Later that night Adam lay in bed in the darkness, listening to Ruth's regular breathing. He felt the evening had gone reasonably well. Maria had been quiet and gone to bed early. He was amazed she looked so good considering the ordeal she had experienced the previous night. They had decided not to tell Ruth about Maria having been lost overboard, as it would inevitably lead to further questions which they would prefer not to be asked. He had suggested a late start the following day which Maria had gratefully accepted.

Ruth lay next to her husband mulling over the evening. Something had happened while they were away. Adam was slightly nervous and Maria was different too. Not nervous, how best could it be described? Empowered perhaps, or changed by an experience. She would leave it for the present; perhaps matters would get clearer with time. She was surprised to find herself so detached from these thoughts. *You don't love Adam in that way anymore Ruth – it's more the way it was when he proposed, a profound friendship. If these are the early signs of Adam truly falling in love, you have been there already.*

A month passed with the fishermen leading a double life; young lovers, when alone on the boat, but only good friends, when on land. Ruth observed the occasional new intimacy at home when they thought they were unobserved; the occasional stroke of an arm or, when passing objects more hand contact than seemed necessary. Ruth doubted anyone in the settlement would have noticed any difference. She felt a discussion with Maria was most likely to tell her what she wanted to know. On a Sunday afternoon, the opportunity for a private discussion arose. Adam had gone down to the lugger to organise arrangements for the Monday. The two women sat on the verandah overlooking the sea.

'Maria, what happened at sea a month ago, that changed your life so greatly?'

Maria looked up, startled, to find Ruth smiling at her.

'Do not fear, little sister, I don't ask in anger. Your world changed a month ago; there is a new maturity about you. You've always been happy, but I sense an added contentment. A particularly large rogue wave perhaps; I wondered if you'd be prepared to talk about it?'

Maria's mind raced. She had prepared some words of apology for her affair with Adam but could not swiftly bring them to mind. It was a kind and caring enquiry, but she knew Ruth must have seen through their attempts to keep appearances normal. Ruth had even given her a possible reason to fall back on – a huge, rogue wave, but she knew a part of the truth would have to be told and, if that led to the remainder, so be it.

'I was thrown overboard by a wave at dusk and it took a long time for Adam to find and rescue me. I have no recollection of the rescue; I was unconscious and almost dead from cold. It was night-time by then and he wrapped us up in blankets and lay with me. He thought I was dead but hoped some heat from his body might revive me.'

Ruth nodded. The story was simply told. She knew enough about their relationship when at sea to imagine the despair Adam would have felt at losing Maria and then finding her, apparently dead.

'He woke up later in the night to find I was alive. When I regained consciousness, I was in his arms and he was kissing me with joy and relief.'

'And then?'

Maria paused. There seemed little point in leaving matters as a half-truth.

'Ruth, I think now, looking back, that I've been falling in love with Adam slowly over the last year. I found I was envying you when we parted to go to sleep in the evenings. I believe I'm responsible for what has happened. We did go on to make love in the wave of excitement that followed great danger. I think we were both lost in a tidal wave of emotion. He tried to apologise after we were spent, but I told him of my feelings for him and that I was a more than willing partner in the matter. We slept for a while and, when we woke, he told me that the feelings I had been experiencing the previous year were similar to his own. We've remained lovers since, when on the boat. You've heard it all now, Ruth, and I'm glad it is out in the open. What will you do with me?'

Ruth's face was impassive. She was silent for a while and then disconcerted Maria with her next comment.

'It must have been terrifying, alone in the sea with the light fading. Did you feel you were going to die?'

Adam appeared at the door, as Ruth had begun to speak. He quietly laid down his satchel and let the conversation take its course.

'Yes, within a few minutes it became obvious Adam's return tack had missed me. I'm sure you appreciate the first chance is the best chance in a situation where high waves obscure the view of small objects. The cold affected me quickly and then I knew I was going to die. I was sad to be leaving the world so early and to be the end of this part of the Ceruso family. I was particularly regretful that I'd not told Adam that I loved him. It was curious, I then started to feel warmer and quite detached from my body and I didn't remember anything more until I woke up,' she paused, 'naked in Adam's arms. At first I thought it was a dream; he was kissing me with a desperate passion. I now know he thought he had lain down with the corpse of the partner he had failed. I hope you can understand how easy it was to return his passion.'

She turned to Adam. I've told Ruth everything.'

Ruth nodded her head slowly and looked up at Adam.

'You must have been in despair, Adam, losing Maria and unable to find her?'

He was surprised at Ruth's calmness and her concern for how he had felt about Maria's loss.

'I had failed her badly and realised that our close friendship had progressed to something deeper. I had to prise her fingers off the water cask and lift her frozen, stiff body from the water. I did think she was dead but hoped, if I could pass some heat from my body to hers, she might revive. In the depths of my mind I knew it was hopeless, but I was simply caring for someone in death, whom I had failed to protect in life.'

Ruth could imagine the situation; she remembered the passions that the fear of Adam's death had unleashed in her just before they were married; how hastily a word had killed the moment and, she suspected, much more besides. She remembered fighting for Jason's life and how easy it had been to give everything she had for the struggle to keep him alive. When he survived and started to recover, she knew she had already given herself totally to him and had no wish to try to change it. She remembered the joyful experience when he told her that he reciprocated her love. The ecstasy that followed when they lay on the soft grass and discarded clothes, consummating their love; an ecstasy that had been inevitable once the battle on the banks of the Styx had been won. Ruth slowly shook her head.

Maria and Adam had been slowly falling in love. Maria's loss overboard and her delayed rescue could only have led to a frantic and desperate outpouring of emotion as they lay naked in each other's arms, miles from land; it could never have ended in any other way. *Ruth Fletcher, nobody understands that more clearly than you.* Ruth saw Adam was concerned by her gesture; she sought to reassure him.

'I can understand the despair you must have felt, Adam, having lost someone who was so close to you.'

'More than that, Ruth, I felt responsible. I've not shared this with Maria, but I planned to lay her out in repose and sail south until my food and water ran out and the cold Antarctic wastes relieved me of life and guilt.'

'And I would have lost you both.'

They fell silent imagining the lugger drifting in the Antarctic wastes with rudder lashed, two frozen bodies laid out on the deck, staring unseeing at the sky.

'I'm glad you know, Ruth, and I'm sorry I have betrayed your love. I had expected anger and recriminations, but you offer none. I'm sure you'll want to think things over and then tell us what you would have us do. Maria and I are passionately in love. No one can tell the future, but I doubt my feelings for her will ever change.'

Ruth smiled. 'I believe you, Adam. Your eyes light up when she walks into the room. You energise each other. I think that fire will not be extinguished readily. Before you came back Maria asked me what I would do with her, now that I'm aware of your love for each other. The real question, I suspect, is what are you going to do with me?'

'I am afraid we will still have to fish far out at sea and that means we'll have to stay out at night, as at present.'

'I will not hold you to promises that two passionate lovers could only fail to keep. However, I think we can all agree that appearances in the settlement must be retained.'

Ruth looked up at Adam. 'Or would you wish that I should go?'

She saw the look of horror on their faces. Adam raised his hand.

'I'd never wish for that to happen. I sought your hand in marriage and gave an oath to care and protect you until death.'

Maria sank on her knees at Ruth's side.

'Never ever suggest such a thing again. Rather I went away to Jamestown or beyond. We're a family brought together by my father's execution and cemented by my mother's death. For the last few years we have faced the world as a trio. I don't know if you can find space in your heart for that to continue in a different way? Ruth, if you feel in the next few days that you cannot allow our love to continue, then I must go.'

Ruth took Maria's hands in hers, smiling down at her. 'And leave everyone heartbroken? That'll never happen, little sister. We'll stay together; I feel there are others in the shadows who are watching us - your father and your mother.'

Tears rolled down Maria's cheeks.

Ruth continued. 'They might be surprised at the turn of events, Maria, but I'm sure they would wish us to care and support each other through this, as for every other threat to our existence. I promised your father and your mother on their deathbeds to care for you until the day I die. I promised your mother I'd protect and support you when you fell in love. We didn't realise where that promise would take us, but I do not seek to revoke it now. We were three against the world and must remain so. I believe that is what Francesco and Carmella would say if they could speak to us. Do you not think so, husband?'

'I agree, Ruth, and can only thank you for the calm manner in which you have discussed the matter.'

She smiled at him and shrugged. 'Of course I would wish it otherwise but I cannot hate you, Adam. We're all bound to our destiny. I love you both and that will never change.'

Ruth rose from her seat. 'Little sister, will you help me in the kitchen, we need to start the dinner.'

That night Ruth lay in bed, the locket gently swinging on her lover's brass lamp. Adam turned down the wick on his lamp and lay down beside her. She leaned over and kissed him gently on the cheek.

'Husband, I would prefer to remain in this bedroom but would not be offended if, on occasions, I found I was sleeping alone.'

Adam mumbled his apologetic thanks, but felt his wife had shown him enough generosity of spirit for one day and chose not to take her up on the offer immediately. He kissed her hand and they settled down to sleep.

Several months later, Adam sat in the stern of the lugger as Maria brought them onto their final tack for Jamestown.

'There are some extra masts in the harbour, Adam.'

'Frigates, I should imagine. The last time I spoke to Sarah, she said a new squadron of frigates is due here to continue the fight with the slavers. The present group was being joined by some from the West Indies and then others will return to England. New customers are always welcome, even if they stay only a short time.'

He placed his hand on top of Maria's and gave it a squeeze, as she adjusted the tiller. She looked up and smiled, nestling into his shoulder. Overall, matters seemed to have gone well since they had told Ruth of their love. She remained caring and loving to them both. Adam felt she was a little more remote with him and did not doubt that he had hurt her very deeply. They were careful not to exhibit too much affection in Ruth's presence, although he did visit Maria's bed fairly frequently. They spent relatively little time in the settlement and their behaviour, on those occasions, had not given grounds for scurrilous talk. They had continued to attend the Sunday services with Adam standing between the two ladies. Adam had been asked to speak twice at the service, since their affair had begun. He avoided subjects involving chastity or fidelity; the congregation could rely on those subjects being covered by Matthew Draper. Ruth had been speaking to Lucy Davies a couple of weeks previously and Lucy had remarked how pleasing it was that the animosity towards Maria's employment and the insinuations of impropriety seemed to have settled. Ruth had shared the irony of the remark with Adam; there had been a tidal wave of accusations of misconduct when none existed only to be replaced by benign acceptance when the two fishermen had become lovers. Even their loyal friend Lucy would have been scandalised, if she had known.

The lugger cleared the breakwater and two weather worn frigates came into view. Maria steered towards the nearest.

'Surely that's the Intrepid, Adam.'

'It is.'

The port authority boat appeared off the starboard beam.

'Ahoy, Bountiful, heave to.'

Maria swung the tiller and the lugger came up into the wind.

'Morning, Mr Fletcher, Miss Ceruso, the frigates have just arrived in from the West Indies this morning and the hospital superintendent has not cleared them for landing yet. I'm allowed to approach. If you would like, I can buy some fish from you and take it to the bottom of their accommodation ladder. If you are here later in the week they will, no doubt, have received their clearance.'

'Is Captain Pickford still in command?'

'Commodore Pickford, now, Adam. A good appointment if you ask me, he has always been very civil in his dealings with the port authority in the past.'

'Yes he's a good man. Do you know who the first officer is on the Intrepid, is it still Jason Hewitt?'

'No, he must have been transferred elsewhere. I spoke to the first officer earlier this morning; it's a Mr George Rutherford. We are to expect a new West Africa squadron within the next two weeks. Commodore Pickford is only here to pick up two of our frigates when they return from patrol. As soon as our new squadron appears, he'll leave for the North Atlantic.'

Commodore Thomas Pickford stood by the window of the great cabin, watching the conversation between the port authority boat and the lugger. He watched fish being exchanged.

'I hope they're for us, George.'

'It looks as though they're coming our way, Sir.'

They heard the marine at the door come to attention. The door opened and the hospital superintendent came in, followed by Captain Jason Hewitt.

'Good morning, Captain. Beg your pardon, Sir, Commodore. May I say in passing that Jamestown was very pleased to hear of your appointment.'

'Thank you, doctor. I trust you've also congratulated the Intrepid's new captain on his appointment.'

'I have indeed, sir, another very popular appointment, Commodore.'

'Now to business, doctor. Captain Hewitt and I consider the crew to be in the best of health and all are keen to be able to get their feet on dry land and sample the entertainments of the town. Have you found any dreadful disease that will divert them from their plans?'

The doctor laughed. 'I've not, sir, all is well. I have signed the clearance certificate. We always worry about yellow fever with the West Indies traffic, but I have no concerns with the Intrepid.'

Jason escorted the doctor to the ladder and watched Adam's fish lifted up from the port authority boat.

'Mr Fletcher sends his regards, sir.'

'Thank you.'

Jason walked back to the great cabin, currently taken over by the commodore. Living arrangements had not changed since his promotion; he still slept in the first officer's quarters and would remain there while the commodore of his squadron chose to remain on his vessel.

'I can confirm the doctor's departure coincided with the delivery of the fish. Adam Fletcher sends his regards, sir.

'He's a good man, Jason. It would be nice to renew acquaintance, but I doubt we'll have the time to go over to Prosperous Bay. Jacob, bring us a glass of wine, if you would.'

The commodore unrolled a map of the South Atlantic on his desk and they held the edges down with sundry objects. There was a vast expanse of ocean with a strip of South America on the left and Africa on the right; St Helena lay somewhat closer to Africa than South America.

'I've been given quite a bit of leeway in terms of arrival at Gibraltar and I wondered whether if the new commander approves, we might combine our squadrons for one massive sweep of the ocean to the east of us. This is, or used to be, the peak of the slave sailing season, when we were last here. They tend to go in convoys and will travel at the speed of the slowest. We might well have eight frigates at our disposal, strung out in a line at maximum range for the lookouts aloft. We could search a huge area of ocean swiftly and bring massive fire power to bear on any convoy. Their faster ships will outrun any ship of the line, but I doubt they'll be able to outrun us. We could then come back here to re-provision for a few days before the trip north to our next assignment. What do you think?'

'It's never been tried, Sir. The slavers would not expect such a large and fast squadron covering so much sea. I hope the new squadron commander agrees.'

'Good, keep it to yourself. The Intrepid is your ship now. I want to give some thought to our new responsibilities in the north. No doubt you'll want to get the ship ready for battle with the slavers and the long haul to the North Atlantic. As we're now free to leave for the shore, we should pay our respects to the Governor.'

Adam and Maria returned to Prosperous Bay and sold the remaining fish. They walked back up the hill with some excellent rock cod which they had set aside for their own use. Adam gutted the fish as Maria showered. Then he opened a bottle of wine.

'Are we celebrating something, husband.'

'Nothing in particular, I just thought it might cheer Maria up. She seems a little down.'

'I can't say I've noticed – perhaps a little more quiet and thoughtful? If I find an opportunity, I'll have a chat with her.'

'Good.'

They were half way through the meal when Adam remembered their visit to Jamestown.

'I forgot to tell you, Ruth, we saw the Intrepid today, back in Jamestown Harbour.'

Ruth's knife clattered onto the plate and she feigned a fit of coughing to cover her confusion. She cast a glance at her husband; he was absorbed in eating his meal; too absorbed it seemed to offer additional information.

'Is Captain Pickford still in command?'

'It's Commodore Pickford, apparently. I didn't meet him; the port authority boat wouldn't allow us close, as they had not cleared medical inspection.'

They lapsed into silence again. If he would not say, she would have to ask, and it had to be now so it could be a continuation of the previous conversation.

'Is Jason Hewitt still first officer?'

'No, he must have moved elsewhere. The current first officer is George Rutherford; I think you may remember him from the dinner aboard.'

'Yes, a nice young man, as I recall.'

Adam nodded. 'The captain had a good team.'

Ruth returned to her food. How easily a ship's name and that of its first officer reignited the overwhelming desire to be back in his arms at the observation point. She had built a wall around her love for him and dampened down the fires of her passion and longing but, with one sentence, the wall had crumbled and the coals glowed as deep a red as ever. She felt heaviness in her chest; they call it heartache, and she considered it well named.

The weekend passed easily. As they went to bed on the Sunday evening, Adam reminded Ruth of their previous conversation.

'Did you get a chance to talk to Maria?'

'No, I'm afraid I didn't, but things were a little unusual this evening. She normally says goodbye to me the night before you sleep on the boat because you leave so early in the morning. Tonight she gave me a long embrace and kissed me on both cheeks. She looked me in the eye and told me she would always love me very much. There was an intensity in her gaze that was heart-warming but also a little disconcerting.'

'She loves you very deeply, Ruth, and is very appreciative of your continuing affection.'

'Perhaps that explains it.'

237

The fishing went well the following day and Adam and Maria sat in the fading light eating a stew which Ruth had cooked.

'Shall we sleep under the stars tonight, Adam?'

'If you like.'

'I would; I'll clean up in the sea first.' Maria laid out their pillows and blankets on the deck. She tied her hair back, undressed and lowered herself over the side to wash off the exertions of the day. Adam helped her back on board and then lowered himself into the water. They towelled themselves dry as the light failed and the stars gradually came into view. A full moon rose from the sea. She lay next to him stroking his body.

'You're very thoughtful tonight, Maria.'

She raised herself on her elbow and looked down at him.

'Do you love me, Adam?'

He held her gaze. 'With all my heart.'

'And you know I love you and that I'll always love you?'

'Always.'

The answer seemed to satisfy her. She started to kiss his body and then she spanned him. The love making was tentative at the outset, savouring each movement and sensation, but rapidly built to a desperate crescendo that left them exhausted and drained in each other's arms.

'Always remember, I love you, Adam.

It is said that seafarers never really sleep; part of their brain is always alert to changes of wind or wave. There are many noises a lugger will make on the ocean which are without hazard and the ever watchful brain will therefore choose to ignore. Adam woke abruptly, his body alert, seeking the reason he had been roused. He heard the noise again; the sound of metal striking metal. He turned to

Maria's side of the boat and found she was no longer lying with him.   It must be near the middle of the night. There were no clouds in the sky and the full moon was well risen, bathing the boat with light. He turned to the stern, from where the noise had come. Maria was naked, silver in the moonlight, her long dark hair cascading down her back with strands across her breasts. She had a leg resting on the stern seat and the anchor, which they rarely used, was propped up against the side of the boat. She had tied a short length of rope through the metal ring at the top of the anchor shank and it had been those muted sounds that had woken him. She was tying the other end of the rope to her ankle.

'Maria, what are you doing?'

The knot tied, she stood up. 'I'm sorry I have woken you, it was not what I had planned. Please stay where you are. I have thought about this a lot, Adam. I have to leave you and this is the best way; lost at sea.'

'What are you saying, Maria?'

'I'm carrying your baby, Adam; in two or three weeks it'll be obvious to everyone that I am with child. I could bear my own shame in the settlement, but I cannot allow you or Ruth to be subject to humiliation and disgrace. The ocean nearly claimed me several months ago. I had no fear of it then, when I was close to death, and I do not fear it now. Thank you for everything that you've done for me and for giving me your love. Tell Ruth I'm sorry and I love her very much.'

She lowered the anchor over the side and swung her legs out over the water.

CHAPTER EIGHTEEN

'Wait, Maria, think of our child.' He hurried on. 'You see the child as a source of shame and humiliation. I see it otherwise; it's a new life, which you would extinguish before it was even born. Several months ago, when you were close to death, you felt a deep regret that the termination of your life would also bring your part of the Ceruso family to an end.'

Adam knew he had gained a short respite, but that he had to build on the temporary advantage with some practical solution.

'I have some suggestions to make, but while we are talking would you pull in the anchor and place it in the boat. And please bring your legs inboard.'

'You won't try and restrain me?'

'If you and the anchor come inboard, I promise to remain here and not to rush you.'

He thought she looked exquisitely beautiful, naked in the moonlight, desperate and vulnerable. She brought the anchor inboard and sat astride the coaming with one leg still above the water.

'What are you suggesting?'

'We both have money, fishing has bought us wealth. We'll have to go away, at least to Jamestown or perhaps beyond. There are charitable societies who support single women in your situation. I believe the hospital superintendent in Jamestown supports a charity of that sort. If you had the baby in Jamestown, perhaps Ruth might be persuaded to adopt the child; we are still childless after six years of marriage and the settlement would not consider it surprising if we adopted. You would have to remain in Jamestown for a few extra weeks after Ruth and I return with our adopted child. Even then there would be talk, but if you allowed Ruth to share motherhood, I think she would be overjoyed and scornful of any criticism. We have tested Ruth severely with our love and she may feel this is too much to ask, but you must give her the chance to support us. If we proceed the way I've described, everyone lives and your family line and mine will continue. All three of us will be parents, if you felt you could share the role of mother.'

Maria looked up at the moon and then at the jet black sea and shivered. 'I would love to have our baby and to share motherhood with Ruth, if she would agree.'

'You're cold, Maria, can I bring you a blanket?'

She nodded. Adam brought the blanket and wrapped it around her, holding her gently and stroking her hair. She looked up at him with a rueful expression.

'You won't try to tie me up?

He smiled and kissed her gently on the forehead. 'No, darling, there are several things that I would want to do with you but restraint is not one of them. May I untie the rope?'

She nodded.

'Now come to bed, there's much we need to talk about and to celebrate. Where you could only see shame, I see great happiness and excitement. Have you felt him move?'

'Not yet, and who says it's a boy?'

'Of course he's a boy but, if not, she'll be a girl as beautiful as her mother and grandmother.'

Maria laughed. 'Adam Fletcher, you're a crazy man.'

He kissed her. 'Forget the shame and share my excitement and happiness.'

She snuggled closer. 'I am already. I hope Ruth can see things the way you're hoping, Adam.'

'Tomorrow night will tell. Well well, it's Maria Ceruso, mother to be.' He kissed her still lean stomach and placed his ear against it.

'Don't be ridiculous, Adam, there'll not be anything to hear at this stage.'

Adam theatrically raised a finger to his lips. 'I think I can hear singing.'

Maria played along with his fantasies. 'And what is he singing?'

Adam looked up, perplexed. 'I don't know it's in Italian – I was expecting an English sea shanty.'

They both laughed.

'Oh, Adam, I feel so much happier now. I shall pray for Ruth's kindness.'

Ruth was immediately aware that some event of significance had occurred whilst they were away. Adam had suggested that he should talk to Ruth first; Maria had been tired and nervous and had retired to bed as soon as dinner was over. Unlike Adam, Ruth had considered pregnancy to be a possibility from the time of their last discussion. He had opened a bottle of wine for no apparent reason and now Adam recharged their glasses. Settling back to the table, Ruth laughed.

'It seems we have something to discuss. Is Maria pregnant?'

'She is.'

'How far?'

'She says it will start to show in a couple of weeks. I have a suggestion to make, Ruth, which may test your love too far. First I would like to tell you how I found out.'

He described waking in the night and finding Maria preparing to end her life, and the discussion he'd had with her before she could be persuaded to stay.

'The plan I put forward was on the spur of the moment. I have thought about it a lot today, but I have not come up with anything better. It all hinges on whether you would be prepared to adopt our baby and be as much a mother to the child as Maria.'

Tears rolled down Ruth's cheeks. 'I thought I had prepared myself for this, Adam, but it seems I have not. We are childless, despite six years of trying and it seems likely we will never have a child of our own. Leave me a while to think this through and, I suspect, come to terms with it. I need to compose myself. No one must lose their life. Maria must not be left unsupported.'

Adam cleared the dishes and quietly washed them and put them away. He doubted Maria was sleeping in the partitioned compartment, but did not disturb her. He heard Ruth call softly from the living room.

'Adam, bring Maria through if she is still awake.'

Maria was standing at her bedroom curtain by the time Adam reached her. She was wearing her nightdress and her eyes were brimming with tears, fearful of Ruth's response.

Adam marvelled at his wife's resilience. In his absence she had composed herself. Seeing Maria's worried face, she rose from her seat and beckoned her into her arms.

'Come here, little sister, don't be frightened or upset. I am overjoyed at your news. Adam told me you nearly did something that would have left us in great sorrow.'

She held Maria out in front of her, looking into her eyes. 'Will you promise me you will never risk your life or that of the baby again?'

'I promise, Ruth.'

'That's good. Adam has opened another bottle of wine. We ladies have a lot to talk about here.

Adam has told me about his plan and I think it makes great sense. Would you consent to me adopting your baby and sharing in the upbringing?'

'Yes please, Ruth!'

'Then it's all agreed.'

Adam watched from the kitchen as Ruth and Maria sat at the table holding hands and Ruth enthusiastically asked about possible names for the child. *I married an exceptional woman, she has been asked to make extraordinary concessions to her husband and his lover. She asks for a mere five minutes to compose herself and then showers Maria with enthusiastic support.*

When they lay in bed later, Adam knew Ruth was crying; he suspected she was grieving at their childless state. He drew her over and held her to him, stroking her hair as she cried into his night shirt.

'I'm sorry we've not had children, Adam.'

'It is as it is, Ruth. There is no blame. Will it hurt you to adopt Maria's child?'

'No, Adam, I love both the parents and I think I'll come to feel this is as close to motherhood as I will ever achieve. It has been three against the world since Maria lost her parents; it is strange – no, exciting, to think that it will soon be four. I'll cope, Adam. Get some sleep, fisherman, we'll start making some arrangements in the next few days.'

They refined their plans the following evening. Adam and Maria would visit the medical superintendent at the hospital, and seek his help. Maria would find some excuse for a stay in Jamestown before the pregnancy was obvious. Reluctantly, Adam agreed he would only be able to visit twice a week in order to preserve his routine in Prosperous Bay. Ruth was pleased to see that Maria was happier; she had spent several weeks dreading the consequences of her pregnancy but now was beginning to share in the enthusiasm.

'Ruth, I forgot to exchange my books with Lucy Davies. She says she has something new she thinks I might enjoy and I would like to have it with me on the boat tomorrow, on the remote chance the captain will not work me too hard.'

'Give Lucy my regards. Are you a slave driver, Adam?'

'I don't need to be. Maria drives herself far too hard for her condition, but will not be told to take things easier.'

Maria walked down into the settlement in the early evening. The scene was tranquil; her long shadow reaching out in front of her on the path. The sea was calm and thin spirals of smoke arose from the houses below, as the settlers prepared their evening meals.

Maria spent longer with Lucy than she had intended and noticed the light was fading fast. She declined the loan of a lamp and walked back up the path lost in her thoughts. *It would be nice if Ruth could be with her at the time of her confinement. What would her parents have made of her situation? Would they be shocked at her disloyalty to Ruth, stealing her husband's love? What would they have thought of her pregnancy? Horror at the disgrace or would they, like Ruth, have come to what was very obviously a genuine excitement at the prospect of new life?*

Maria was almost at the top of the path and could see the lamp by the front door in the gloom. She heard a noise behind her and half turned but too late to avoid a heavy blow to the back of her head. Stunned, she fell face forward onto the path and then strong arms rolled her onto her back. The hands moved to her throat, gripping firmly so she could not breathe. Her assailant was strong and she was unable to release his grip. Her head spun and she lost consciousness.

When he judged she was senseless, John Logan released his grip. He pulled her dress up to the waist and removed her drawers, leaving her legs splayed out below him. He paused to savour the situation; a beautiful body – perhaps a bit fatter than he had imagined.

He laughed. 'I've waited a long time for this young lady, I never got to your mother, but why not fresher goods. Then it'll be drawers back on and a fall from the cliff – a tragic accident. Your family caused me to lose all I had and there's only you to pay the price.'

Maria drifted back into consciousness; she did not move, slowly gathering her wits. She could see the man standing over her, talking to himself. She could feel sharp pebbles against her buttocks and thighs. As soon as he had started to speak, she recognised him. He started to loosen his breaches and move closer. She knew, at best, she had one chance to save herself using the benefit of surprise. He was starting to move his right leg forward to meet his left, which lay at the level of her knees. She waited until all the weight of his body was carried on his left leg and then swiftly drew up both her legs, brought them together, and drove them at his left knee. All the anger and hate she felt for the man who had destroyed her family exploded into the forceful movement. The blow hurt her feet, but she had the satisfaction of hearing a loud crack and felt the knee move backwards beyond straight. Logan fell on his back with a howl of pain. He tried to move, and she drew up her knees to protect herself. However, with a groan he sank back onto the path.

Maria staggered to her feet and stumbled the remaining distance to the house. She pushed the door open, holding the frame for support. Adam rose from his seat by the table.

'What's happened, Maria?'

'It's Sergeant Logan, he attacked me on the cliff path and tried to rape me.'

'Where is he?'

'Unconscious on the path; I've probably broken one of his legs so, even if he comes round, he'll not be able to move quickly.'

'Ruth, look after Maria, while I go and restrain Logan.'

He took some rope, a stick and a lamp and ran down the path.

'He came up on me from behind and struck me on the back of the head and, while I was stunned, strangled me until I lost consciousness. I had not recognised him in the dark but when I regained consciousness he was talking to himself and I recognised his voice immediately. He planned to rape me, then replace my drawers and throw me off the cliff so that it would look like an accident. Fortunately he gave me time to get my wits together and I kicked him and I think I've broken his knee. He fell backwards very heavily and I managed to escape.'

Adam returned and put the stick in the corner. He had picked up the book Maria had dropped and put it on the table. Ruth saw he still had the length of rope in his hand.

'Has he escaped, Adam?'

'No, he's still there. He's dead, Maria. There is some blood coming from his ear. His head is near one of the larger rocks on the edge of the path and I think he must have struck it as he fell. He's not in uniform; perhaps he's on leave. I didn't even know he was still on the island.'

Ruth burst out in anger. 'That man will destroy us all.'

Adam closed the door. 'We can leave him where he lies for the moment but we'll have to come up with an alternative before people start moving at dawn.'

'He was going to throw Maria off the cliff. Could we do the same with him?'

'No, dear, if he fell from there into the ocean it might be different, but there are rocks beneath. We cannot have a marine found dead on our cliff path or on the rocks below. The only place he could have been visiting would be us. We have to try and keep his death separate from us. We cannot afford any attention until we have Maria's baby recognised as Ruth's adopted child. We'll leave it a couple of hours and then I'll carry him down to the settlement and lay him on the stone steps onto the north shore and hope people do not find him until after we've left in the morning. We never go that way to the lugger; people know we go on the other path to the beach. If we leave at the normal time we should be at sea for a couple of hours before he's found.'

'I'm going to Lucy's for tea tomorrow morning, Adam, at 11.00 o'clock and I'll try and find out what people are saying. Maria, there's a bit of bruising coming out on your neck, you'd better wear a neckerchief on the boat. I have a high collar dress that would hide it on Sunday.'

Adam gave Maria a hug. 'Do you think you'll be fit to go fishing tomorrow?'

'Yes, Adam, I have to go; everything must be as normal. I know it's a risk for us, especially as I'm pregnant, but I can't afford anything that delays me leaving the settlement. I'm glad he's dead. I bet he murdered that poor marine. I felt immense hatred and anger when he came forward to rape me. I know it's wrong to hate and kill, but I can't regret it.'

'Set the table, Adam, if you would, we need to eat. When you've carried him away, Maria and I will clean the path of any evidence of his presence. You are fishing closer in tomorrow, as usual?'

'Yes, we'll be back at about four, and we'll try and glean as much information from our customers as we can. Most settlers loathed him; let's hope his death is a one day wonder and it does not upset our plans for Maria.'

Late into the night the two ladies helped load John Logan's body over Adam's shoulder. They threw a long coat over the corpse to disguise the load, knowing that it would never pass close inspection. Logan was small and thin but Adam knew it would be difficult walking downhill on an uneven path. The moon was mainly obscured by cloud as they wished him a safe and secret journey. He moved quietly down the path with one hand supporting his load.

The settlement was quiet and deserted; he moved cautiously through the village, pleased he had not disturbed the dogs. He released the body at the top of the stone stairs that led to the north shore. It settled half way down, Logan lying on his back with one leg at an abnormal angle so that it looked consistent with an accident. He put on his coat and quietly retraced his steps through the village without incident.

Ruth and Maria had finished clearing up the path when he joined them in the house.

'Some rum, husband?'

'Thank you, Ruth'.   He supped the generous mug of neat rum.

'I think it went alright; I saw nobody. The dogs were quiet and Logan lies half way down the steps in a position that should suggest an accident. Try and get some sleep, Maria, we leave as usual in the morning.'

All the houses in the village had detached privies close to them.   The aroma in the enclosed area was never particularly pleasant, especially in warm weather. Many settlers were in the habit of leaving the privy door open when using it at night; the air was fresher and no one could see inside. The view from one privy gave out onto the path Adam had used.   There had been one witness to

Adam's passing with such a strange load. The coat had shifted on his journey down revealing a head limply hanging down his back, as a gap in the cloud offered a few seconds of illumination. Elizabeth Mott completed her needs and returned to her house.

The settlement was quiet as they walked to the lugger. The body had not been found. They moved the boat swiftly out onto the water in the pre-dawn haze.

An hour later, the marines were woken by their corporal. After Francesco's execution those seconded to the settlement had been chosen with more care. The sergeant was an experienced man, close to retirement. The corporal knocked on his door.

'Reveille, Sergeant, and I found this note pushed under the barrack's door.'

The sergeant swung his legs off the bed onto the ground, unfolding the page. The message was short and unsigned. *Adam Fletcher is the killer, I saw him carrying the body.*

'Delay breakfast, Jim. This is probably nothing but you know the previous history here. Inspection in fifteen minutes; side arms only. The men are to work in twos. I will divide up the settlement into sections; I want the whole area searched before most people are out and about. Do not tell anyone about this message or its contents, even our own men. If they find a body, one is to return with the news and the other is to stay at the scene. Adam Fletcher is not my idea of a murderer; I don't want a riot on my hands.'

The body was found within the hour. The corporal brought the news to his sergeant who had remained in the barracks.

'Is he one of the settlers, Jim?'

'No, Sergeant, one of ours, or used to be; John Logan.'

'How the hell did he get here? He lost his stripes shortly after the last trouble and was dismissed from service earlier in the year. Are you sure it's him?'

'He's a bit thinner but there's no doubt it is Logan.'

They walked slowly down the steps. The sergeant agreed.

'Leave two men here, Jim, recall the rest and give them breakfast. Relieve these two every couple of hours. I'll speak to the Davieses and Mr Draper and I'll put up a notice asking for information.'

He scanned the beach. Adam Fletcher's boat had gone, but there was nothing necessarily unusual about that.

'Jim, I want you to take the anonymous note to the Governor, for his eyes only. It's possible Fletcher might be sailing there, in the hope of catching a ship. The Governor may wish to notify the harbour master. I will visit Mrs Fletcher, but no-one must know Adam Fletcher is the suspect. I hope they'll send Captain Doyle to deal with this; the settlers respect him.'

At four in the afternoon, as the lugger was nearing the beach at Prosperous Bay, the Governor was convening a meeting. The marine corporal sat outside.

'I'm sorry to drag you into this, Commodore Pickford, but you and your flag captain have previous knowledge which could be helpful to me. Ah, Captain Doyle, thank you for coming. Do you know these two?'

Benjamin Doyle laughed as he shook their hands. 'Not at their current ranks, Governor, but we have served together in the past. Congratulations to you both.'

'Be seated, gentlemen. I've had a message this morning from Prosperous Bay. Perhaps the simplest thing will be to invite the corporal in to explain.'

The corporal recounted the arrival of the note and the finding of the body.

'Are you sure it's Sergeant Logan, Corporal?'

'No doubt, Sir. He was demoted to private when in Thompson's Bay and released from the service a few months ago. There is no doubt it is him.'

'Who is the marine sergeant in the settlement at the moment, Ben?'

'Albert Fischer. He's close to retirement, a good man. He's popular with the ranks and I should imagine with the settlers. He's a safe pair of hands for the moment.'

'Who knows about this note, corporal?'

'Sergeant Fischer and us, Sir; the sergeant insisted the information was not shared.'

'Excellent. Thank you, corporal, you can wait outside.'

Thomas Pickford shifted restlessly in his chair. 'Adam Fletcher is no murderer, but I could well imagine that, if there was one person whom he might kill, it would be John Logan. Logan had Adam's partner executed for a crime he almost certainly did not commit.'

The Governor passed the note around. 'He'll have to be questioned.'

Benjamin Doyle walked over to the window. 'Of course, Sir, but it'll have to be handled with care. The settlement considers a great injustice was done when Francesco Ceruso was executed. They believe it arose because of corrupt marines and a reckless Governor and to be honest, Sir, I think they were right on both counts.'

'Yes, I heard some of the details before I left London. I appreciate the sensitivity, Ben, so how best to proceed?'

Captain Doyle took the initiative. 'I suggest we do nothing today, Sir. It would mean a night arrival with torches and there is no need for that. With your permission, I will leave at first light with two sections of marines to further Sergeant Fischer's investigation, seeking to identify the murderer, if indeed there is one, and the source of the anonymous note. Ceruso was executed on uncorroborated evidence from the person who quite

252

possibly was the real murderer and we cannot permit a re-run of a previous injustice.'

The commodore intervened. 'I agree with Ben, Governor. Would you mind if Jason joins you, Ben? He knows the Fletchers extremely well and that might be helpful.'

'The repairs to the Intrepid are not quite complete, Commodore.'

'Ye Gods, Jason, I may be a commodore, but I've not forgotten the duties of a captain. Leave the ship to me; you'll have, say, four days. We'll not be sailing before then. Help the Fletchers all you can; I'll always be indebted to that family.'

'We'll leave at dawn from the barracks, Jason. I'll get a horse for you.'

'A docile one please, Ben. You are dealing with someone more suited to the water.'

Ruth decided to wait at the house for Adam and Maria's return. The early morning news at Lucy's had been reassuring. An accident while drunk seemed the likely explanation. Sergeant Fischer had visited the Davies while Ruth was present. The conversation generally had gone well but she was disconcerted by the direction of some of the questioning. There seemed no interest in her or Maria, but she was closely questioned about Adam's movements; *had he left the house after sunset and what time did he leave in the morning?* She gained the impression the Sergeant was not completely satisfied with her answers. She chose a gap in the questioning, as he was writing in his note book, to offer an additional statement.

'Sergeant, you were not here in 1838 and frankly if you had been, I believe an innocent man would still be alive today. You will know that my family has cause to hate John Logan. I loathed him. However, I promise you my husband is not a murderer.'

The sergeant closed his notebook and smiled at her. 'I could well believe that is true, Ma'am, thank you.'

Adam and Maria walked through the door looking tired. They compared notes over dinner and agreed their plan appeared to be succeeding. An accident seemed the likely explanation, although no one had seen John Logan arrive in the settlement and the reason for his appearance was baffling.

'You must expect close questioning of your movements, Adam. I've already said you did not leave the house from dusk until you went with Maria in the hour before dawn.'

'They're bound to be interested in me, Ruth. I'm a man and, of all the people in this settlement, I have the most cause to dislike Logan.'

There was a knock at the door. Mary Tate stood in the darkness, looking agitated.

'I am sorry to visit so late, but I wanted to leave it until after dark.'

They brought her in and sat her by the fire. 'Elizabeth Mott visited me this afternoon and told me in confidence that she saw you carrying the body last night. She's frightened and she says she has not told anyone else, but she put an unsigned note under the barrack's door identifying you.'

'When?'

'I don't know, but I presume before the troops were up. I know she hates you, Mr Fletcher. I was embarrassed by her outburst when you brought Silas and her son to land. You had your reasons to support Maria and I respect that. Everybody knows Elizabeth is not a reliable witness in matters concerning you, but I wanted you to be aware of her mischief.'

'Thank you, Mary; I'm grateful you've warned me.'

Her message delivered, she withdrew and silence descended on the room. Adam looked up at Ruth.

'Who found the body?'

'The marines did.'

'When?'

'I don't know, about 8 o'clock I think.'

'After dawn?'

'Yes. Does it make any difference?'

'All the difference in the world; if the body was found and then the note arrived from Elizabeth Mott it could easily be mischief from someone who is known to hate me. But if the note arrived advising them of a body to find, it greatly increases the likelihood that it's authentic.'

'Then why haven't they come for you?'

'They know I'm going nowhere; perhaps they want to pick me up in Jamestown in two days' time, when we bring in the fish. I don't think anything will happen tonight but it cannot be long before I'm called to account.'

Adam brought a bottle of wine from the cold shelf in the larder and pulled the cork. 'This may be our last opportunity to be together. There are many matters we need to agree before Maria and I go down to the boat tomorrow morning at dawn.'

CHAPTER NINETEEN

Maria spoke first.

'I am responsible for Logan's death, Adam. I will go to Sergeant Fischer and explain the circumstances. There is no need for either of you to get involved.'

Ruth reached over the table and grasped the younger girl's hand. 'Maria, you have to stop talking and thinking that way. You have no responsibility for his death; you simply resisted an attempted rape. John Logan brought about his own death.'

Adam agreed. 'Ruth's right, you may have been on the path, but you are no more blameworthy than Ruth or me. Logan sought you out, assaulted you and would have raped and killed you if his plan had succeeded.'

Ruth shook her head. 'Even in death this man persecutes our family.'

Adam turned to Maria. 'I don't think you should go to the Sergeant for two reasons. In the first instance, you're not a suspect and I'm already linked to Logan. I think we have to keep attention away from you and get you to Jamestown or even Cape Town, if the medical superintendent advises. I am linked to the crime and the marines probably only found the body because of Elizabeth Mott's anonymous note; that'll increase its credibility. I think the best course of action is if I take on your role, Maria. We will bring the attack an hour earlier to fit in with the testimony Ruth has already given. That will give you an alibi, talking with Lucy in the settlement. He attacked me from behind and in the struggle we both fell badly and he struck his head on a boulder. He died swiftly and I panicked and hid his body. When you and Ruth were asleep I slipped out of the house and moved the body. I was frightened people might think I had murdered him because his perjury caused my partner to be executed quite wrongly. Probably I will be taken to Jamestown for questioning, but the new Governor is a fair man and is quite likely to accept my story.'

Maria became distressed. 'Adam you can't take responsibility for this.'

Adam turned to his wife. 'Ruth, what do you think we should do?'

For a fleeting second Ruth displayed her true emotions. Tired, and experiencing conflicting loyalties, she raised her hand as if to indicate *do not ask me to adjudicate which of the two people I love best in the world should put their lives at risk.* She regained her composure, looking first to Adam with concern, and then more brightly to Maria.

Adam is right, Maria. We have to keep you out of it and get you away. Adam's story will hold up well; moving the body is obviously a criticism but, in the circumstances, anyone is allowed to panic. He is well respected in the community and it's very unlikely that he would be penalized. Logan no longer has the support of the marines, quite the opposite it seems. It has to be as Adam suggests, Maria.'

'Do you really think so, Ruth?'

Ruth answered briskly and with confidence. 'I do; the matter is settled then. When will you speak to them, Adam?

'Not now, we're not supposed to know about the note and I don't want Mary Tate drawn into this. I'll tell them when I'm questioned, either in Jamestown or on my return here. So we are all agreed; good. It shouldn't be a problem, Maria.'

They retired to bed early. Ruth and Adam lay in the darkness both sensing the other was still awake.

'Is there any other way to do this, Adam?'

'I don't think so, can you think of an alternative?'

257

'No. You spoke lightly about the risk, Adam, and I supported you in front of Maria, but in the privacy of our bed, you must realise I'm a lot more worried about the outcome.'

'I know, so am I, but I don't feel I can do otherwise.'

'Adam, I know I have lost your love to another woman. I've come to terms with that. I do worry this might be our last night alone together. For just this night would you love me as you have done in the past?'

'I still love you, Ruth.' He took her in his arms and did her bidding.

Ruth rose with the fishermen the following morning. They joined together in a tight embrace. Adam and Ruth were again publically confident of the outcome.

'I'll stay up here, Adam. Good luck, I'll see you tomorrow night.'

She watched the lugger clear the bay and then returned to the house. The vegetable plot required work and she spent the morning weeding and planting. She had returned to the kitchen and was cleaning some vegetables when she heard a footfall on the porch and then a knock at the door. Drying her hands on a towel, she opened the door to find Jason Hewitt looking down on her.

'Jason!'

Her hand flew to the locket around her neck.

'It's nice to see you're still wearing it.'

'I'm never without it.'

'Might I come in?'

'I'm sorry, of course.'

He carried a satchel on his shoulder and placed it on the table, closing the front door behind him.

'Is everything alright?'

Ruth burst into tears and flew into his arms, burying herself in his embrace.

'No, Jason, things are not well at all.'

'Are there things you can tell me?'

'Only that Adam is not guilty of murder.'

'You know he is a suspect?'

'There is a rumour in the settlement. This family has cause to hate Logan most; we've seen a gross miscarriage of justice here in the past and I worry that this odious man, even in death, will cause us harm.'

'Captain Doyle says Adam will not be back until tomorrow and he'll await his arrival. Commodore Pickford relieved me of my duties so that I could offer you and Adam support. He sends his good wishes.'

'Would you come up for dinner, Jason; I would like company this night.'

'It would be my pleasure. Would it help to go for a walk, Ruth, we could talk of pleasanter times.'

Ruth laughed. 'Those days weren't without their worries – you nearly died.'

'But I didn't, and we'll get you through this business equally successfully.'

They walked south along the cliff path and eventually came to Bay Point. The observation post was at the very tip and lay about a mile to the east of the Sentinel. The sheer face of rock glinted in the sunshine, as waves crashed against its base. Jason held her in his arms and kissed her.

'Have you put those times behind you, Ruth?'

'No, Jason. I am as much in love with you now as I was the day you sailed away. Your locket is with me at all times and you're never far from my mind. And your feelings?'

'The same; I meet some ladies when in port but, in truth, I have no interest. You fill a space in my mind that leaves no room for others.'

Their embrace became more intimate and then Jason hesitated.

'Do not hold back, Jason. You should not worry what happens now or later on this evening. I'm yours, Jason; do with me as you will.'

The catch had been sparse when the fishermen settled down to supper in the evening light. Adam threw out the sea anchor, as Maria took down the sails. He noticed an object in the water which slowly drifted towards them.

'If your father were here, Maria, he would be invoking god's blessings and protection.'

'Why?'

'That's a dead albatross. Sailors consider it bad luck to kill an albatross, or even to see a dead one.'

The broad wings were outstretched, as if in flight. The large bill hung down in the water, with small fish feeding off the carcass.

'It's sad to see such a magnificent bird in that condition, Adam. I do hope it doesn't bring us bad luck; we need all the good fortune we can find.'

They watched the bird drift away into the darkness to the east. The air seemed cooler and they were grateful for the warmth of the bow compartment, out of the evening breeze.

'Maria, I made love to Ruth last night.'

Maria paused from stirring the stew on the small oil stove.

'Why?'

'She pretended to be confident when talking about Logan's death, but she is worried all may not be as simple as we would hope. When I make a statement, we'll become a hostage to fortune; we no longer have control of our destiny. When that happened before, a gross injustice followed. She asked me to love her as I had in the past and I did.'

'Thank you for telling me, Adam. I understand her need; I cannot complain if a wife in need requires a husband's love. Do you share her worries?'

'I do. I hope for the best but I worry about the outcome.'

She smiled. 'In that case, my love, we need to ensure we have a special night together.'

Both woke abruptly in the early hours of the morning. The moon shed limited light on the boat and the ocean around it.

'What was that noise, Adam?'

'I'm not sure.'

They scrambled out of the bow and swiftly scanned the horizon for other sailing craft.

'What is that smell?' When free of the enclosed space in the bow, they had both become aware of a strong smell of marine life. Adam was about to reply when a dark shape loomed up on the port beam and they were engulfed in spume as a whale vented.

'We're in a pod of whales on the surface.'

Adam grabbed a boat hook to fend off any whale that might come too close. Almost immediately the boat struck the back of a whale and was thrown up from the water. As it fell back into the sea, the timbers groaned under the load. Adam was still holding the boat hook and ran to the starboard side of the boat as the whale passed beneath them. As if in slow motion, Maria saw the whale's tail fin rise out of the water on the port side behind Adam, striking the boat again as it slid back into the ocean. Adam was thrown forward; the tip of the boathook failed to clear the counter and bowed under the momentum of Adam's body. The shaft snapped and slid into Adam's stomach, its bloody tip protruding from his back. He sank to his knees with head bowed, grasping the counter with both hands.

Within seconds there was silence and they were once again alone on the ocean.

Maria ran to his side. His face was pale, contorted with pain. 'Help me to the stern, Maria.'

He half stumbled, half crawled to the seat, blood slowly seeping down his shirt onto his legs.

'Check for damage, something cracked on the first collision.'

Maria lifted a lamp and worked swiftly through the boat. 'We're not taking on water, Adam. The tabernacle is shattered at the base of the mast. It is no longer held securely, and it's about 10 degrees off vertical.'

Blood dripped slowly off the brass hook onto Adam's knee.

'Shall I pull the shaft out, Adam?'

'No, Maria, I've seen injuries like this before. I'm afraid there is no hope for me; if the shaft is pulled I will bleed to death in minutes. The handle causes great pain, but its presence reduces the blood loss. I may live for a day or two if it is left undisturbed. My sole interest is getting you back to land safely. You and our child, whom I will never see.'

Taking care to avoid causing him pain she held him, kissing his cheek.

'Is there nothing we can do to change this?'

'I'm afraid there is not. Bring me my blanket and some water, my mouth is dry. Erect our smallest sails fully reefed as though we were in a gale. Bring the compass and we'll start the journey home. I pray the reduced canvass will not dismast us.'

Maria did his bidding and they slowly sailed west and south, as the clouds obscured the moon.

Dawn revealed the extent of the damage. The lugger had buckled amidships with a slight curve to port. The socket in which the base of the mast should lie was shattered, and as the wind rose, they could see it shift its position slightly. An hour after dawn they sighted Diana's Peak.

'Let me take you to Jamestown, Adam. Perhaps the medical superintendent could save you.'

'No, my love, believe me it will be futile. Take me to Prosperous Bay. I want to die with you and Ruth. I know you'll take care of our baby, and when he is old enough tell him of our love – I hope he understands.'

Maria squeezed his hand. 'I'm sure he will. A child who is already singing Italian is bound to understand. I will make sure it is so.'

The wind had been shifting throughout the night. Initially from the west, it had swung south and was continuing to veer to the east and gaining in strength. By noon they were off Barn Long Point; its contours so familiar in what now seemed such carefree times. They were obliged to make, what Adam hoped would be, the penultimate tack to get them back into Prosperous Bay. The change in loading proved too much for the damaged craft and with a loud crack the base of the mast broke free and fell overboard into the sea, leaving the boat captive to currents and the wind.

'Cut them free, Maria, they are no more use to us now.'

When the last stay was cut away, the lugger moved more freely.

'Can you control the rudder, Adam?'

'I think so.'

'The current south will take us to Prosperous Bay in the fullness of time but the wind will have us on the rocks long before we get there. If I keep rowing to the east I should clear the Sentinel and then we can run on for the beach.'

As she spoke, the wind tugged at her hair.

'Yes, Maria. It's the best we can do.'

She released the oars from their bindings and placed the rowlocks in their sockets and began rowing. Adam swung the tiller to port and Maria started her long pull east to safety.

Her hair, broken loose from her band, blew across her face as the wind rose and buffeted the bow. Adam tried to look astern, but the pain was too severe. Maria could see the drift was taking them slowly to the south as planned. She could not convince herself that she was yet clear of Black Point or, more particularly, the Sentinel. She knew her hands were bleeding but maintained her steady rhythmic stroke. Adam stared straight ahead into the wind; he coughed and was wracked with pain. A trickle of blood ran from the corner of his mouth. The Sentinel rose steadily on the starboard beam. Maria's efforts were gradually drawing them to the east of the jet black edifice, and to safety. The leading edge of the Sentinel slowly began to cross their stern. Exhausted, she sat with head bowed, hair blowing in the wind.

'There's nothing more you can do, Maria. Come back to the stern and let us take our chance with that rock together.'

As she moved back towards the stern, Maria noticed a slight irregularity to the ocean to the east.

'Adam, can you look to the east?'

He turned his head and followed the direction of her gaze.

'Yes, Maria, it's a rogue wave.

'It's quite large and about seven waves to port. It will strike us before we have crossed the face of the Sentinel.'

'It's not a problem if we pass over the top of it before it breaks, we'll then slide down the back slope and still get through to the bay. If it breaks before it reaches us, we're finished.'

Maria cut a length of line and passed it swiftly several times around her left calf and his right leg near the ankle.

'Whatever happens, Adam, we stay together.'

Adam suppressed the pain and turned to watch the Sentinel passing on their starboard beam. The air seemed startlingly clear with light reflecting off the smooth cliff face. He experienced an increased awareness of sight and sound, the waves crashing against the rock and gulls circling above them in the updraught created by the easterly wind against the Sentinel's surface. Adam's right hand held the tiller and Maria placed both her hands on top. He lifted her hands to his face and kissed them. She snuggled into his side as the wave approached. They braced themselves as the final normal wave passed beneath their stricken craft. Almost immediately the sea dropped away beneath them as they entered the trough of what was now a huge wave. They watched as water fell away from the jet black rock to reveal a large defect in the middle, perhaps 30ft from the surface. Water poured out of a large, deep, oval shaped cave. The temperature had dropped abruptly and there was a smell of rotting vegetation. He could see the debris of previous boats which had foundered against the cliff; broken keels and rotting ribs, the only evidence of previous tragedies. The water boiled around them and it seemed inevitable their damaged craft would be dashed against the rocks on the sea bed, in company with the other wrecks, before the rogue wave reached them.

Abruptly, the boat began to rise as the wave towered above them on the port beam. They were half way up its leading slope when the crest curled and broke. The boat was again surrounded by boiling water. The lugger tilted to starboard in response to the inclination of the wave and swiftly picked up speed. White water surrounded the lugger as they were catapulted towards the darkness of the cave.

'I love you.'

'I know.'

CHAPTER TWENTY

Jason and Ruth had been standing on lookout point since the late morning. He had been following the lugger's progress through his telescope as it made its way slowly back towards the safety of the bay. Two marines from Benjamin Doyle's detachment stood with them; one, with a larger telescope on a tripod, and the other with signal flags. Captain Doyle stood on the beach with the remainder of his men.

'The boat is damaged, Ruth, it looks twisted and the mast is not straight. They are sailing on reduced canvas and I suspect Adam is afraid the mast will not cope with additional sail.'

Several minutes later the marine with the telescope reported the loss of the mast.

'Maria is cutting it away, Ruth. Adam remains in the stern; perhaps he is injured.'

They witnessed Maria's attempts to clear the Sentinel and then watched her return to the stern.

'Will that be enough sea room, Jason?'

'Probably.' Then Jason saw the rogue wave.

'Corporal, is your rifle loaded?'

'Yes, Captain.'

'Please discharge it to get the attention of the beach party. Advise them to clear the beach.'

By the time the message was sent there were only three normal waves remaining. The beach was cleared at the double as the water began to recede and the rogue wave gained height. Attention returned to the lugger. As the crest of the wave began to break, Ruth looked up at Jason questioningly.

'I am sorry, Ruth, they're too close to the Sentinel.'

He stood behind her with his arms around her, holding her hands as the boat surged forward towards the cave. They lost sight of it abruptly as the sky at the base of the Sentinel filled with spray. The surface of the ocean slowly returned to normal. Ruth turned and buried her head in Jason's chest.

'Is there any chance they will have survived?

'I'm afraid it is unlikely, Ruth.'

'Do you see any wreckage, Corporal?'

'No, Sir, none, and no sign of the fishermen but there was a cave near the base of the rock.'

'Yes, I saw that too. Captain Doyle will not have had a view of this at all; he will need to know what happened. Do you agree that no one could survive such an event?'

'Yes, Sir.'

'And that Adam and Maria must be dead, even if we can see no bodies. They may well lie with the wreckage in the cave.'

'Yes, Sir.'

'Please signal Captain Doyle, Corporal, and say we are coming to the beach. Would you prefer to go to your house, Ruth?'

'No, Jason, I should also like to come to the beach and tell Benjamin what I saw.'

Ruth made her statement and was then released to the care of Lucy and Edmond Davies. Jason walked with Benjamin to the settlement barracks. They sat at the mess room table.

'Some rum, Captain Doyle?'

'Thank you, Sergeant.'

Two glasses and a bottle appeared between them and the sergeant withdrew.

'I did not want to persist with the matter in Ruth's company, Jason, but is there any doubt about the deaths?'

'None whatsoever, Ben; survival would not have been possible. The final second or two were obscured by spray, but the lugger was in line with the cave and I think the boat and its occupants have been driven deep into the rock. They may float free in the next few days, but even if they don't, there is no doubt they have died. What are you going to do about enquiring into John Logan's death?'

'Accept any additional testimony which settlers might wish to offer; if I have nothing new by tomorrow lunchtime, I'll return to Jamestown and report that I consider his death to have been accidental.'

'I will join you for the return trip, if I may?'

They walked to the Edmonds and were invited, with Ruth, for dinner.

'Ruth, I have men on the Intrepid who are good swimmers and can stay under water for several minutes. If Adam and Maria's bodies are not found in the next couple of days, would you like my men to try to enter the cave to look for them? We would need calm weather, but I'm sure they would be happy to try.'

Ruth shook her head. 'Thank you, Jason, but no. If they are lodged deep within the Sentinel then let them remain there. Few people would have such an impressive monument to their lives.'

She stared out of the window as the wind rattled a loose pane; *far better Maria's secret died with her, safe within the Sentinel under several fathoms of water*.

The Edmonds said they would organise a memorial service for the following Sunday and Jason promised to attend. As planned, Captain Doyle reassessed matters the following day at noon. No bodies had been recovered from the sea. No additional testimony was forthcoming and the officers returned to Jamestown.

Ruth climbed the lane from the settlement and then walked slowly along the cliff path to the look-out point. All the fixed points in her life were laid out before her. She could see the roof of the house in which she had been born and had lost her parents whilst still a young girl. Her brother had sold up and moved to Thompson's Bay three years ago. She could see Adam's house, now hers, on the cliff top with the settlement spread out below. She could see the rock on the beach with the heavy metal ring, where the lugger used to be secured, and the stone steps where John Logan had been found. Beyond the settlement she could see the graveyard where Francesco and Carmella were buried. The sea was calmer now with small waves lapping against the smooth black surface of the Sentinel; a monument to Adam and Maria. She remembered her uncertainty when Adam had made plain his interest in her and her discussion with her brother; love or affection – a passionate need or a simple friendship? All too starkly life had shown her the differences between the two in the last few years.

'There is nothing more for me here.' She slowly walked back to the house.

A longboat from the Intrepid swung into the bay shortly before the memorial service. George Rutherford had been left in command. Jason, Thomas Pickford and the Reverend Wilkes disembarked with several crew members, including Daniel Bates. Ruth greeted them in the square.

'Good morning, Commodore. Congratulations on your new appointment.'

'Thank you, Ruth. It's a sad day that brings us together.'

'Thomas, if I may call you that, the Fletchers have always had a row in the church near the front – I used to share it with Adam and my brother, and then more recently

Adam and Maria. I would not wish to stand alone. Would you both stand with me for the service?'

'Of course, Ruth.'

'I gather you are due one final patrol, Thomas, before you sail north?'

'Yes, at present we have seven frigates and plan to do one extensive sweep before I take my squadron north. We have a little flexibility concerning our arrival in Gibraltar. I plan to re-provision in Jamestown for the voyage north in about two weeks' time.'

When they took their places, she turned to Jason.

'After the service would you escort me back to my house?'

'Willingly, Ruth, there are things I would wish to say to you privately and I was concerned the opportunity would not arise.'

She turned to the commodore as the Reverend Wilkes brought the congregation to order.

'Thomas, would you mind if Jason escorted me back to my house after the service?'

'That creates no difficulty, Ruth. We have plenty of time to get back to Jamestown before nightfall.'

Edmond and the Reverend Wilkes spoke warmly of Adam's contribution to the community and Ruth and Adam's kindness in taking Maria into their family at the time of her father's death. Edmond felt her parents would have been proud of their daughter; a beautiful, accomplished, young lady and a masterful sailor. Ruth's mind roamed to other more private times, as their family had shrunk in size with the loss of Francesco and then Carmella. Now there was only one. The congregation stood for the final hymn and then the naval officers escorted her to the door onto the square. The settlers filed past offering their condolences.

Ruth turned to the commodore. 'I'll say goodbye to you here, Thomas.'

''Of course. I hope, despite your losses, you'll find happiness and contentment.'

The commodore turned to his flag captain. 'You have plenty of time, Jason.'

They walked up the hill in silence. Ruth led Jason onto the rear porch, overlooking the sea. The longboat was drawn up on the beach. She could see the commodore talking to the Davieses in the square. Jason stood behind her with his arms around her waist and she felt comforted by his proximity. He spoke tentatively. 'Ruth, please do not feel insulted by the timing of this declaration, I know it could not come at a less appropriate time. However, it must be said today, for there would probably be only one chance for us to meet again in this life and I must leave you time to think matters over, so you can come to a measured decision. I love you. I have loved you since you fought for me on the banks of the River Styx. I was not frightened of the journey the boatman was offering; there was calmness and tranquillity. I remember your fierce love as you held our naked bodies together and begged me to stay. I want you to come away with me and to be my wife. Thomas knows there is nothing left for you here or in Jamestown and he has allowed me to offer you accommodation on the Intrepid. I avoided any discussion of love or marriage, simply a passage to Europe. I suspect he knows my feelings for you. Would you consider my proposal while I am on this final sweep of the southern Atlantic before we sail north? I am embarrassed by the timing but would never forgive myself, if I failed to make my feelings clear.'

Ruth turned around and looked up at his face, which was clouded with uncertainty and apprehension.

'Thank you for your declaration, Jason, and I thank God you have had the courage to speak to me today. You can have my answer now. I mourn the loss of my husband who was the best friend I ever had. I married him in the hope that friendship would grow into love. Just before we married, I probably killed that chance with a momentary error of judgement. Through rectitude I failed to grasp the moment then, Jason, and I will not make that mistake today. Life has an urgency which cannot be denied. Since the time of your illness, I have loved you passionately. Had he lived, I would have remained with Adam, as our marriage vows dictated. I have lost all the people I loved here in Prosperous Bay and, it's true, there is nothing to hold me here. Take me with you when you leave St Helena. When a decent interval has passed, I would be honoured to become your wife.'

He kissed her.

'Thank you, Jason. When will you come back for me?'

'I will send word by long boat or by land. Be ready to leave any day beyond two weeks from today. It will either be by longboat to Jamestown or the Intrepid will come for you directly.'

He kissed her again, stroking her hair. 'You've made me a very happy man, Ruth.'

'Take care of yourself, Jason.'

'Always.'

With one final embrace they parted; he moved swiftly down the path to the beach. She watched him board the longboat and she followed it north as it passed her husband's grave.

With excitement and trepidation in equal measure Ruth began her preparations for moving away. The following week, she visited her brother Robert, at Thompson's Bay. He was now married with two children and ran a small herd of dairy cattle, providing milk to the settlement. Robert and Edmond Davies promised to oversee the sale of the house and land and transfer the funds to Ruth. It was almost three weeks before word came that the Intrepid would visit Prosperous Bay the next day. Ruth was packed and ready as the frigate swung into the bay and dropped anchor. The longboat came to the beach, followed by Jason in the captain's gig. The sailors moved through the settlement towards the cliff path, with Jason following on behind. Daniel Bates led the men to the house.

'Are you packed, Mrs Fletcher?'

'Yes, Mr Bates, all is ready. Will there be space for the beautiful furniture you made for us?'

'Yes, ma'am.' he surveyed Ruth's belongings. Two trips will do the job. It'll be nice to have you on board, ma'am.'

Jason appeared on the porch and they sat on the bench overlooking the sea.

'She's a beautiful sight, Jason. You must be very proud. I have the remains of a bottle of wine in the pantry. Would you share it with me and drink to our future?'

'Of course.'

'Did your last sweep of the ocean find any slavers?'

'Yes, the commodore had us out at maximal distance from each other. Only the sailors in the crow's nest could see the ship on either side. We covered a huge expanse of ocean and, by the time the slavers realised they were being pursued, there were frigates appearing on the horizon from port and starboard. None forced an action and none escaped. We escorted all five of them into Rupert Bay. All the slaves will be released and the ships burnt.'

Ruth filled his glass. 'So Captain Hewitt, what accommodation are you offering me on your magnificent vessel?'

He laughed. 'It will be small and cramped, I'm afraid. The commodore has my cabin, I have George Rutherford's cabin and he has taken over the third officer's bed, leaving you the cabin he used to have as a second officer, before

Thomas became a commodore. Daniel Bates has tried to make it as comfortable as possible.'

The sailors returned and the remaining possessions were removed. Ruth walked through the empty house. The rooms contained so many memories; the walled-off area in the kitchen where Maria had slept. She paused by the front door, a boundary in the weeks when Jason's life had hung in the balance. Ruth had held back the bedside lamp that Jason had given her.

'Will I be able to use this in my cabin, Captain?'

'Of course, it's designed for use at sea.'

'I will always want it close by, when I sleep.'

He kissed her. 'It will not be long before we reach Gibraltar and there will be the chance to be together in private. Until then, my darling, the lamp will have to suffice.'

They walked slowly down the hill into the settlement. Lucy Davies bade her a tearful goodbye.

'I shall miss you, Ruth, but I understand your need for a fresh start. Edmond will deal with the sale of your property and make sure the money catches you up.'

Ruth declined the offer of the boson's chair and was greeted warmly, as she climbed the accommodation ladder to the deck.

'I've had the bags you wanted put in your accommodation, Mrs Fletcher, the rest is stored below.'

Jason led her to her quarters. It's very small, Ruth. There's a hook on a beam there that will serve for your lamp.

'All will be fine, Jason. I feel at home already.'

They could hear the chanting of the sailors manning the capstan, as the anchor cable was shortened.

'Is there a place on deck where I could stand, Jason, and not be in the way, as we leave the bay?'

He placed her by the port bulwark in sight of the binnacle and wheel on the quarter deck. Jason ran lightly up the steps to the quarter deck and took command of the frigate from George Rutherford.

She was surprised by the absence of noise. Some sailors scampered up the rigging to release sails, whilst others adjusted lines on the deck. As the anchor rose from the seabed, the sails unfurled and were sheeted home. The frigate healed gently in the wind and picked up way. They moved swiftly out of the bay and the houses in the settlement slipped out of sight behind the Sentinel. She noticed the commodore had appeared on the quarter deck. He stood by the port rail to attention, along with Jason and those who were not at the helm. All the sailors not sheeting home had assumed the same position, as the mighty edifice of her husband's grave slowly slid by.

Within the hour they had cleared the north of the island and were now exposed to the full force of the westerly wind. Daniel Bates had lashed a chair to the bulwark for her convenience and the third officer had presented her with a thick cloak. She watched the island sink below the horizon. In the Intrepid's wake, three other frigates took up station and followed in line astern. She pulled the cloak more tightly around her; it was a new life and she knew she was ready for it. She looked out to port, her eyes half closed in the strengthening breeze; two thousand miles of ocean to South America and a thousand miles behind her to Africa. She watched the sun set on the last day of her life on St Helena. There was a riot of colour in the western sky as the crimson disc sank below the horizon. She promised herself that she would return to the deck early the next morning to watch the dawn of her new life. Daniel Bates joined her to ensure the chair was suited to her needs. They heard a cheer from a group of sailors near the bow.

'Now there's a sign of good luck, Miss Ruth.' He pointed to an albatross effortlessly soaring high above them in the evening sky. It was still illuminated by the rays of the sun.

'It's rare to see one this far north. The crew think he has come to wish us well for our journey.'

Several of the sailors had been apologetic about the size of her accommodation, but she had immediately felt at home in her cabin; a small part of their wooden world. It was as if she were still living in a settlement, but one that roamed the seas. Lost in her thoughts, she did not hear Jason walk up behind her.

'I see Mr Bates is spoiling you already.'

'He's very attentive, Captain, and all your crew are very kind.'

'You look very fetching in that cloak. You'll need it in the early evening and more frequently as we sail north; the wind off the great oceans is often cool, even near the equator. I bring commodore's orders, Mrs Fletcher; we are to attend his cabin for dinner at the start of the first watch. In case you don't know, that's eight o'clock. Are you available to attend or do you have a prior engagement?'

Ruth laughed. 'No, please thank the Commodore. I would be delighted to attend. You must teach me the time keeping on board; the watches and the system of bells.'

He smiled down at her. 'You'll have plenty of time for that. I will come for you at the appointed hour.'

She placed her hand upon his sleeve as he turned to go.

'Thank you, Jason.'

'I am the one who should be thanking you. Gibraltar will come soon enough.'

She turned and took one final look at the sky. The albatross had swung south, returning to the cold, remote ocean, south of St Helena.

She smiled. 'The destination is immaterial, Jason. I care not whether it is Gibraltar, England or wherever; I would follow you to the ends of the earth.'

Lightning Source UK Ltd.
Milton Keynes UK
UKHW011248190721
387406UK00004B/1295

9 781785 074844